"We're all lonely travelers, wandering empty roads under a weight of cosmic indifference."

- Kevin Lucia

Jeff's Long Weekend In The Backrooms

***

A Journey Through The Liminal Abyss

Christian Meteor

ALSO BY THE AUTHOR

The Patterns of Existence

The Patterns of Existence II: The Subsequent Fate

Jeff's Long Weekend In The Back Rooms: A Journey
Through The Liminal Abyss

ISBN 13: 978-1-7369663-4-1

To understand the liminal abyss, consider a dreamscape. It is a dynamic world created from the memories of the dreamer; an environment built from past experience. Dreams are inherently liminal; they are solo ventures in spaces that are inevitably temporary, and despite the presence of other beings and environments that are familiar or even recurring in them, the very existence of the dreamscape is rooted in the constantly shifting human consciousness. This impermanence shares a close relationship with the experience of liminality.

"Purgatory" may help describe the liminal abyss as well, but there is a key distinction between the two; liminal implies a familiar space, while purgatory is often an alien or ethereal place. The location and experience of the liminal abyss is certainly similar to the traditional descriptions of purgatory, but its structure is recognizable to humans in some way.

Consider an empty airport; it is not dilapidated, but is noticeably under-decorated and entirely unpopulated; you are the only living thing there. Place yourself as far from any exits as possible, and picture nothing but infinite runway outside all the windows. . .This is the abyss; a boundaryless, transitional environment that offers only enigma beyond your perception. Dreams can be thought of in the same way; islands of experience surrounded on all sides by not-yet-developed environments. This "dough" of the undeveloped dreamscape forms into the liminal abyss by building from one's experiential island, or, in other words, a person's immediate experience of an environment repeats itself unconsciously into oblivion, almost like a cancer, reproducing and deforming as it grows.

Liminal spaces are immersive and encompassing. They are strange but familiar, and alluringly haunting, stoking a peculiar curiosity in the human mind. They parallel with the half-developed aura around the edge of dreams because they are places that are familiar to the mind, but yet lack the details of common human experience. They are incompletely rendered spaces that are not designed for human presence, displaying themselves as distorted versions of familiar places that seem to stretch infinitely into oblivion. They are the kinds of environments a mind corrupted by the effects of dementia might create; horribly lost and confused in a world that touches familiar parts of the mind, but yet disturbs with a bleak emptiness and appearance of forsakenness.

Jeff's
Long Weekend
In
The Backrooms

Chapter 1

Clocking Out

My last job for the week was to find and fix the source of a leak in the HVAC system of the Delta wing of the Caius government complex. I had worked in the building plenty of times in the past since our company had a big contract with them, so I immediately recognized the secretary at the front desk. She was immersed in her computer screen when I walked in, and after lingering behind the counter for a moment, I cleared my throat to get her attention.

"The permitting department is closed. You'll have to come back Monday." she snipped, still staring at her computer.

"*Amyyy*, come on now; we don't have to do this every time." I jested, leaning my elbows on her desk. Her eyes shifted towards me beneath a furrowed brow before looking back at the computer.

"Mm," she muttered. "Maybe you guys wouldn't have to come in here so often if you did your job right the *first* time."

"But then I wouldn't get to see your lovely face anymore," I teased, causing her to roll her eyes and let out a fed-up sigh. She then pushed back in her seat and stood up with a groan before waddling around the desk and towards the elevator on the edge of the room. I walked slowly over to where she waited with her hands on her hips as the droning noise of the elevator grew closer. A loud ding sounded as the doors opened, and then she stepped through and put a key into a slot on the pad before looking over at me with a tired expression.

"What floor?"

"Uhm," I stuttered before quickly pulling out my phone to look at the map I had downloaded of the building's venting system. "Delta wing is on floor. . .E." I replied.

"Don'tchu know this building like the back of your hand by now?" she said as she pressed the floor button.

"I don't think I've been down to Delta before," I said, still looking at my phone. A few uncomfortably quiet moments passed before I realized she was waiting for me.

"Oh, hah., thanks!" I laughed before scurrying past her into the elevator. Familiar music then began to play as the beige cube-interior of the elevator drifted downwards for a few lulling moments before coming to a gentle stop. The doors opened to an unfamiliar and empty part of the building, and after a brief look at the map, I followed the quiet hallway to a junction and then towards a metal door that opened to an office.

I was greeted by another secretary—this time a much prettier one, with bobbed, silky brown hair and a soft face—and informed her that I needed access to the Delta wing to fix the heating problem. She told me that I had the wrong floor, and to head to the other end of the hallway where a staircase would take me to that section. I thanked her, and then followed the hall past a dozen or so offices before finding a heavy steel door that opened into a beige stairwell. The steps only led down, and I hadn't seen floor F listed on the elevator buttons, so I figured it was a private floor for secure meetings and maintenance purposes.

The stairs ended at a landing with another insulated door, which opened to the floor that was noticeably colder than the one above. For jobs like this, I would typically locate the furnace and trace the venting back to the source of the problem. The map showed it on the other end of the wing, so I followed the silent hallway, taking a couple turns before I noticed the floor getting warmer. The problem was most certainly in one of the offices nearby.

I slipped through the closest door into an unlit room that had rows of desks aimed towards a projector screen at the front, and began searching for any damage to the aluminum HVAC piping overhead. After a few minutes, I noticed that one of the vents to the room was frosted over, so I checked my map for the location of the floor's air conditioning system. Strangely, it was back up on floor E; I had seen buildings designed like this before, where they try to skip a secondary heating and cooling system for private floors by just piggybacking off a different one. The system was probably malfunctioning because it was overloaded, but my job was just to get it back up and running. I'd have my boss give the administration a call later and tell them they needed an upgrade, but I figured I would wait until after it was fixed so that he wouldn't make me spend another hour here talking with an edgy manager about their flawed system.

Back on floor E, the map showed access to the furnace and A/C in the office of the pretty secretary I spoke with. I made my way back into the stairwell and then down the white hallway before opening the office door and greeting the secretary once again. By this point, the office was mostly empty, spare for a few straggler employees organizing papers in their cubicles. The door to the utility closet was on the backend of the room, and after opening it, I immediately spotted the problem: a corroded c-clamp on the air conditioner was leaking coolant into the venting. These things broke all the time, and I kept a full supply in my work van. It was a quick and easy fix. All I had to do was run back to the parking lot to get my supplies. Then I would be off for the weekend and could even meet my buddy Grant for happy hour.

I trotted back from the utility closet for a third encounter with the secretary, who now appeared a little sick of seeing me.

"I've got to clock out soon. You gonna be quick?" she said impatiently.

"I need to run back to my van for some parts, but the job will just take a couple minutes." I explained. "I'll have to go to the front for the master key if you lock up."

"Just go get it, I'll wait here." she said, folding her arms. "Most of the administration has already left for the weekend, and I'd rather you fix the air now rather than Monday.".

"Oh, thank you. That makes my job easier." I said happily. Usually, I would get the master key ring from the front, but that was always a headache with government buildings because of their tight security standards and general lack of haste.

I scurried back to the elevator and rode it up to the main floor. As I was heading out to my van, I felt my phone buzzing and noticed it was my boss calling.

"Jeff, have you finished that job over at Caius yet?"

"Just about to. I'm grabbing some parts from the work van now. Should be a quick fix."

"Great. I bet you'll be happy to get off on time this week. It's been a hell of a month, but at least you've been getting good overtime pay. I'm gonna be busy tonight, so just send me a text when you're done, and I'll log your hours."

"Yep, alright. Bye."

As if overtime pay was worth the 65-hour weeks I'd been working for the past two months. At least things would slow down soon in the shoulder season.

I rummaged through the van for the equipment before tossing it all in a canvas tote bag. Then I texted Grant that I was on for drinks at 5:30 at the Orange Inn.

"Finally! Hell yeah!" He quickly sent back. He'd been bugging me to go out for weeks and complaining about my lousy boss, and though he wasn't wrong, I needed the money. Plus, with the new year coming up, I was eligible for a raise.

I worked my way back down to the office on floor E and then smiled as I saw the cute secretary at the door to the office still waiting for me. I jogged over to her and then said a half out of breath "thanks" as she propped the door open.

"You're welcome. I hope you get that air fixed." she said half demandingly.

"I'll do my best ma'am." I said, glancing over my shoulder at her as she lingered in the doorway.

"Good," she said with a wink. "Have a good weekend, Jeff!"

"You too!" I said, flustered by the encounter that now somehow seemed sensuous. I stared at the curves in her tight dress as she turned to walk down the hallway, daydreaming about what it might be like to feel them. Her form then disappeared as the gray door closed with a secure thud, and then I was left wondering if I should have asked her to come with me for drinks.

The office was empty and dark now, so I flipped on the lights which made a soft buzzing sound. I passed the dozen rows of cubicles as I headed to the end of the room and then opened the thick metal door to the appliances. I removed the old clamp and sopped up the refrigerant before noticing a hairline crack a few inches long down the feed tube to the unit.

"You gotta be kidding me," I said with a heavy sigh. Not only did they need a new clamp, but also a whole new section of pipe had to be installed, which I had not brought with me. As matter of fact, I didn't have any in my van either, so in order to fix it, I would need to make a trip back to the company warehouse to get the part.

I wrapped some of my insulator tape around the leak before affixing the clamp. This was a temporary fix, and though I *could* make the trip for the part, that would take at least another hour and then I would miss happy hour *again*. Instead, I figured I'd just call my boss and tell him about the building's need for a new unit and repairs for the existing one. I dialed him up, and after a few long rings, I got his voicemail, and then a text shortly after.

"Can't talk now. Did you finish up?"

"Did a quick fix. System should be okay for another few days, but they need a new A/C pipe."

"Quick fix? Why didn't you just install a new piece?" he texted back.

I paused for a moment. He wants me to work overtime again. No way.

"I'm already on my way home for the day. I can fix it

Monday."

I stared at the screen while contemplating the risky text; maybe I should have just told him I was going to fix it. I hadn't made a fuss about any of my other overtime work because of that raise, and I hoped he would cut me a break.

A few more long minutes passed before another text came through.

"That's alright. You've been working really hard. Take care of it Monday. Enjoy your weekend bud."

Thank goodness. I smiled as I noticed the time was only 5:10. The job was done, and I had just enough time to get to the bar for happy hour. I did a once over of my repairs, and then collected all my tools into the bag before exiting back into the room full of cubicles. I made my way past them to the front door before shutting off the fluorescent lights. Daydreaming about my weekend and wondering if I might even be able to catch up with that secretary in the parking lot, I pushed to open the metal latch on the door, which sent my entire body into it.

I laughed to myself; of course, the key! I slipped my hand into my right pocket and quickly pulled it out, only to find that it was my house key and a half dozen others on a ring. Still holding them in my hand, I reached into my other pocket and had a split second of panic before my fingertips found metal. I pulled it out, only to find that it was a quarter.

I slapped my back pockets, palmed my shirt pockets, and unfolded my wallet to see if it had slipped in there. Nothing. I thought deeply for a minute about where I had put it, and then it dawned on me that I had left it in the bag. I opened it excitedly and quickly rummaged around before emptying the whole thing onto the floor and separating all its contents into piles. Still no key. I dug through all my pockets again before jogging back to the appliance room and using my phone's flashlight to reveal all the nooks and crannies between the appliances.

I spent ten minutes going over every part of the room before noticing the bottomless furnace drain. Dread percolated in my stomach.

"I would have to be a fool to drop the key in there."

I pushed out those thoughts and continued rummaging. I searched the path between the exit door and the furnace room three times, reinvestigated my pile of tools, and went over my pockets one last time before heading to the secretary's desk to search for a spare. I went through every drawer, lifted every paper, frisked for secret compartments, and palmed the underside to see if there was one taped. Still nothing.

Then a text came through from Grant: "Got a rum and coke waiting here for you. Better get here before I down it."

My mouth watered as I thought about kicking back in a plush red booth and sipping the fine drink, but then it finally dawned on me that I had never even *gotten* a key from the front desk. I let out a laugh mixed with anger and sadness, kicking myself for being so lazy that I hadn't even gotten a master key. That secretary had distracted me.

I figured I needed someone to come get me now, so I texted Grant: "I got locked in the Caius building. I need someone to come get me out."

A few seconds passed before Grant called my phone.

"You bastard!" he shouted. "You're working overtime again. Get down here!"

"I told you man; I'm locked in here!"

"Bulllllll shit! You better be here in five or I'm gonna

burn your boss's house down!"

"I'm not kidding man. I got to call the front desk or something to have someone let me out."

I could hear people hollering in the background and Grant telling them that I was my boss's bitch, before he got back to the phone and said loudly: "Well if *I* can't convince you, maybe one of these *ladies* can."

There was more babbling in the background before I heard Grant's voice again, this time so close to the phone that it crackled with static,

"This girl wants to meet you. Her name is *Jaaaasmine*" A loud crash of static followed before I heard a woman in the background say annoyedly "My name is *Jeniffer.*"

"Tell him what you were gonna do" Grant demanded drunkenly from the background as I heard the phone change hands.

"Hello? Is this Jeff? Grant says you like *dirty* stuff, and baby let me tell you, I can do *whatever* you want."

"Miss, I'd love to see what you can do, but could you PLEASE tell Grant that I'm locked in the Caius building, and I need someone to get me out?

"Sure thing, honey."

Her voice got further away and I heard her say "He says he wants you to come get him. He's locked in the *Klaimus* building."

The phone got traded violently again and then I heard Grant's voice.

"Klaimus? You said Caius! You can't even keep your story straight! Way to lie to your friend!" he accused.

I pleaded as I heard his voice get further away, before

hearing "what a dick." amongst the babbling of the bar. The phone clicked, and I stared in utter disgust at my screen that now read 5:26.

Alcohol always made Grant a real piece of work; I probably should have just called the front desk in the first place. I searched up their number on my phone, which took a terribly long time to load, but eventually it came up and I raised the phone to my ear.

"Thank you for calling the Caius building. If you would like to continue this message in Spanish, press one."

A short but frustrating pause was followed by the continued robot message.

"Please note, due to the recent COVID restrictions, our office will be requiring face masks until further notice. . .For hours, press two. . . Did you know, you can find our hours online, and much more information about our building by going to www.caiusbuilding dot com. That's www. C-A-I-U-S-B-U-I-L-D-I-N-G. . . dot com. . . For accounting, press three.

With excruciating patience, I continued listening to the menu options.

"For marketing, press four. For all other questions, please press five.

I brought the phone away from my ear and immediately mashed the five key before bringing it back up to listen.

"If you would like to schedule a meeting, say "meeting." If you are calling about a permit application, say "permit." You can also find information about the status of your permit by logging into your mygov account on our website. . . If you would like to speak with an agent, or have any other questions, say "agent."

"AGENT!" I shouted.

"I'm sorry, I didn't get that. Did you say, "main menu?"

"AY-GENT."

". . .we're directing your call now."

Soft elevator music began to play over the phone with god-awful interludes about the building's policies and website access. This went on for four more stupid minutes before a human voice came over the line.

"Hello, you have. . ."

"Hi, yes I'm locked down in the Delta wing and I need someone to come get me out."

". . .reached us outside of our office hours. We are open from 9am to 5pm, Monday through Friday. If you would like to leave a message, please leave your name and number, and someone will get back to you during our normal business hours." *click*

I slammed my fist into the metal door, leaving a large dent and even bigger throbbing in my knuckles. The next best option was my boss, who I had just lied to by telling him I was going home. Still, better to face that then be stuck here until I scare the janitor at 2am.

My phone rang four long dial tones before, to my great relief, my boss's voice sounded on the other side.

"Already gotcha clocked out bud. You can fill me in on the details of that job Monday. I can't talk now; our food just got served."

"Wait, please just a second. I got locked down at Caius and I need you to come get me out."

"You what? You told me you were on your way home a half hour ago. You're not supposed to be there." he said irately.

"I know. I messed up. I wanted to try to finish the job, so I ended up getting the part from the warehouse after I texted you. Then I got locked in." I lied.

"I'm in Florida all week Jeff; there's no way I can get there, but I can call Tommy and see if he's able to get you out tonight. No promises though."

"I'm sorry, I don't want to be stuck here all night. Please just send someone."

"Like I said, no promises. Call the fire department if you want but say goodbye to your job if that happens. We do a hell of a lot of work for those guys, and if they see one of our employees screwing up this bad, I know we'll lose that contract."

"How long until he gets here?" I asked.

"I don't know, a couple hours at least. He should be able to break you out though."

"*Break* me out? Why don't you just call the building's administrator?" I questioned.

"Did you not hear what I said? If anyone high up gets wind of this, we'll lose a bunch of our contracts. Just sit tight and I'll see about Tommy's rate."

"Rate?" I snapped.
"It ain't cheap breaking into secure facilities, so be ready to pay." My boss said coldly. Then the call ended. My phone went back to its home screen, listing the time at 5:38pm.

Chapter 2

Stuck

I scanned the office to see if there were any emergency exits I had overlooked. Even if it meant climbing through a service tunnel, that was better than spending another three hours stuck down here and paying an escape-artist's fee. I also knew that my boss was being stupid paranoid; did he actually think he would lose contracts because of my tiny mistake? He's a neurotic son-of-a-bitch for threatening my job, and I'm sure whoever's in charge of this building would *prefer* it if my boss just told them to let me out. Who cares if I accidently got stuck down here?

Despite how ridiculous it was, throwing away my job because I couldn't wait for a couple hours would be foolish. If Tommy didn't come tonight, my only way out was calling 911 or trying to find a janitor or a security officer, and in either case, my boss would find out. There was no way I was waiting until Monday when the building opened back up, so realistically, I had to either find a way out or wait for Tommy. But, there was a major flaw with all of it: the van. Security patrolled the parking lot at night and if the work van was the only vehicle parked there, they would probably know I was inside.

My phone began ringing from an unknown number and

I immediately declined. Dealing with a telemarketer was the last thing I wanted right now, and I was thinking I'd call my boss back to ask him about the van. The plan didn't make sense if Tommy wasn't going to get me out before night security started patrolling the lots. Then, my phone rang again from an unknown number, which I cursed at before declining and calling my boss. 5 long dial tones were followed by his voicemail. Annoyed, I recorded a message.

"Hey, it's Jeff. It's almost 6 and security is going to find my van. They are going know I'm down here, so I'm just going to call 911 and have them get me out. I'm really sorry about this." I hung up the phone and took a few deep breaths, preparing to talk to the 911 operator. My boss's plan wouldn't have worked anyway; maybe he would realize that and not fire me. Or he was just looking for a reason to screw me, and I gave him the perfect opportunity. At least I'd be out of here soon.

I was just about to press the last digit in 9-1-1 when my phone started ringing again from that unknown number. This time I picked up and said: "Never call this number again or I will bomb you and your miserable family!"

There was a brief moment of silence before I heard the telemarketer scoff.

"I don't want to buy anything. Quit calling me!" I snarled.

"Alright, but I think you'll want to know that your van is moved from the lot." they said in a deep voice.

"You did *what?* Oh. . .you're the guy my boss is sending. Tommy, right?"

"Yeah." he said curtly. "I called security and told them that a van had died in the lot and needed to be towed. They

14

think you got a cab home."

"So, you're coming to get me now then?" I asked.

"Yes, but I need to know your exact location in the building. Read me your IMEI number from your phone settings and then I can ping you."

"Sure," I said, opening my phone. I read aloud the sequence of 15 numbers and heard some typing before Tommy's gravelly voice came back.

"Well, you're a ways in. You'll need to get up to the first floor before I can get to you."

"First floor? I don't think I can even get out of this office. How am I supposed to get there?" I said, dumbfounded.

"Looks like the only way out of that room is a ladder down to floor F. From there you should be able to take the stairwell up."

"There's no ladder in here. I checked over the whole room"

"Under the fourth desk from the north wall. There should be a latch on the floor. It shouldn't take you long to get to the first floor. Also, use that HVAC map on your phone—it's easy to get turned around in Caius." The call ended abruptly and then I was left back in silence

I had more questions, like where was I supposed to go when I got to the first floor? And what was I to do when I got there? I also didn't know what Tommy looked like, so how was I supposed to tell the difference between him and a janitor? I figured he would probably call me when he saw I was getting close, and the fact that he had my GPS location gave me some solace. If I did get stuck or lost, he would know. I still didn't have any way to call *him* though, but, worst case scenario, I'd just call 911. Though, I figured I should at least try to make it out without getting any first responders involved; I'd keep my job that way and wouldn't have to deal with a bunch of firemen.

I gathered all of my tools into the canvas tote bag before doing a once over of all my pockets, half-hoping that a key had somehow magically found its way onto my person. I wasn't that lucky, so I shuffled over to the desk that Tommy had described on the phone. At first glance, there was nothing out of the ordinary; just a gray desk that was indistinguishable from the dozens of others in the office. It was, however, devoid of any personal items or decorations, and after inspecting it for a moment, I pulled out the wheely chair and noticed the carpet beneath the desk had a 2ft indent in the shape of a square. There was also a small latch that blended in with the carpet. I stared at it suspiciously for a moment and then pulled it up to reveal a 6-foot steel ladder that led down to what looked like a yellowish room with old carpet.

I carefully climbed down the ladder and stepped onto the dingy carpet that I immediately noticed was a bit squishy. The room around me looked abandoned, like some kind of an old backroom to an office building, but it was large. There were at least half dozen corridors off of the main route that trailed off into separate hallways, and a few out-juts of rectangular walls that pieced up the space. It was empty, too; no desks or faux plants like in the office above me; just a bunch of hallways surrounded by yellow-tinged wallpaper.

I glanced up through the trapdoor at the fluorescent lights before slowly lowering it closed. It had a lever on the bottom in case someone got stuck below, so I figured as long as I kept my sense of direction, I could do some exploring and just climb back up into the office later if I didn't find a way out. I pulled up the HVAC map on my phone, and after a few minutes of tapping through the different floors of the building, I eventually found floor F. The map was being glitchy, though, and seemed to be having trouble loading the entire floor. This resulted in large areas of unrendered space that just appeared on my phone as gray-grids over a white background. I figured this was probably because phone service was spotty down here, and even considered that it might just give out entirely in some sections for "security" reasons. That said, I had already been to a different section of this floor earlier while inspecting the piping; perhaps these yellow rooms could lead me to one of those offices and then I could take the stairwell up.

I headed away from the ladder down the main hallway, and the first opening I passed was on the right. It jutted at a sharp 90 degree angle a short way down, appearing to connect to a different room. The second hallway was a bit further down, opening to a large room with a wide center and two hallways trailing off it that led to more sections. The map showed this hall as the way towards the exit, but there was a lot of unloaded space between where I was and the exit-pin, so I decided to just investigate more of the main hallway before taking any out-juts.

The third hallway was a bit further down, this time on the left side, and was just a straight line towards a sharp turn, 200 feet or so down at the end. It was less lit than others, illuminated by the overhead glow of a single white, fluorescent light at the turn. I stared at it for a moment, feeling a strange, creeping anxiety that was almost attractive. It felt like I was trespassing, as if I was a kid that had broken into his school at night. The feeling was novel, like I was being naughty, but I snapped out of it when my ears finally recognized the dull buzzing that I had been hearing since I got down here. It was these damned fluorescent lights; they were all over the main hallway. A bunch of the bulbs were probably burnt out in this abandoned section of the building, and it gave the whole hallway a shadowy appearance that was undeniably eerie.

Two more openings sat directly across from each other on the back end of the hallway. The one on the right appeared to lead backwards, while the one on the left just looked like a dead end. Strange; what was the purpose of a short, narrow hall that just stopped abruptly with no doors or turns back? At least I could take it off my list of halls to check. . .From what the map showed, the second opening I had passed back by the ladder looked like the most direct route towards the exit pin, so I tracked back down the main hallway towards the rectangular opening in the wall.

The room had a large amount of empty space that was highlighted by gradients of light along the yellow floors and walls from the burnt-out overhead lighting. I followed what looked like the natural progression of the hallway towards a door-sized opening that appeared to be the way out. The map still wasn't loading though, and when I ducked to walk through the short doorway, it opened into a room with a tall ceiling and a half dozen corridors beneath a ledge that hung over the entire perimeter of the room. I knew for sure now I was on some kind of "secret" floor designed for the government. Your average architect would not plan a building with irregular ceiling heights and so many looping rooms. The place looked long abandoned, too, appearing to have been out of use since it was constructed in what I guessed was the 80's; probably as some kind of cold-war era design. With that in mind, it made perfect sense now why Tommy had sent me down here; this was one of those hidden levels in a building that granted access to different sections for secretly moving high profile individuals.

I refreshed the map on my phone to get a better sense of direction and to my surprise, a large section around my position had been loaded. However, the path leading back to the main hallway was now blurry. . . It appeared as if my phone was having trouble storing the data of where it had been and was only capable of rendering a small perimeter around its current location. This was unsettling, to say the least. If I were to get lost, I would have to retrace my footsteps by memory or hope to wander somewhere where my phone loaded something familiar. It was also running a little low on battery; 46%, which I figured was probably a result of it roaming for service. I only had one bar down here and was almost certain now that there was some kind of material in the walls that was interfering with cellular signal.

I looked around at the tall ceilinged room, taking note of the details that set it apart from other sections of the level. I wanted to remember this room in case I got lost and made it back here. After spending a few minutes trying to differentiate between the six doors set beneath the ledge surrounding the perimeter of the room, it dawned on me that I had a pencil in my bag of tools that I could use to just mark the door back to the main hallway. So, I drew a big "X" next to the doorway before taking the third door on the west wall towards the exit. It led me through a hallway that immediately turned into a junction that looked like the corner of a much larger area. Two long hallways leading opposite directions sat on the far ends of the junction, along with two more door-sized openings a few feet in front of me on the right wall.

The map hadn't shown these doors, and I wondered if they might just be dead ends. But, my curiosity got the better of me, and as I peered into the first dark opening, I immediately realized that I had misread the map—this was a big room. I couldn't quite figure out how big because of the lack of lighting, but it felt expansive. The only light in the room was above a wood door on the back wall of the room, maybe 100 feet away, but I couldn't help but give in to the eerie feeling the room gave off. I was sure it was empty; there was nobody down there, but the expansive dark space and door on the other side of it was just unnerving. Where did it even go?

My impulse was to follow the hallway that I had originally seen on the map, but I wouldn't have any confidence in my direction with the existence of this large room. I was certain I had not seen it on the map, and wondered if I might have taken the wrong door in the tall ceilinged room. I *really* wasn't trying to get lost, so I loaded up the map on my phone again, which showed the opposing halls, but not the empty room with the wooden door. Curious, I looked up from my phone back through the doorway into the darkness and thought it must be blocked from GPS for security reasons; it was probably some kind of encrypted data room.

It would be foolish to start "exploring" this level, particularly because I was trying to get *out* of here, but I could not deny that curious anxiety once again percolating in my stomach. Nobody would know if I took a little peek into the room, so I convinced myself that I would only look around for a minute and then get back to finding my way out. The twin openings to the room were set a short way apart, and after slinking towards the one closest, I reached in and palmed the wall for a light switch. It was coated in a moist, old wallpaper, but I didn't find a switch. I walked over to the second opening and once again frisked for a light switch, but still had no luck.

I waited for a minute, staring across the dark room at the dimly lit wooden door, before deciding it was probably for the best that I left it alone. Who knows what kind of security measures they have down here anyway; maybe entering would have set off a silent alarm. It was probably just another big empty room that's lights burnt out. . .or maybe it's a top-secret laboratory from the 80's with nuclear technology and bioweapons. . . either way, checking it out was probably a bad idea.

I turned back towards the two hallways leading out. Then something moved. I jolted my head back towards the room, convinced I had seen the dimly lit door open, but nothing had changed. My heart thumped in my throat as I gawked at the still door. Why was I so scared? I took a few deep breaths, chalking the experience up to a peripheral hallucination that was not so uncommon in the darkness. It was strange that I had gotten so spooked, but I figured the fear had also probably come from the sense that I was somewhere I wasn't supposed to be.

I didn't even know if this was true, though. My theories about this being some sort of "encrypted government sector" were just explanations that had popped into my mind. As a matter of fact, the whole eerie vibe was probably just something I was creating to add novelty to the drab experience of being locked in an old ass building. Creeping myself out was probably not wise, and for all I knew, this whole place was just extra storage space that wasn't being used.

I was still a bit unnerved, though, and ready to get away from the dark room. The map showed the long-left hallway as the next step towards the exit, so I followed it, occasionally glancing back over my shoulder at the square area I had just been in. I couldn't kick the feeling that I had somehow gone the wrong way; it was the same one I got when I originally discovered that empty unlit room. The tall ceilinged room I had come from had a bunch of doors anyway, so if this hallway was a dead end or, god forbid, put me *further* from the exit, I knew that was where I had made a mistake.

The straight hallway continued for a while before ending in a "T", with each path opening into larger rooms and more hallways leading off of them. The right path had a 90° wall that sat a little ways into the room, separating two openings that led to hallways with doorways scattered down the length of them. The left path of the junction led to a similar 90° wall that was deeper in the room, but the halls leading off of it were significantly less lit. I could see these hallways were long because of the fluorescent lights that were sporadically illuminated down the length of them, but I could not see the end or how many doorways sat along it. The sparse lighting also created completely black zones of the hallway that made it impossible for me to tell if they were parts of the wall or openings to more sections.

My mind was spinning from trying to map where all these dark out juts could possibly go, and I quietly prayed for the map to show the well-lit path of the "T" as the way to go. Even though it looked just as confusing, at least I could see, but sure enough, the map had me take the dark one. I knew now that this level was much larger than I had originally anticipated, and wondered if I might have been too far zoomed out on my phone's map to realize it. I wasn't a stranger to big buildings from all my years of HVAC install, but this place was certainly one of the biggest I had been in. It also was emptier and more abandoned than any occupied buildings I worked on, almost as if this wing had been under construction for decades but was never completed.

I used a little flashlight in my toolkit to start navigating down the dark hallway. It was a bit dimmer, and I was sure it had been months since the last time I had replaced the batteries, but it was better than nothing. My flashlight illuminated only a small section of the pale-yellow walls, but it was enough to keep me moving. The map showed a doorway a hundred or so feet down that led to a large room near the exit, so I walked carefully through the darkness, keeping an eye on the blue dot on my phone's map that showed my position.

I must have walked by at least a dozen more dark doorways and jutting corridors before reaching the oak door that the map showed as my next step. I breathed a sigh of relief; I was finally coming out of this weird dingy-yellow section of the building. I twisted the brass handle on the door and had a split second of panic as it put up some resistance; was it locked? I wrenched on the handle again which caused it to break loose and turn.

The door opened to a medium-sized, square room, covered entirely in tan wallpaper. In the center of the room, there was a small lamp hanging from the ceiling over a round table and single wooden chair. I stared at the dimly lit furniture, unsettled by their presence deep into the floor. Who would sit in this room, completely alone, a dozen turns away from any exit?

It looked like some kind of interrogation room, and the dusty brown color made the room feel especially claustrophobic. I didn't even want to step into it, particularly because I didn't see any other doorways. Once again, my map was wrong, or I had taken a wrong turn.

I left the doorway of the room back into the dark hallway and began walking back the way I came, watching the map on my phone. It showed me getting further and further from the correct path, so I reluctantly turned back towards the oak room and continued looking at the map. Sure enough, this was the right way. I was entirely dependent on the map at this point with no idea how to get back to the ladder, so I really had no other choice but to investigate the oak room and see if I had missed something.

Inside the room, the claustrophobic feeling increased, as did the temperature. The round table in the middle was empty with some wear on the edges, and the chair looked splintery. I scanned the perimeter of the room, looking for any handles or secret latches, when my phone started ringing. It was coming from an unknown number, so I stared at it suspiciously for a moment before remembering Tommy. I answered the phone quickly, greeting with an uneasy "hello" before immediately feeling better when I heard a voice on the other line.

"Looks like you made it to the manila room; gets kinda confusing down there, huh?" Tommy said in a smug voice. I remained quiet, entirely not in the mood for jokes.

"Yeah, I don't blame ya; that building is a damn labyrinth. But listen, you've made some progress—you'll be out of there in no time." he said cheerfully. I didn't believe him.

"Well, I'm at a dead end, and my phone keeps on

glitching, so I hope you got something for me." I said curtly.

"That's not a dead end; look for a loose wall. You know how the government is, with their hidden doors and all. You think they would just put the entrance to a top-secret facility out in the open?"

"Top secret? I. . .I'm not even supposed to be down here. I'm an HVAC guy, not a god damned spy. It's creepy down here, too." I said tiredly. "Just. . . tell me how to get out of here."

"The signal down there is a bit spotty, but it's not a complete dead zone. Just keep following your map up to the first floor and you'll get out." Tommy assured, unaware that my phone was nearly dead. "As for the room you're in, just feel around on the wall. There should be one that gives with a little push."

Before I could scold him, Tommy hung up. Then I was left alone again, 5 floors down in a creepy interrogation room.

Chapter 3

On The Way Out

The sound of buzzing fluorescent lights stuck out from the otherwise entirely quiet building. I figured it was probably getting close to dark outside now; my phone read 8:04 pm. I'd been stuck down here for nearly 3 hours now. This was as depressing as it was uncomfortable; I had no idea how much further I had to go before I would make it out, and pictured myself sneaking past security in the parking lot after another 4 hours of wandering helplessly through this place. What then? Would I call a cab or start walking home? And *where* was I going to come out of the building at? It might be pitch black by the time I made it out, and the Caius complex was huge.

I tried to replace my doubts with the fantasies of getting home and falling into bed, but I had become inescapably disheartened. I hated the fact that I was stuck down here, and that nobody seemed to care if I got out. If I had just called 911 in the first place, I'd have been out of here hours ago, and though it would have cost me my job, there were plenty of other trade jobs in my city. Besides, this incident had soured the little bit of enjoyment I got from the solitude of this sort of work; I was completely alone down here, and the thought of waking up

Monday morning and doing it again was repulsive.

If it took much longer to find the exit and my phone got close to dying, I planned to just bite the bullet and call 911. Without a map, all hope of finding the exit would be gone, and I would be almost completely lost, spare for the X's I had drawn on the walls. My only hope then would be finding my way back to the ladder and returning to the locked office door, waiting until someone found me. Who knew how long that would take? I planned to go a bit further, and then if there were still no signs of escape, that's when I'd make the call.

Tommy called the place I was in the "manila room" which I thought might be in reference to its wallpaper, but the walls were darker than your average manila color. Maybe it was just old and dirty? Whatever it was, I was done being in here; the claustrophobia was oppressive. I began to feel around on the dry and dusty walls, starting on the left end of the room and working my way around clockwise. The idea of a "secret door" seemed far-fetched because I couldn't find any seams in the wallpaper, and after palming the whole perimeter, I found nothing.

I stood in front of the doorway, staring at the table and chair dimly illuminated in the center of the room. The darkness of the dingy yellow hallways I had been wandering through crept into the room through the open door, and I quietly dreaded going back out there. Not only would it be back tracking, but I had to admit to myself that I was good and lost. If I were to go back, I would be entirely dependent on my phone, whose low-battery I was now very conscious of. I needed to find the way out of here, and I had grown impatient and weary before noticing a discoloration in the ceiling where the cord of the hanging lamp was attached. It was the only part of the room that wasn't perfectly uniform wallpaper, so I walked over and stood beneath the buzzing lamp, staring up at the circle of lighter toned color.

There was no way I was going to be able to fit my body up through that small of a gap in the ceiling, but I had to investigate. I climbed up on the table and just as I was standing up, I bonked my head on the lamp, causing me to lose my footing. As I was falling, I instinctively reached out for something to break my fall and grabbed the light cord. It wasn't strong enough to catch my whole weight, but it did slow me down. Just before I hit the floor, I heard a metal clunk, and then the dampened thud of my back against the ground.

I had ripped the cord out of the ceiling, and I was now laying on the ground next to the lamp. The whole room was dark, and after wincing and taking a moment to catch my breath, I slowly stood back up, unable to see anything. I felt around for my toolkit for a moment before rummaging around it blindly for the flashlight. I aimed it at the ceiling before clicking it on and then saw a small hole where the cord connected, along with some frayed wires. I had no way of getting the lamp hooked back up, and wondered what would happen when someone discovered it had been broken. Would there be some kind of mass investigation into the building because there was now evidence of a breach, or would the broken lamp never even be discovered down in a place so far away from the main offices?

With the manila room now completely dark, I had lost all chances of finding some secret exit. My flashlight was too dim, and I had already searched the whole thing, so with a heavy sigh, I turned to head back into the yellow hallways. As the oak door slowly came into view, I froze in place. It was closed.

I stared at it with wide eyes before saying loudly: "Hello? Is someone else down here?"

There was no reply, sending goosebumps down my arms. Despite being desperate for a way out, the thought of coming across someone down here was horrifying. What in the hell were they doing down here? This was far too deep in the building to be a part of securities patrols, and, who, or whatever it was, decided to play a prank on me and shut the door.

"That's not funny!" I shouted again into the silence. Again, no response. I reached for the box cutter in my tool bag before going back to the door and reaching for the handle. I did so slowly, ready to tear open the door and confront whatever was on the other side, but when my hand went to turn the knob, it didn't give. I wrenched it from side to side before throwing my shoulder into the door.

"No, no, no!" I begged. "Please, no, no, no!"

I continued slamming my shoulder into the door, pounding it with my fist. I kicked it as hard as I could, numbing my toe and sending me into a rage. Tears filled my red face as I slammed both fists against the door. I couldn't take it anymore; I was done.

My phone was at 28%, and I breathed for a moment while staring at it before dialing 911 and bringing the phone to my ear. I continued to try and catch my breath and calm down, and began rehearsing what I would say to the operator.

"I'm stuck in the Caius building in the manila room. It's down a ladder in one of the offices. What floor? The floor is . . .? Wait, what floor was I on? Don't they know where the manila room is; that floor. What would I tell them? I had just walked through a dozen yellow, dingy corridors? *That's* the best I could give them? They're gonna think I'm crazy! I can't remember what floor I'm on. . .but, they should be able to get to me. The manila room; just remember to tell them about the manila room"

The dial tone to 9-1-1 rang for 5 tones before I heard the line pickup and then I immediately began jabbering.

"Hi, my name is Jeff. I'm an HVAC worker and I'm locked in the Caius building. I tried to find my way out but now I'm locked down in a place called the manila room. Please send help!"

There was a long silence and then I said pitifully: "Hello? Is anyone there?"

It took me a moment, but when they spoke, I recognized the voice on the other line; my despair turned to rage.

"Why are you calling 9-1-1? I already told you, you're on the right track. Just keep moving."

"What? Why didn't my phone go through to 911, Tommy! What the fuck did you do!"

"You shouldn't even be on the phone right now; my computer says you're at only 20 percent. You best keep moving."

"I shouldn't be. . What?! You've got to be kidding me! Call the cops! I'm gonna die down here!"

"You better calm down; getting all panicked is gonna turn you catatonic. I told you, there's a door out of that room." Tommy said calmly. I hung up on him and attempted to re-dial 911, only to hear his hollow voice on the other side once again.

"That's not going to work, and I can explain it to you, but that would just use up more of your time and phone battery. Get a move on; it's going be a lot harder to get you out if your phone dies."

Astonished, I stood in silence. I couldn't believe what

was happening. Not only was I stuck in some labyrinthian building, but now I was Tommy's prisoner. I couldn't get through to 9-1-1, or anyone for that matter if he could just intercept my calls. I didn't have a choice now; I had to find the way out.

I turned from the oak door that had sent me into full blown panic and illuminated the table and chairs in the middle of the dusty manila room with my flashlight. It was far more eerie now; there had to be *some* way out here. I shined the light around the perimeter, keeping my eyes peeled for any signs of exit. Then, like some kind of sick joke, I noticed a white string protruding from the wall; I was **sure** it had not been there before, but when I walked over and pulled on it, the wall gave way and opened to a large concrete ramp. I immediately recognized it as the Caius parking ramp, and a great wave of relief crashed over me. I was almost out.

Being stuck down here for this long is enough to drive anyone mad, not to mention the fact that Tommy had somehow cut off my phone from reaching emergency services. *That* was the most unsettling part of this whole ordeal, but at least I had made it to the ramp; now all I had to do was follow it down.

The door out of the manila room had opened to the middle part of a ramp, and I immediately turned left and began following it down. I was still riding the high of almost getting out of here, but I couldn't help but reflect on the weird-segmented yellow rooms I had come from. I wasn't one to get easily scared being alone in "spooky" places; my job had desensitized me to them, but this particular building just had an uncanny vibe. I figured this was likely due to it appearing mostly abandoned, but the layout was so unusual that it almost seemed *intentionally* confusing. Maybe I would look into some history of the building once I got home; all I really cared about right now was getting out.

I figured I was close enough to find the way outside without using up the precious last bit of my phone's battery, so I followed the slow descent of the ramp to the first turn, where it doubled back and led lower into the garage. I had half hoped I would see a car when I made the turn—*some* sign of civilization—but there was none; just a long concrete tunnel illuminated by cold-white lights. I sighed and continued down the ramp, wondering how many floors I would have to climb. I had made it all the way down to the second bend and was turning the corner when it dawned on me that I hadn't seen any windows or openings in the ramp; this was a subterranean parking garage.

What was I thinking; of course it is! How in the heck would I have gotten into an above ground garage when I'm five floors down in Caius? I laughed at my mistake, shaking my head. Just about every parking garage I had been in reached into the sky, not the ground, so my instincts had just told me to go down. Down was **definitely** not the right way, and I was sure glad it wasn't; the next floor was much darker. The next turn was just barely visible, enveloped in abyssal darkness. It was probably just overflow parking with power-saving motion sensor lights; pale-white concrete pillars and yellow parking lines disappearing into an oppressive darkness.

Who knew what was down there anyway? Government vehicles and armored cars? Maybe. I bet there's even more secret levers and buttons down there too, like in the manila room, but I had no interest in doing anymore snooping. I turned to head back up the ramp and figured that my best bet was to find a doorway to one of those stairwells that climbs the height of the building. I hadn't seen any on my way down where they usually are at the bends in the ramp, but I attributed this to the section likely having some kind of a security clearance. If I climbed high enough, I thought I would make it to the gate for government employees, and then I could find one of those stairwells.

I passed back by the door to the manila room and climbed to the next bend, keeping an eye out for any more doors. Once again, there were no cars; just more wide-open concrete tunnels illuminated by fluorescent light. The ramp was a bit echoey too, with each of my footsteps lingering in sound space, but this was better than the mind-numbing buzz of fluorescent lights from the yellow rooms. My direction was also a lot more clear here than it was in those rooms: just keep going up. That plan fell apart when I made it to the next bend and the ramp plateaued.

I fumed, cursing every person who couldn't be bothered to help me out of here. I had been stuck here for **hours** now, and who knew how big this fucking parking garage was? Tommy, apparently—the guy who was now the reason I had to struggle my way out. If I just called 911 instead of my stupid boss, I'd be out of a job, but at least I wouldn't be "HERE!" I screamed, sending echoes throughout the garage. This was God damned dreadful; I was tired, hungry, and filled with absolute disdain.

My rage seemed to fuel me, so I marched forward into the long and straight parking garage that spanned further than I could even see. I knew it had to bend at some point, but the plateau had attracted a low-hanging fog that covered the entire level and obscured my visibility. It wasn't the worst I'd ever been in, but it did make the space that was already cold and unfeeling feel much larger. Plus, the concrete pillars that were supporting the roof were now slowly revealing themselves from the fog and kept tricking me into thinking they were a person—just a split-second dread followed by calm as I realized what it was. I don't know why I was getting scared either; coming across someone would be a good thing; they could help me out.

As I trekked further into the pale concrete garage, I grew more despondent as the floor revealed itself to be far larger than I had initially thought. It seemed like a simple way out, but now I was in the middle of some seemingly endless parking tunnel. Then, out of the fog, a white double door appeared on the right side of the garage, and I cheered as I ran over to it. I had begun to think I would have to turn back and absolutely dreaded the thought of going down deeper into the dark area.

I opened it up to a white rectangular hallway that was about 200 feet long with a very tall ceiling and a white double door at the end, along with another hallway halfway down on the left side. I pictured a stairwell on the other side of those doors and jogged down to the end of the hallway. I yanked on the metal handle and prepared to run up the stairwell before, to my immense disappointment, it opened to a medium sized work room with no other doors. There was a metal desk and two chairs, some lockers along the back wall, and a gray shelf. It looked like some sort of break room that was either abandoned or rarely used, so I immediately turned around and decided to check the hallway I had passed on the left.

I let the metal door to the break room slowly shut, which made a thud that echoed for an unusually long time. I was already halfway into the hallway when this happened, and the noise sent shivers down my spine. There was another white double door at the end of the hall, illuminated by fluorescent light. I ran over to it and began to pull on the handle. Then the lights flickered and turned off, followed by a loud crash that echoed from the bowels of the lower parking ramp, sending a violent jolt through my body.

I frantically searched through my tote bag for the little flashlight, feeling pencils, a tape measure, pliers, and screws before finally getting to the flashlight. I yanked it out of the bag and immediately clicked it on, illuminating the hallway with dim, beige-light. Movement at the junction to the break room and garage, like the shape of a dog, flashed from my sight. I stood, staring wide-eyed at the blank white wall, trying to convince myself that I had been hallucinating. Shadowing from my flashlight and the fear brought by the loud crash and everything going dark; that's what it was. What in the hell had made that noise anyway? It sounded like a transformer blew. . .The dark hallway was extremely uncomfortable, so I shook my head and turned back towards the doors before something moved in my peripheral *again*. I spun around, staring at the empty junction with the pitiful beam of my flashlight.

My heart was racing, but there was nothing there; just a blank white wall and the corners of the hallway. My mind spun with hazy images of apparitions in the dark, but I worked to keep myself together; **nobody is down here. . .**Or, if they are, they're here to help. Security, that is; why would anybody else be here? Why in the hell else would anyone else be down here?

One thing was for sure: **I was not turning back**. If the loud bang wasn't enough to deter me, then the pervasive image of the murky lower level of the garage was. I don't know why I couldn't get it out of my head, but it kept popping in; a dark expanse of old concrete tunnel leading god knows how far down. It haunted me. I didn't even care if that *was* the quickest way out; I would find a different route. I figured there had to be more than one way out of this place, and I was going to find the exit that *didn't* take me through hell's dungeon. I didn't care if my phone directed me to go down or if Tommy told me to; I was NOT going down there. Besides, why would the exit be *deeper* underground?

I turned around to open the double door, praying to God that it wouldn't be locked. It wasn't, and the first thing I saw was stairs, so I leapt through the doorway and immediately began running down. My mind filled with images of the starry night sky above the Caius parking lot and began painting a rough picture of where the garage was on the complex. I had probably climbed down three floors, noticing doors on each of the landings, before I stopped at a platform to catch my breath. Just as I was ready to start running again, I paused before letting out an agonized groan; I had done it again. These stairs were taking me **down.**

I turned and ran back up the stairs as fast as I could, picturing the level I had come into the stairwell on. It had a double door, not singles like all the others I had passed, but then I realized it didn't really matter; I was just going up. I continued climbing, finally making it to the floor I had been on, and then screamed; the stairs didn't go up any further. I threw my hands over my face and then pulled my hair. I was finished. I wanted out, and I wanted it now. Tommy would have to come find me here; I wasn't going any further.

I sat down next to the double door and wrapped my arms over my knees, looking down at the stairwell. I was avoiding the sinking truth in the back of my mind that I needed to go back into the parking garage to keep exploring, but I had been so convinced that this was the way out. I hated it out there, and even though being stuck in here wasn't much better, it felt kind of safe. Out in the garage, the fog made everything feel bigger, and now I really thought *something*, or someone, might be out there. They had followed me from the manila room and hid when I came into the white hallway.

My phone began to ring, and I answered it immediately to stop the ringing.

"I'm done. I'm not going any further. You'll have to come find me here." I asserted.

"How do you expect me to do that from Florida?" the voice on the other line said wryly.

"Who is this?!" I shouted. "Put Tommy on, that fucker!"

"Woah tiger, good luck getting anybody to help you with that attitude." the voice retorted. "Tommy is already on his way in. He wanted me to tell you so that you don't think he's security."

I tried to respond, but fumbled my words into a sigh. I now recognized the voice as my boss's, and after a moment of silence, I said resignedly: "I. . .I'm sorry. I've been losing it down here. This building is massive and my phone's almost dead. I started to think I was gonna be stuck down here forever."

"Yeap; Caius is some place. Lots of winding hallways and abandoned sections. Don't worry though; Tommy is a professional. You'll be out of there in no time. Just sit tight and he'll get to you soon." my boss said reassuringly. I had so many choice words for both him and Tommy, but they seemed unimportant now that I was close to rescue. I had a lot of questions for my boss, and though his tone of voice was sympathetic, I could tell he wasn't in the mood to chat.

"That's. . .good to hear. I'm glad he's almost here. But, I have to ask, why didn't Tommy just call me instead of you?" I asked curiously.

"The section he entered at is a total dead zone for phone service, but he checked your location before entering. Tommy knows his way around Caius pretty well, so I wouldn't be surprised if found you in the next couple minutes." my boss explained. "Alright? All good then?" he asked impatiently. I was about to ask him about Tommy cutting off my service, but figured it best to leave that part out; I could still keep my job.

"Yeah, all good then. Thanks." I answered, holding back any more questions.

"Good, glad to hear it. Alright, you take it easy now and enjoy your weekend. We'll see you back Monday."

The line clicked and then I was once again left in silence. Despite the rage I had towards my boss for getting me into this situation, I couldn't deny that hearing his voice had calmed me down. He seemed unconcerned with the whole deal, and though at first, I thought this was because he didn't care, I supposed now that was just because he had faith in Tommy's skills. I didn't realize how massive this building was when I first got stuck down here, or how deep into it I would have to go, but at least Tommy was coming. I still didn't understand why my boss was so concerned with keeping emergency services out of it, but it seemed like he didn't know I had tried to call them earlier. Maybe Tommy hadn't told him, or maybe he didn't care because the call never went through, but one thing was for certain: something else was going on.

Their story had seemed plausible at first—that this was a secure government building, and it would be a bad look for the company—but I knew there had to be more. There was no way they would go to these lengths just for my simple mishap, and I had the feeling that I just got unlucky enough to get caught up in whatever this was. I sensed that neither Tommy or my boss were all that interested in answering any questions, and probably just wanted me to keep out of it. Despite my curiosity, all I really cared about was getting home; I had no problem batting an eye to their shady business.

I collected my composure in the quiet, beige-colored stairwell before standing up and stretching my neck from side to side. Tommy was probably the reason I thought I had seen someone following me, and I figured he would probably have a better shot at finding me if I went back out and called for him. So, I pushed open the heavy metal door to the white hallway that was now lit again, and walked back down to the fork. After looking back at the door to the break room, I decided Tommy was probably out in the garage searching for me. So, I went to open the door back to the concrete ramp, which was just as foggy and unsettling as before.

"Hello? Tommy? I'm over here!" I shouted, sending echoes through the garage. "I think I'm up on the 3rd floor." I wandered a bit further into the dimly lit ramp, before shouting again: "Tommy! Yell if you can hear me!"

My voice echoed further this time, seeming to travel all the way down to the lower level of the garage. This once again brought the image of the gloomy base level of the ramp into my head, which I tried to shrug off. I had no plans to go any further and risk getting lost, especially if Tommy was on his way to my last location. I figured I would search for a bit longer and see if I could find Tommy before heading back to the stairwell.

The fog seemed to have thickened since I had originally come in, and was now creating more illusions in the dark. The concrete support pillars were almost entirely obscured now, so when I saw what looked like one that had fallen over, I went a bit closer to investigate. I figured it was probably some kind of a wheel stop, but I hadn't seen many of them down here, so I wondered if it might have been blocking a window or another stairwell. Once I got closer, I noticed that it was hollow in the middle, followed by a long bar spanning across the top, like a fence-barrier. Then it moved.

I stood in terror, staring at what looked like some deformed apparition of a hairless dog. Its body was bony and lanky, standing hunched over on all fours, with the knobs of its spine protruding from the withered pale skin on its back. Only once I saw its grotesque face look at me, with its empty white eyes covered by scraggly black hair, was I able to move my feet and run. I could hear it chasing me by the sound of its feet smacking through wet puddles, but its bone chilling howl is what filled my body with primal horror. It was the sound of bellowing death from static and drums, and I could feel its frothing snarl just on my heels.

I charged headlong into the darkness, refusing to look back; even a split second of hesitation would mean my end. I had no idea where I was going, whether it was in circles or deeper, but the creature's piercing bark seemed to grow closer by the second. I had nowhere to hide; all I could do was run. I had no capacity to think of what it was, only to sprint as fast as I could. My legs felt like jelly, but kept working without any thought. To stop is to die, but then from the fog a shape emerged, a door!

I crashed into the door's push handle, slamming it against the concrete wall before rushing behind it to force it shut. It was closing too slowly; I could see the gnashing fangs of the disgusting beast growing closer and closer with every second. It was running and howling, and its dead-white eyes were the last thing I saw in the gap in the door before it smashed into the metal, causing me to fall backwards. I immediately scrambled to get back on my feet, and threw my body back against the door, bracing for another impact.

Ready for the beast to charge, I forced all my weight into the metal panel of the door, but instead of a thud, I heard the ear-splitting, scratching of its claws against the metal. It was still trying to get in. I looked around frantically for something to brace the door or clobber the creature with when, the scratching suddenly stopped. I stood against the door, ready for another attack, but the room remained quiet. My heart was throbbing, and I couldn't stop gasping for air. I laid my head against the door, trying to catch my breath.

For what felt like an hour, I braced against the door in silence, ready for the creature to charge at any moment. It never did, but I still lacked any faith in the doors ability to stop the beast if it decided to attack again. There was nothing around to brace the door with, and though something in my toolkit might have worked, I had left it back in the stairwell. I shuddered at the thought of going back out to try and find the door to that white hallway and my tools, but it was then that I realized that's exactly where I was; by some miracle, I had found my way back to the *same* white hallway while running. I was no closer to escaping, but this did mean that I was somewhere familiar, and I hadn't lost all my tools.

What in the hell was that thing? Some sort of human-canine hybrid experiment gone horribly wrong? And what was I supposed to do if it got in? Bludgeon it with one of the tiny hammers in my tool kit? Maybe I could craft some rudimentary weapon out the junk that had accumulated in there over the years, but I doubted anything in there would be all that impactful in the grand scheme of fighting to death with a fucking *hellhound*. My best bet was blocking the door; I needed to get to the stairwell and take inventory.

I spent a great deal of time convincing myself that the beast was gone and that I was okay to leave, all the while thinking the minute I walked away, it would burst through and maul me. Its face haunted me, and I pictured it crashing through the door with dead white eyes and a frothing muzzle. I hadn't ever really thought about how I would die, but three floors down in a subterranean parking garage, lying in the middle of a bleak white hallway, being eaten by a grotesque hound-like creature was certainly not what I imagined. I also could not stop thinking about what in the hell it was; the only plausible explanation was a feral wolf with mange that had somehow gotten this deep in the building, but I could not deny that its face had looked disturbingly humanoid. The scraggly, long black hair hanging from its head was also very uncharacteristic of any wolf *I* had ever seen.

Eventually, I decided I had no other choice; I had to leave. I would walk as quiet and fast as I could away from the door to get back to the stairwell for my toolkit. There was no way I was going back into the garage, whether Tommy was out there or not, so I decided I would have to go through one of the doors down the stairwell. The idea of going *deeper* into this hellish place was appalling, but it was the only way forward. So, very slowly, I moved away from the door, walking backwards with my eyes locked on it. If it were to move, I would charge back at it and slam the beast in the crevice, but if I was more than halfway down the hallway; then I would turn and run towards the stairwell door and hopefully make it in time.

The door did not move an inch, and once I had made it to the fork in the hallway, I stared at the door to the ramp for a long couple of seconds before sprinting towards the stairwell door. Every hair felt like it was standing on end as I hurried towards the stairwell, whose door looked like it was getting further and further away, but then I made it, and jumped through the doorway. Sure enough, my toolkit was lying on the ground right next to where I had been sitting when my boss called, so I grabbed it and propped my weight against the door, searching for something to secure it closed.

A few things caught my eye: A set of screwdrivers, some Allen wrenches, a pliers, a couple of drill bits and a spool of 20 gauge wire. I thought for a moment about forcing a drill bit into the lock to see if I could jam it, but then I looked at the handles on the door and thought I could just wire them closed. I had about 50 ft of wire; a dozen wraps or so would do it, so I wrapped a loop in the wire and threaded it through itself before pulling tightly and spinning the spool around the handles. I didn't want to use it all, but I **had** to use enough, so I tested the door after wrapping it, and spun around the handles a few more times to make it tight. Once I was satisfied with the strength, I clipped the wire and plopped the precious remaining bit back in my toolkit.

I felt a bit of relief as I stood back to stare at my work,
feeling mildly safe from the hound. I could rest here for a
minute before going down and exploring further, but then
it dawned on me that if Tommy was in here, he couldn't
screen my calls anymore. I had no interest in waiting for
him or accommodating my paranoid boss any longer. I had
nearly been mauled by a hellhound minutes ago, and Tommy
intercepting emergency calls was criminal. Now was as good of
a time as any to call.

Chapter 4

Pipe Dreams

Somehow, I was now in a complete cellular dead zone. My map wasn't loading anything, and I couldn't make any outbound calls. I couldn't make sense of it; my boss had been on the line with me in this **exact spot** no less than 30 minutes earlier. Maybe my battery was too low, or maybe getting a signal had just been lucky, but my hopes of firemen bursting through the door to save me quickly died. All I wanted was to just be home.

I was hunched over my knees, wallowing in self-pity, when the sound of a metal door crashing open jolted my head up.

"Tommy?" I shouted, praying that I would hear a reply. Nothing; it was the hound coming into the first hallway. I had to move. I pushed myself up off the ground and took a shaky, deep breath before grabbing my toolkit and paying a silent homage to the cold stairwell that had served as a haven. Then, I hurried down the stairs and took the door on the first landing. I didn't know where it went, but one thing was for sure: I wanted to stay as high up as I could in this place. Going down meant going deeper, and I needed to reach the surface.

The door opened to a grayish concrete tunnel with

pipes spanning across the ceiling and walls. The path was long and straight, stretching as far as I could see without any bends or turns, and was dimly lit by overhead amber lights that filtered through the metal pipes. It looked like some sort of maintenance tunnel, but I was glad that it went straight, not down. I figured it probably would take me to another part of the Caius complex, far away from the dreary garage with the hellhound. I did wonder, though, if there was any chance of running into Tommy now that I had moved and wired the door shut behind me.

The straight hallway brought me deeper and deeper into the level. No turns, juts, or bends; just a long, straight rectangular tunnel that gave off the convincing impression it was going *somewhere*. Amber cones of light shined down from the square bulb-covers on the ceiling, illuminating the long stretch of tunnel. Patches of darkness from burnt-out bulbs chopped up the space, but this section felt better than the garage because it was not nearly as open and exposed. Perhaps this was just because it was different from the murky expanse of the parking ramp; the impending claustrophobia would get to me eventually.

I wandered deeper, wondering how long my wire wrap would keep that devil-dog out of the stairwell. I had gotten in the habit of looking over my shoulder every couple minutes to see if it was behind me, all the while trying to cope with the reality that there was nowhere to hide in here. If something started chasing me down here, it was a game of who fatigued first, and I didn't have high hopes for myself. My best bet was to put as much distance between me and the door back to the stairs as possible, and pray that this tunnel was bringing me closer to the exit. I had no map or cell service, though, so for all I knew, I was just going deeper into Caius. This building had already revealed itself to be a labyrinth of strange rooms and hallways, but I really had no other choice but to press on.

I estimated that I had walked over two miles now, and having passed no doors or turns, doubt began to fester in my mind. Surely the building couldn't be *this* big; perhaps the tunnel was taking me to another facility? I hated to admit it, but I had most likely wandered into some kind of secret subterranean passage for government personnel. . .The thought of winding up in a whole other building that I had to find my way out was revolting, but maybe, just maybe, that one would be less fucking elaborate. Maybe I would stumble upon a security guard there who would pull his gun on me and have me arrested for trespassing in a top-secret facility. That would be fine. Matter of fact, it would be preferred to *this*.

The tunnel became less and less lit the further I went. Long patches of darkness stretched between the sections of dim lighting, and I knew I was starting to lose it when faces began to appear in the darkness. They were all white with wide eyes and grinning teeth, and appeared to be moving. They floated in the void, but seemed to disappear when I made it to the light. I knew they were a hallucination, but I hurried through dark sections of the tunnel, wary of letting my paranoia run wild. They were getting to me, and it almost felt like I was being chased. My jogs through dark section turned to sprints, and then I spotted something ahead in the tunnel; a turn.

I ran to the turn, eager to find a stairwell, ladder, or anything to get me out of here, but then my soul sank when I realized what I had found; a 4-way intersection in the tunnel. Each way looked just like the others: an endless, dimly lit tunnel with pipes spanning the walls and ceilings into oblivion. I had no clue which way to go, and as I stared into the darkness, those damned white faces started appearing again. Grinning, as to mock me. Maybe I should just keep going the same direction; it had to end up somewhere eventually. One thing was for sure, I wasn't going back, and if any of the paths led me that way, I knew that was the wrong. Or. . .perhaps they would take me to a different section of Caius? Standing here wasn't getting me any closer to home, so I just kept going straight; whether it would dead end or open to more tunnels of pipes, at least it felt like I was making progress. I did wonder where the left and right ways went; to more subterranean government facilities and parking garages with demented hounds? I wondered, but I was not especially interested in finding out.

My nearly dead phone listed the time at 2:48AM, sending chills down my spine. I'd been lost for nearly a full twelve hours now. I knew my mental state was degrading from the sleep deprivation too, but the most uncomfortable thing was the time itself. The feeling worsened the more I thought about it. I was alone in a dark concrete tunnel in the middle of the night, hopelessly isolated and lost. I wished I hadn't checked the clock; the time made me feel like I was surrounded by an enormous hellscape that I could not see; trapped in some section of a maze that blinded me to the true scale of my dreadful fate. My predicament was an object of horror, but I told myself that this was just paranoia. The time of night didn't change anything, and with no sun or sky to tell me it was the devil's hour, I ought to just continue on as if I was oblivious to it.

A pit dropped in my stomach at the sight of something filling the tunnel a few hundred feet down. I froze in place, staring at the motionless being when its shape then became familiar. It was a human. I couldn't believe my eyes. Excitement welled in my heart as the thoughts of finally getting home danced in my mind, and I was so glad I had chosen the straight path. I had finally picked the right direction, and though I knew this person would have a lot of questions, I was eager to tell my story. I couldn't just start running at them and scare them off though, and I wasn't sure if they had seen me yet, so I shouted "Hello! I need help!"

I started walking towards them, expecting my voice to grab their attention, but they remained in place. Maybe they had headphones in? A janitor rocking out while cleaning the tunnel? I could see it.

"Can you hear me? My name's Jeff. I'm an HVAC technician and I've been stuck down here all night."

I could tell I caught their attention this time as their head turned towards me, and so I waved and kept walking towards them.

"Do you know the way out of here?" I said meekly. "I have no clue where I am."

The person still had said nothing, but was now headed in my direction.

"He. . .hello? Did you hear me?" I said warily, coming to stop. The person had entered a patch of darkness between the lights, but I could still make out their silhouette. My heart was thumping, and I moved to take a step back because of their strange behavior. I thought they might be a security guard trying to get cuffs on me, but when they stepped into the amber light, their vile image was revealed. Their skin was pale and yellow next to sunken white eyes that glared down at me from a tall stature, stunning me with disgust. I forced my legs to move and nearly fell over trying to turn around as the abomination began to charge, roaring with guttural horror.

The image of the creature thrashed about in my mind as I ran with everything I had. I quickly reached the intersection and tore around the corner. The gurgling roar of the creature echoed through the tunnels, shooting mortal panic through my core like lightning. I sped past dozens of overhead lights that flashed through the steel piping, pushing as fast and far as I could into the tunnel. It appeared to be growing narrower, with the ceiling getting lower and the pipes getting closer. I must have been approaching a dead end; this is it. I kept running; maybe I could run far enough in that the tall beast couldn't fit.

My vision narrowed, seeming to shrink by the second. A circle of darkness was closing in around my peripherals, but then up ahead, something caught my eye. Another hellhound?! No, it's on the wall! A climbing creature; wait, it's a door! An elevator! Would I make it in time? I glanced over my shoulder to see the beast racing down the tunnel, flashing in and out of the lighting. This was my only hope.

I skidded to a halt at the elevator door and frantically mashed the button. One. . .two seconds passed. *DING!* It works! The noise of the bell is proof! Hurry! Faster! The doors began to open, and I slipped in as soon as I could fit. There was only one button on the pad that I punched immediately before my eyes darted to the opening. Why weren't the doors closing?!

"Go, go, go!" I screamed.

The doors remained unmoving, and I could hear the heavy footsteps of the creature approaching fast. It was too late, and I began to say my prayers when the bell dinged again, and the doors started to close. They were *so* slow, and then terror flooded my body as the creature came into view. Just a smidgen of opening remained when the creature turned its head and stared into my soul with its gaunt, entirely white eyes. It shrieked and reached its long, sucker-ridden arm towards the opening, but the doors sealed, and I could hear the beast scratching on the other side. I stood frozen in panic; was the elevator going to move? The floor lurched, and I half expected it to go into freefall before it began moving up.

My heart pounded violently in my chest, all the way up to my ears. All I could hear was the thumping. Then, music started to play; was I hearing things? Had I fully lost it now? I put my hands over my ears and shook my head. Then I took them off and the music was. . .still there. Elevator music. My breathing was rapid, but my vision was starting to come back, and the elevator was still moving. Where was I going? The music continued to play, and it was old, like something out of the 40's. I slowly looked up towards the ceiling, and stared at the circular grid-covering over the speaker producing the sound.
More sick jokes from the evil god that had put me in this place. Who would put that music on at a time like this? I was still in shock, but then the elevator came to an abrupt stop, knocking me off balance. The music crackled with static before turning off, and then the bell went off again, making me jump. The doors opened, and then I was left staring into an empty office building.

Chapter 5

The Abandoned Office

The floor immediately unnerved me; everything was gray and unfeeling, and I most definitely was not supposed to be here. I had no choice though; face the unknown or stay in the elevator and risk being brought right back down to the tunnels with that horrifying creature. I stalled for a few seconds, but once the elevator bell rang again and the doors began to close, I quickly leapt through them into the office space. All my sense of direction was gone; I had no idea if I was even in Caius anymore, much less any closer to getting home.

The office looked completely abandoned, lacking any furniture or decorations, with white walls and grayed carpet. Its architecture was all very square and uninteresting, and though I had already spotted a half dozen doors and hallways, the thing that caught my attention most was the *windows!*

"Thank GOD!" I shouted, running across the empty room to look outside. I hoped to see a parking lot, metropolitan area, or just *something* to show me a sign of civilization. I knew it was the middle of the night, so I figured I would probably just see streetlights. But, when I got there, it was pitch black. I rubbed my eyes and looked outside again before running a short ways to another window on the wall. Once again, pitch black.

I was astonished; how were there NO streetlights? Was this office building in the middle of the wilderness? I couldn't see how far down the ground was, but I strongly considered forcing the window open and finding out. But then what? Would I just wander into the blackness and hope to find someone's cabin? Or a street? That seemed better than wandering around an abandoned office building, so I forced open the window and then the sound of heavy rain surrounded my ears. It was pouring outside, and I could even hear the distant rumble of thunder.

This caused me to stop and stare out into the darkness, filling my mind with thoughts of running soaking wet through the forest. It sounded exceedingly unpleasant, but at least I would be outside and closer to home; or. . . even more lost. I took some deep breaths as I tried to muster my confidence, but when I looked down into the pitch black, the thought of breaking my legs stopped me. What was I doing? I had no idea how far down it was, and my only hope if I got injured was my phone.

My phone, that's right! I closed the window and pulled out my phone, anxious to see if I had any service. The battery was at a disheartening 3%, but I was immediately dejected when I saw the top right list, in big, tormenting letters, "No service."

I shook my head and sighed. Jumping out the window might be suicide, and I wasn't willing to take that chance. I was making it out of here, if only to tell the story. This place was insane, more expansive than any building I had ever been in; not to mention the deformed creatures here that looked like the product of some twisted experiment. I was still trying to process what that thing even was down there, and I knew for fact that

I had stumbled upon something that was being hidden from the public. This was undoubtedly some secret testing facility, and that might mean I could never tell my story. Maybe the fact that I was even here in the first place meant I was bound for the grave, whether that was by some vicious creature, or by whoever made this place. Or, maybe they would pay me to keep quiet?

Despite the terror of this wretched building, I could not deny that I was curious. How many buildings did those tunnels connect to, and why did so much of it seem abandoned? When was the last time anybody was even here, and what were these human experiments gone wrong? I wanted to know more, so I mustered my resolve and kept on. I figured there was probably another elevator or stairwell that would take me down to the base floor from here, but I was wary of letting myself believe I was almost out again.

I passed by a half dozen black windows through the unnervingly quiet office space, and took one of the doors at the far end of the room. I planned to use the straight wall of the windows as my reference point and stay along it as long as I could. The door opened into more empty office space, but this time there were two chairs sitting in the center of the room. There were also four more doors which quickly extinguished my plan of staying along the window wall; each of them sat along the wall directly across from the windows.

I opened the closest one first, which led into a small, square room with nothing but an empty desk set against the wall. I went to the next door over, and could now hear rain more clearly; maybe I was near an exterior stairway or fire exit? I tested the doorknob, which was locked, and sighed before walking over to open the third door. The knob stuck again, but then released and opened to a much larger room that had a dozen or so rectangular support columns scattered throughout the empty space.

The size of the room was particularly unsettling and brought flashbacks of the foggy garage. The space was well lit, but the hairs on my neck stood on end as I walked towards the center of the room. I felt like I was trespassing, like someone was watching me. It was as if I had stumbled into a vacant retail building. This place felt completely desolate and looked like it had been abandoned for decades. Dark spots on the carpet showed the outlines of furniture that had once been here, and I now noticed sparse bits of trash around the floor. Scraps of crumpled paper and pen caps along with bits of food debris were almost mixed into the carpet, and I even noticed some patches of fuzzy green mold. Whoever *was* here appeared to have left in a hurry.

I scanned the perimeter of the room for any doors or hallways, but there were none; just black windows that were partially covered by damaged, rectangular blinds. I turned to head back towards the door I came in from, and then felt a creeping sensation up my spine, causing me to sprint out of the room. Something just felt wrong in there. Whether it was my fear of seeing another creature, or just the chilling space, I wanted to distance myself from it. I went back into the room of four doors and sighed; it was as if I was walking on eggshells around every corner, just waiting to be ambushed by God knows what's next, yet I had literally no choice. I had to keep going. I decided to check the very last door before backtracking towards the elevator. It was near the end of the room, and I got a sick feeling when I noticed it partially propped open

I stood frozen in place with wide eyes, staring at the dark crack of the door. There was no light coming from behind it, and I thought I should just leave it alone. Whatever opened it is probably back there. Maybe it's sleeping, or waiting to attack someone. I didn't know what to do. It could be the way out, or another seven-foot-tall abomination. If I don't check it, it will fester in the back of my mind; the creature could wake up and lurk around the office while I'm exploring. But, if it *is* something, what do I do? Race back to the elevator, or just run as far away as I can. There was no good option, but I knew it would torment me if I left it. I had to check it; there was no way I could deal with the fear that something is in there while I'm wandering the level.

I took slow breaths, and quietly paced towards the door. My heart pounded in my chest. It was all I could hear as I reached the tips of my fingers towards the edge of the door. I pressed lightly, causing the door to slowly drift open. My breathing had grown shallow, and my entire body was tense, ready to bolt at any sign of movement. The door was now over halfway open, revealing a room that was still entirely black. I slid a tiny bit closer so I could open the door further, now in a full lunge.

With the door open and the room still pitch black, nothing had attacked me. I wanted to just leave it alone, but I had to see if it was the way out, so I inched closer to the doorway. I stared into the blackness, and then reached onto the interior wall and immediately found a light switch. I flipped the switch and jumped back, ready to see the charging figure of a grotesque beast, but instead it was another small, plain office room.

Parts of the room remained blurry for a moment, as my

eyes seemed to be oversensitive to the light, but then I noticed a small fridge plugged in next to the desk along the wall. I was dumbfounded at first, and thought I was certainly hallucinating, but when I went over to investigate, the fridge remained. I could not, for the life of me, figure out why someone would have left this here. I could tell it was running, too, from the soft electrical hum vibrating through the room.

"Tsk! What are the odds?" I spat, shaking my head. Whatever is in there is certainly rotten and full of mold, but I was curious, so I popped open the door. Sure enough, sitting on the middle shelf were three glass bottles filled with a beige tinted liquid. They each were covered with an old looking label, like something from the 40's, and had a photograph of a queen above fancy lettering that spelled "Almond Water."

I was as stupefied as I was curious; was almond water even a *thing* back then? And why was it in this office; why now? It was as strange as this place, and despite my initial impression that the fridge would only be filled with things that were old and moldy, I was thirsty. As a matter of fact, the last drink I had was a lukewarm sip of coffee from the bottom of a styrofoam cup in my work van. I had run God knows how many miles without even taking a sip of water and couldn't recall seeing any drinking fountains. Besides, who's to say the water would even be running in this building?

I was parched, and knew that was probably contributing to my declining mental state, so I decided to see if I could find an expiration date on any of the bottles. I mean, they appeared decades old, so I wasn't especially hopeful, and after failing to find a date on any of the bottles, I thought hard about whether or not to risk it. If I opened it and it smelled bad, then it was for sure a no go, and if it tasted bad, I would spit it out. But, I had to drink *something* soon.

I grabbed one of the bottles from the fridge and loosened the cap. It popped open with a bit of force, and gave me hope that, at the very least, the seal was still intact. I brought the open bottle to my nose and took a slight whiff; it smelled faintly of vanilla and rose water. Not bad. I sniffed it again before bringing the bottle to my lips and pouring a sip into my mouth to swish around and taste. The flavor was light and sweet, like coconut water with less cream. It was actually pretty good, and immediately began quenching my increasingly apparent thirst.

I ended up guzzling down the whole bottle, and planned to slip the other two into my tool kit when I realized I had dropped it down in the tunnel when I saw that creature. Damn, there was NO getting that thing back. I grieved the loss of all my tools, perhaps my best asset here, but the hydration from the strange liquid seemed to help calm me down, increasing my lucidity and slowing down my thoughts. I was finally able to take a refreshing deep breath, which slowed my heart rate and gave me a second to think about everything that happened. I put my hands on my head and stared out of the doorway into empty office space, weary but mildly sedated. I wondered where Tommy was; if that thing I had seen down in the tunnels had actually been him and if I was just hallucinating. I tried to remember where he had told me to go, and whether he had any way of knowing where I was now.

I looked around the office room for anything else that might be helpful and considered breaking off one of the desk legs to use as a weapon. Maybe I could lock a door with it too, but I figured my efforts were better spent trying to find the way out of here. I decided to head back into the room with four doors, and immediately noticed that the storm had gotten louder. The idea of jumping from a fourth story window in the middle of a storm seemed even more foolish now, and though I hated being here, at least it was sheltered. Plus, now that I had checked all the doors, I could take this large room off of my to-do list and enjoy a little satisfaction in making some progress.

I walked past the third door that I left open to the expansive room, and got a chill as I glimpsed at the vast space. It was still just as uncomfortable, even with some of my sanity back, so I hurried out of the room back to the long, rectangular office space where the elevator doors were still closed. My vision almost seemed clearer now, making me think I had been suffering from dehydration worse than I thought. The clarity I had gotten from the almond water was, while noticeable, still not cutting the eeriness of this space. It all felt so empty and desolate, like whoever had been here before packed up and left without any thought of ever returning. I wondered how long it had been since this office had been occupied by anything other than janitors and realtors. When was the last time people actually gathered here for work and why had it been abandoned so abruptly?

There was a white hallway staring at me from across the room that appeared to turn, along with some more doors along the elevator wall. I decided to go investigate the hallway first, figuring it was probably the most likely place to find a stairwell. The turn led to a narrow hallway with more doors scattered along the opposing walls. Sure enough, just like the others, this building was revealing itself to be expansive and convoluted, but I decided to follow the main hallway as far as it went before checking any of the doors.

The hall seemed to be taking me deeper into the office away from the wall of windows, which dampened my hopes of finding a stairwell to the outside. I figured I was at least three stories up in the building and wondered if the levels below me would be just more abandoned office space. I also wondered why the elevator I had taken up didn't have any other buttons for more floors. This only added to my suspicion that I was somewhere I wasn't supposed to be; a secret floor that was only accessible from the tunnel below.

I took the narrow hallway to the end and wound up in a room that appeared nearly identical to the one I had come in on. The only difference was that this one had some vertical support columns. I checked the first two doors, which were locked, and then opened the third one to a big, unlit gymnasium. It was so terribly out of place in this building that it haunted me. Not to mention the single door on the far end of the empty space that made my stomach bubble with a curious dread. I hesitated for a moment before slamming the door and turning around to keep following the main hallway. A gymnasium was far too strange and eerie to be wandering through right now. My mind couldn't take it; that door on the back end of it would just have to remain unopened. Besides, there was probably just basketballs and janitor stuff in there anyway.

I could still hear the sound of thunder and rain outside, and wondered if the halls might just loop back and force me to investigate more doors. There seemed to be so much of this level to explore, and with no maps or signs to an exit, I felt like I was just flipping a coin on getting out of here. It was sickening, like I was completely lost with no means of communication or any clue how far I was from home. I had heard stories of people getting lost in the woods and national parks, but never would I have thought someone could get lost in a building. The concerns of finding shelter and building a fire weren't in play here. Instead, it was about keeping my mental state intact and hoping to come across another human being or a clue as to how to get out of here.

The hall I was following stretched on for a while and appeared to be getting dimmer. Either the fluorescent bulbs were close to burning out, or I was just starting to lose it again, but then I saw hall turn at the end with bright light coming from the other side. I figured it was just more office space, but the hope of finding something different made me jog to see where the light was coming from. When I rounded the corner, a large, brightly lit room filled with cubicles filled my view. They appeared to stretch on to infinity, with the furthest parts of the room masked in a light fog.

My instinct was to turn back; this did not look like the way out, but I was interested because so many objects were still left in here. The desks had laptops, papers, and pens lying on them, along with black office chairs that made the room look like it had been in use recently. It was the closest thing to active civilization I had seen in the last 12 hours, and I wanted to see if I could find anything here that might point me towards the way out. That, or clue me in to where in the hell I was.

I walked down the center pathway through the cubicles, peering over the low walls onto the desks to look for any leftover documents or keys. I had passed a few rows when I realized that I had not seen a single personal effect; no family photos, plants, or decor; just work supplies. This part of the building was also warmer—humid even—and I could feel sweat beginning to stain my shirt. It reminded me of the office back at my job, except much larger, and I couldn't help but be reminded of the busyness of the place. "Check emails, call customers, file for permits," it all seemed to be coming back, and I thought this might be the real reason I was beginning to sweat. Maybe it wasn't warmer at all; I was just stressing about work. The aroma of stale coffee even percolated through the air, probably from decades of spilled cups of the stuff in the carpet and desks.

I had passed two dozen cubicles when I thought I was probably further in than I could have seen from the entryway, figuring the light fog was just obscuring the back wall, but all I could see ahead of me was more cubicles. Wherever I was, it was an absurdly massive operation; too big to lack any kind of fire-exit or easy way out, so I knew at some point, I would *have* to come across an exit. The humidity of the office was beginning to fatigue me too, so I decided to open another bottle of the almond and sip on it while I kept exploring the cubicles.

The further from the entrance I got, the wearier I felt. If this wasn't the way out, I would have to go all the way back, and then I would still be at a complete loss at where to look next. I eventually grew tired of looking into every cubicle and ended up just walking while staring up at the tall ceiling filled with square tiles. It seemed to stretch on forever, covered with square fluorescent lighting that filled the whole space with a sterile, white light. The almond water was keeping my head level, but not quite enough to ward off the audible hallucinations I was having of shuffling papers and typing keys. The whole place felt restless, stuck on an endless coffee high and monotonous work cycle.

I was probably over a half mile in when I noticed the floor began to get less clean. The carpet now appeared dingier, along with the cubicle walls that had light brown splotches, like someone had splattered coffee on them. Even the ceiling was beginning to look less intact, with displaced tiles, loose hanging wires, and discolored trim. The office appeared to be growing more decrepit the further I went, showing signs of mildew and wear on the carpet. Patches of fuzzy blue mold dotted the cubicle walls, which were now dark with rot where they met the floor. These all came along with a growing musty smell, amplified by the humidity, and eventually made me stop going any further. I should have listened to myself; this was not the right way.

I dreaded turning back and returning to the office, with my suspicion now growing that some kind of creature was in those empty rooms. My instincts had been screaming at me to **get out** when I was in there, and now I began to think it was for a reason. I knew I was probably just being paranoid, but my god was it intrusive, and I really wanted to just find the end of the cubicles. I had to just stop and think for a minute. I needed to breathe and sort this out.

I found a cubicle that wasn't completely filled with mold, and sat in the office chair, leaning over on my knees. I rubbed my face and stared across the pathway into the cubicle on the other side, overwhelmed by a growing sense of hopelessness. I knew it was probably close to morning now and I was exhausted. I wasn't any closer to home, and with no service and a phone that was basically dead, I was completely on my own. I had no idea where Tommy was, or if he had any way of knowing where I was, but the 5th floor office I had gotten locked in in the first place was now miles away. It's not like that even mattered at this point; I didn't know how to get back, and even if I did, the hell spawn was enough to keep me away. The only reason I had gone wandering in the first place was Tommy, and, more importantly, my boss. Had I just called 9-1-1 before giving Tommy my phone information, I could have been home safe last night.

Though I knew it was probably close to sunrise outside, time didn't feel real anymore. This whole cubicle section had no windows; just bleak, white walls. . .*but*, if I could make my way back to the windows, I could see if there was anything, or, anyone, outside. Even if it didn't necessarily put me any closer to an exit, seeing the sun would be comforting; just a little reminder that the world outside still existed.

I realized then that I had been oblivious to what was sitting right in front of me; a *computer*! I'd never heard of an internet chatroom for 9-1-1, but at least it was some kind of communication. I could post on a forum or something and let somebody know that I needed help. I flipped open the laptop and was immediately dejected when I saw the screen ask for a password. I wasn't surprised, with my luck being as bad as it had been, but then I saw a guest option, and immediately clicked on it, which brought me to the computer's desktop. Joy flooded my heart as I quickly clicked on the internet explorer and waited for it to load. The cursor spiraled for a few seconds, before a gray screen popped up that read: "No internet."

Determined, I pulled up the available Wi-Fi tab and discovered a single network labeled: "Level 4.3" It was, of course, password protected, and after a dozen guesses, including "kill me, almond water, and Caius 69," I started searching the desktop for any clues. There weren't many programs other than what was installed on the computer by the factory, but I did notice a folder labeled "emails" and clicked on it before finding a single document titled "Employee Letter - 6/17/2001."

> *"Good morning section 4.3,*
>
> *We are writing to inform you of this week's progress report (please see attached), as well as to give you an update on the status of construction in the west wing. Due to concerns raised by employees with our H.R department, we are now implementing a mandatory parking policy, effective immediately. From now on, employees are required to park in the McCrahn ramp, accessible from the eastern side of the building.*
>
> *The active construction on the western ramp poses a safety hazard, and though we have permitted access to employees because of its proximity to the office space, any employees seen passing through that section now will be suspended without pay. The ramp is scheduled for completion within the next 6-8 months, and we ask for your patience and compliance during this time.*
> *We understand the inconvenience this may cause but ask that you please schedule your morning commute times accordingly.*
>
> *Sincerely,*
> *Dan Weston"*

Standard, cold-hearted bureaucracy; not sure what I was expecting. The email was almost giving me Deja-vu, as the company I worked for had just sent in half of its fleet vehicles for service, and was now making us drive old vans with broken A/C and lousy suspension. I was almost ready to just turn the computer off and keep exploring, but then a familiar detail in the email caught my eye: the sender's last name. Weston; that was my bosses last name. I didn't know who Dan was, but the spelling of the last name was correct, and I couldn't help but wonder if the two were related.

Before closing out the email, I decided to open the progress report to see if I could find any more info about the company. From what I could see on the spreadsheet, it looked as though this was a carpet manufacturing company, and in the top right, the address read as:

> *BMC Inc.*
> *778 Industrial Pkwy*
> *Seymour, IN 47274*

Reading the address gave me a bit of relief, as it showed I was still in Indiana, and not far from where I lived. I'd never heard of BMC, but I knew where Industrial Parkway was, and figured I was probably just turned around inside the manufacturing complex. The email was old, though, and I wouldn't be surprised if the company had gone out of business. A bunch of venture capitalists had moved their businesses here in the late 90's and then quickly sold after struggling to find labor, so I thought there was a good chance this office space had already changed hands a few times since 2001. The last owners probably just defaulted on their mortgage and decided to take everything they could before the bank foreclosed on the building.

This made the building feel even more desolate. The office's state of disrepair looked like it had been years since anyone had been here, and now the space was just in an abandoned limbo. I knew for a fact that this was not the only foreclosed property either, because at least a dozen other businesses had gone bankrupt in the area. Most of them were just filler industries that jumped on Seymour's boom in the 90's and struggled to stay afloat before finally deciding to cut their losses and sell. The boom had brought a bunch of development to the town, bringing in a new mall and some restaurants, but 90% of those places had closed in the last decade and now just sat as empty retail space. I was quite literally in a complex of foreclosed industrial buildings.

My boss's last name in that email made more sense now; his family was one of the groups that bought up a lot of the real estate in the town and developed it; this building was probably just one of their failed ventures. This did beg the question though; why did their building connect the Caius complex underground? The tunnel did not appear to be "new" construction, and I didn't recall any major excavation operation when the companies moved in, so maybe it was just some kind of nuclear-era design. It seemed like a major security flaw, though, connecting a government building to some abandoned office. Maybe most people didn't know about it and the government decided to just keep it secret.

This whole night had been beyond strange, and despite the small shred of normalcy that I found in the email, the weariness brought on by this place was inescapable. Staving off panic while being thrown between hopelessness and delusions of escape was driving me mad, and I knew I was beginning to lose my sanity again. In all honesty, I didn't even trust my memory anymore, particularly about those weird creatures.

They seemed too horrible to even be real, and whether this was to calm myself down or simply cope, I told myself they weren't real. Sleep deprivation was likely a major contributor to everything going on, and I knew its effects would only worsen with time. I needed every edge up as possible to get the hell out of this place; trying to retrace my steps back to the windows while being groggy and paranoid seemed like a bad idea. Sleep was the smart choice, despite the sleeping arrangements being nothing more than the floor of this rotted cubicle, but at least it was quiet. Even a few hours of shuteye would help.

Rest was fleeting. My dreams were filled deformed creatures chasing me through vast, empty spaces, and all I could think was that I was only getting deeper into the labyrinth and further from escape. I think I only slept a few hours before I started fading in and out of consciousness and tried laying on my side to see if I could get comfortable. Time lost more of its meaning the longer I laid there. With no windows or changes in lighting, everything just felt stuck, like it was frozen in time. It didn't matter how long I laid here; nothing in this place cared. I could turn into a skeleton and the space would sit unchanged. The feeling haunted me.

I was beginning to wake up now, feeling irritable and no less rested, when the silhouette of a humanoid figure began to take shape behind my bleary vision. I didn't pay much mind to it at first, brushing it off as sleep hypnagogia, but when it persisted through some long blinks, I focused on it a bit more, watching its details reveal themselves. Its face was. . .red, charred almost, next to wide open beady eyes, staring directly at me. It was too freaky to even be real; like some horrible burn victim standing on all fours, smiling at me from the center aisle of the office. Its body was skeletal and sickly, with visible muscle sinew and ligaments.

I was frozen in shock, stuck on the floor and staring at the lidless eyes of this wretched creature searching my body. I squeezed my eyes closed and tried to make it go away, but when they opened back up, the creature was now closer, crawling towards me. Unable to move and still in shock, my only option seemed to be to play dead and hope that it would go away. I sorely doubted my chances of success; this thing wanted to eat me. I could hear its congested, heavy breathing as it grew closer, and even began to smell an acrid rot.

I had accepted fate by the time it was at arm's reach, and the last thing I saw before closing my eyes was the leathery red skin of its hand reaching out with pale black fingernails. Then I heard a metallic thud, which sent a jolt through my entire body. It was just enough noise to make me move, and I scrambled to push myself backwards from the beast, but when I opened my eyes, I saw it running off into the cubicles, shrieking like the devil. I stared with wide eyes, disturbed by the thought of that creature now lurking somewhere deeper in the building, when another figure caught my eye, standing in the aisle next to my cubicle. It was a tall man, probably 250lbs, bald with a grimace, wearing a navy car mechanics suit. I couldn't believe my eyes; it was another human being.

His large hand was extended out towards me, and as I took it, he jerked me to my feet and then took a step back. He was wielding a crowbar, and with a million things running through my head, I did not know where to start.

"Took me all night to find you; it's a good thing I did, too. That thing almost killed you."

'I. . .thank you. You don't know how good it is to see another human being." I said gratefully. "I've been stuck here for. . .wait, find me? Are you. . ."

"Tommy; and yes, I know. I've been here all night and morning too, trying to catch up to you." he said with a twinge of irritation in his voice. He then slid a backpack off his shoulder and tucked the crowbar into a pouch sewn to the side.

"Then maybe you can tell me what in the hell is going on?" I shot. "You cut me off from emergency services; I could have been out of here yesterday!"

Tommy raised his eyebrow before dropping his crowbar into a holster on his belt and folding his arms.

"Not my call; that was the **bosses.**"

Astounded, I stared at him with my jaw hanging open before rubbing my face and throwing down my arms. "Well I guess that just makes it okay then? Leaving me in this hellscape to fight off science experiments gone wrong."

Tommy, staring smugly at me, shook his head and then turned and started walking away.

"Where are you going? Come back here!" I shouted. This had no effect on him, so I ran out of the cubicle and stopped in front of him.

"You're going to tell me what's going on." I demanded, glaring up at him. He looked at me with a tired expression before pushing past me and continuing down the aisle. Fuming, I spun around and grabbed his shirt, causing him to turn and swat my hand away.

"We have a *very* long way to go. Now, you can wait around here for that wretch to go and get his friends, or, we can start heading back. I'd suggest we keep moving." Tommy said calmly. Right as I was about to protest, a blood curdling, cacophony of screeches echoed from far off in the fog of the cubicles, causing Tommy to tilt his head at me and purse his lips. Fear crept through my bones, and so I shooed Tommy along and kept close behind.

"You said that thing was a wretch?" I asked sheepishly. "What. . .is that?"

"It's what happens when someone gets lost in here for too long—dehydration, lack of sleep, and loss of overall sanity—it turns you into a wretch." Tommy said matter-of-factly.

"Are there lots of these things? How many people are getting lost and turning into wretches?"

"Depends. No one knows exactly. Most estimate they are somewhere in the thousands."

"*Thousands?*" I said, flabbergasted. "How have I never heard of this?"

Still walking, Tommy began shaking his head. "People go missing all the time, and, more often than not, they end up here." he said like he expected me to believe that people vanishing into rabbit holes was normal.

"Right, everybody who goes missing ends up in an old office building in Indiana. Why don't you tell me what's really going on?" I sneered.

"You still think you're in Indiana? Ha!" Tommy scoffed. "We're in The Back Rooms, bud."

Chapter 6

The Back Rooms

"The *Back Rooms.*" I said wryly. "So what, we came across some *secret* hallway in a department store and now we can't get out? Give me a break; tell me where the hell we are." I demanded.

"I mean, you aren't far off. The Back Rooms is where you go if you happen to no-clip out of physical space. Kind of like in a video game if you glitch out of the terrain; you end up in a weird in-between sort of space that you aren't really supposed to see." Tommy explained. We were still walking down the aisle of cubicles, but I could see the interior beginning to improve. It wasn't nearly as degraded or damaged as where I had laid down to sleep, and I could now see the hallway back into the main office.

"Yeah, I'm not buying it. I know you and my boss are into some sort of shady stuff; that's why he sent you to come get me in the first place. I don't care why; what you two do is your own business, but don't talk to me like I'm a child. The *Back Rooms*; what a load of nonsense." I spat. He didn't really think I was going to believe him, did he?

"Call it what you want, and tell yourself whatever helps you deal with it, but I'm just telling you the facts." Tommy said, stopping at the entrance to the dark hallway. "If you'd like, I can tell you that we're in *fairy land*, and that those creatures are just big meanies." Tommy traipsed down the hallway, beginning a condescending monologue.

"Yes, we're on a big quest to save the princess. And all these rooms, they are magical puzzles with all sorts of surprises!"

"You can stop now; let's just get out of here." I said, fed up with his foolery.

We continued through the empty hallway, passing by the office doors and gray walls until coming to stop at an unassuming room with the door propped open. Tommy then turned around, looking at me with a wondering expression.

"What? Is this the way back?" I asked impatiently.

"I don't know, what do you think?"

"What do *I* think? You're the one they sent here to rescue me! Why in the hell would I know the way out?" I shot back. What in the heck was he thinking?

"Does it seem like the right way to you?"

"I have absolutely no idea! My thinking is what led me into the middle of a decaying office building that is apparently infested with wretches!" I yelled.

"Alright then; we'll go this way." Tommy said smugly, ambling into the room. I peered over my shoulder once more at the desolate office before hurrying through the doorway to catch up with Tommy.

"What? You don't know where you're going?" I asked angrily.

"At some point you're going to realize that we're in the same boat." he said earnestly. The room we had entered was very similar to one I had come into from the elevator; vertical support columns scattered around wide office space without any furniture.

"So what? We're just wandering around here, hoping that we find an exit before we come across another entity?" I said in disbelief. Tommy continued walking, leading us towards another door at the end of the room.

"Not exactly," he said. "There's an exit somewhere around level 10, but I'm not sure how to get there." he said, sending me into a fury.

"We might as well go make friends with one of those wretches then, since, according to you, we're on the path to becoming one." I spat. Tommy had just gotten to the door and was about to open it, when he turned around and grabbed me by the collar of my shirt with two meaty hands.

"I'd have gladly left you to be eaten if it weren't for the fact that I was specifically sent here to save you. Now, you can piss and moan the whole time I'm doing so, or you can shut up and try to deal with the fact that we are lost." Tommy snarled, glaring at me with furious eyes. "No, I do not know where we are; I have never been this deep before. I know people who *have*, and most don't come back." He then released his grip and turned back to open the door. "It's a damn miracle you made it past level 3, anyway."

Shaken, and still confused, I followed Tommy into the room, and shortly after spotted an elevator at the far back wall. It was starkly different from the one I had come in on. This one was ornate, like something out of a hotel from the 1930's, with a cherry wood frame and burgundy velvet on the door, along with brass trim. I couldn't help but notice how out of place it felt against the drab white environment of the office, but it brought a glimmer of hope in that it was finally something different.

"I've been tricked into thinking I was almost out enough times to be skeptical, but I have to ask: is this. . .the way out?" I said resignedly.

"Level 5; The Terror Hotel. I've heard stories; never thought I'd have the chance to see if they were true, though." Tommy replied. "Keep your wits about you; this level isn't the most dangerous, but it wears on your psyche."

"I think crawling humanoid zombie creatures are pretty taxing on the psyche." I scoffed. "As long as there aren't any more of those, I think we'll be alright."

"It's not the entities here that you should be worried about, Jeff."

Tommy pressed the large golden button on the elevator, causing a mechanical rumbling in the floor. It was almost like white noise, and then a loud "ding" sounded, causing me to jolt backwards. Tommy looked back at me with a canted expression, but my eyes were locked on the doors as they began to slowly open.

"You're going to need to get a hold of yourself. Being all jumpy like that is going to drain your sanity in there. Try and stay calm; I'll tell you if we need to run." Tommy said. I wasn't assured, wondering about what could be worse than the horrors I had already seen, but at least Tommy seemed like he knew what he was doing. Although displeased, he didn't seem all that scared, and kept a neutral expression as he stepped into the elevator. I took a deep breath and stepped through the doors onto the red carpet floor. Then, Tommy pressed the only button on the pad, and after a brief pause, the doors shakily closed. Old music began to play from the speaker above, causing us both to look up as the elevator began moving down.

"I don't think this is right; we're in the lower levels of the building. Shouldn't we be going up?" I said, puzzled.

"Hmph, I thought you would have learned by now; this place isn't like the buildings back home. Places don't always go from A to B."

"What? Like there's a different way up? I guess I should have figured that out when I went through the tunnel with pipes all over the wall." I said, recalling the expanse of dark, lengthy hallways.

"Not exactly. The Back Rooms are a non-Euclidean space, so while it may appear you are moving in a straight line, you might be moving in circles, or vice versa." Tommy explained. "It's part of what makes escaping so challenging."

"So, what you're saying is there isn't a defined way out? What in the heck are you supposed to do then?"

"Keep moving and hope an exit pops up. While the paths to them are changing, the characteristics are the same. You're pretty lucky to have gotten this far. Level 3 is a major barrier to further exploration." Tommy said with a twinge of admiration in his voice.

"Those pipe tunnels? Yeah, I got chased by some 9ft tall bloodthirsty humanoid thing. It would have gotten me had it not been for that elevator."

"Skin-stealers; they're common throughout The Back Rooms. Best bet is to move quietly so they can't hear you." The elevator came to a stop, followed by another loud ding. It startled me again, but not as severely this time. Then Tommy looked at me and said in a grim voice: "We're here."

The doors opened to what appeared to be an old hotel

lobby. There were ornate couches and fancy wooden tables atop a beige patterned carpet. In the center of the room sat a large, patterned Persian red rug, illuminated by a hanging brass chandelier overhead. The walls were covered in damask wallpaper, dotted with wooden-framed artwork and candle sconces, and the whole vibe of the place was antiquated. I half expected to be greeted by a bellhop, but there was nobody at the front desk. Brass luggage carriers were organized neatly next to the elevator, and faux plants decorated the lobby, but it was clear nobody had been here in a very long time.

"Come on, let's get moving; no use wasting our sanity standing here." Tommy said, stepping out of the elevator. I couldn't help but keep looking around as we walked through the lobby, noting the architecture and antique decorations. I had never been in a hotel this old, but it felt strangely familiar, like a remnant of the past that had somehow found its way into my memory; a relic of a past society. The lobby itself wasn't very large, so we quickly ended up in the hallways of hotel rooms. Red ornate runner carpets dotted the ground, and at this point I was just following Tommy; nothing in this place looked like it was leading out.

"You hear that?" Tommy whispered, sending a chill down my spine.

"No, what?" I hissed.

"The whispers; you don't hear them behind the walls?"

I stopped walking for a moment and listened. At first there was nothing; maybe just some music, but then the faintest voice spoke from behind the door we were standing by. I couldn't make out what it was saying, but it was unmistakably there.

"Yeah, I hear it. Think someone's in that room?" I

asked, reaching for the handle. Tommy's eyes were wide, and as he saw what I was doing, he grabbed my hand.

"No," he snapped. "Don't check the rooms."

"Why not?" I asked, off put by his sudden fear. "If someone is in there, they could help us."

"There's nobody there; it's a hallucination." Tommy said ominously. "Like I said before, I'd heard rumors about this level. It's best just to ignore it; the rooms don't lead anywhere good." I stared at the door with wide eyes, wondering what he was so afraid of, before deciding to defer to his judgment and keep walking.

The whispers continued as we walked, seeming to come from deeper in the hotel. It almost sounded like the rabble of a cocktail party, but there were no signs that a soul had been here in the last century. There were no modern upgrades, either. No video cameras, keycard doors, or fluorescent lighting. The whole place felt like it had been frozen in time 100 years ago. Now, here we were, wandering around it; some lonely slice of old society that was long forgotten.

We must have walked past 3 dozen doors before finally coming to the end of the hallway, where it opened up to a wide room with a vaulted ceiling. At the end of the room were two red-carpeted staircases, leading up to a landing where a set of French doors sat, covered with curtains. Tommy continued towards the ornate staircase, and I followed him to the landing, before he paused and looked back. This spooked me, more than it should have, not because something was wrong, but because of the growing look of fear on his face.

"What? Do you see something?" I asked anxiously.

"You see that painting?" he said, nodding his head

towards the wall. On it was an old picture of a woman in a ruffled dress against a farm background. The color was quite faded, which gave the background a dusty, weathered hue.

"Yeah? What about it?"

"I swear the eyes followed me as I walked past it." Tommy said uncomfortably.

"You're losing it worse than me now! Just keep going; I want to get out of here." I said, motioning him up the stairs. Tommy glanced back at the picture and exhaled before continuing up the stairwell. As I followed, I could not help but notice the same thing; the eyes of the picture following me in my peripherals. I peeked over my shoulder once we made it to the landing and saw that the picture hadn't changed. Tommy was starting to scare me.

Long, straight hallways stretched from both sides of the landing deeper into the hotel, but I knew we were investigating what was behind the French doors first. Tommy brushed the curtains aside to peer in, and I stood a little ways back, growing restless.

"What do you see? Any exits?" I asked, slinking towards the doors.

"It's a ballroom." Tommy answered, pulling open the doors.

We both stood still, staring into the large, quiet room, where a small table and chairs sat in the center as the only pieces of furniture in the otherwise empty space. A bright crystal chandelier hung in the center of the room, illuminating most of the patterned red carpet and vaulted ceiling. The light didn't reach the walls, though, which caused the edges of the room to be fully shadowed.

"I don't like it." Tommy said, turning towards me. "Let's go somewhere else."

"What do you mean? There's a double door on the backend of the room. It's probably the way out." I replied.

"You don't know that. There could be a whole nest of wretches back there." Tommy snapped. He started to close the doors, but I stopped him, grabbing the frame.

"You said we didn't have to worry about entities here. Now you're telling me there's nests of wretches?" I hissed. Tommy glared at me, still holding the door, before pulling it back open and motioning into the room.

"Go ahead, if you're so sure. I'm just saying we should be careful. This room feels off."

"It's a double steel door that looks totally out of place; we might as well check it." I said, walking past him into the room. I took a few paces into the room before looking over my shoulder at Tommy who was still lingering in the doorway.

"What are you waiting for? Let's go." I hissed.

"You go ahead and check it; I'll be here when you come back." Tommy replied. This sent a creeping dread up my spine at the thought of being alone, which got worse as I looked across the dim ballroom at the partially lit steel doors. The room looked darker and larger now, and I could even hear the faint sound of a staticky gramophone playing old jazz. All my senses screamed to get out; I wasn't going alone, so I jumped back through the doorway next to Tommy.

"What do you propose then? These hallways just lead to more hotel rooms with whispering ghosts and paintings with eyes that follow you. At least this looks like it goes somewhere different." I said, glaring at Tommy.

"All I'm saying is something is off in there. I know you feel it too."

"It's just an empty ballroom. Those doors could take us *home*. I don't want to be here anymore than you do, but we have no choice but to try and get out." I insisted. I didn't understand why this level had shaken him so much. It was unsettling, sure, but so was everything in these so-called "Back Rooms." Maybe he was losing his sanity, or was just especially afraid of hotels, but either way, we had to keep moving. Lingering here on this balcony was making me weary. I was beginning to notice more paintings with wandering eyes, while the distant whispers were beginning to sound sinister. The very architecture of this place seemed like it wanted us gone, and as I glanced over my shoulder at the hallway back the way we came, I saw something dart into one of the rooms.

"Come on; let's just go check it out. Standing here isn't getting us anywhere." I said, tugging on Tommy's sleeve. I was done standing here; this hotel seemed to leer at us with malice, as if we had desecrated it with our presence. Tommy peered into the ballroom, and then at me, before reluctantly stepping through the doorway. The sense of dread immediately came back, as the whole room seemed to grow colder once we passed through the French doors. Tommy had taken the lead, despite his increasingly apparent fear, and was hurrying through the room. The bright light of the chandelier grew more glaring as we moved from the shadowy edges of the room, and once we were standing beneath it, Tommy stopped to inspect the table.

"Anything helpful?" I asked, walking up next to him.

"No, but look at this," he said, pointing to a blotch of purple slime on the tablecloth.

"What is *that?*" I exclaimed, leaning in to get a closer look. Tommy reached out with his forefinger and smeared a glob of the goo onto it, before bringing his finger and sticking into his mouth.

"Yuck! Are you crazy?" I shouted.

"SHH!" he hissed. It's moth jelly." Tommy then lifted his head and squinted, looking around the room before pointing towards a dark object in the corner. "Look, over there."

I followed his gaze and immediately felt a pit in my stomach when I saw it. Attached to the dark wall was an enormous moth, colored black and gray with a fuzzy abdomen and waving antennae. Its wings pulsed slowly, detailed with markings that looked like skulls and bones.

"Oh my god!" I hissed. "What in the world. . ."

"Death moth; looks like a female. That would explain the uneasy feeling. They rapidly drain your sanity." Tommy said with a grimace, eyes still locked on the large insect.

"What do we do?" I asked, frozen in place.

"Just move quietly. It hasn't sensed us yet. Keep your eyes on it, and if it starts flying, run." Tommy said, before beginning to slink towards the steel doors. I crept close behind him, growing wearier by the second. The creature was repulsive, like something out of a nightmare, and I could only imagine what it's face would look like before latching onto me. It wasn't really moving though, and looked almost like it was sleeping, but its drain on my sanity was becoming increasingly apparent. The room seemed to be growing darker, and I had to keep my eyes locked on Tommy to make sure I didn't get off track.

We had made it to the edge of the chandelier's light, and the death moth was almost completely out of sight now, hidden by the darkness. I could barely make out a couple of its features, but then I began to see faces. White eyes and teeth in the dark, emerging from my peripherals. It was the same thing I had seen down in the tunnels; evil faces that were laughing and multiplying, like a plague, filling my soul with horror. My whole body seemed to weaken, and when I looked for Tommy, he was gone. All I could see was white smiling phosphenes in the dark. I didn't know what was happening, but I couldn't walk anymore. I stumbled and was now propped up by my elbows. Had the moth got me? If not, it was only a matter of time. Then I felt something tighten my shirt collar and pull me. The carpet rubbed against my clothes, making it feel like I was being drug through sand. I tried to resist, but the thing dragging me was stronger. There was a growing ringing in my ears, and the laughing faces in the dark swarmed around me. Then everything went white, followed by a loud thud.

Something forced my mouth open before I felt liquid hit my tongue. I coughed and sputtered, trying to fight the creature before I heard Tommy's echoing voice shout, "Drink!" I was completely disoriented, but I obeyed. The liquid tasted familiar, with a light coconut flavor. Then things started to come back. I could see a beige ceiling with fluorescent lighting, and Tommy, kneeling beside me. The room began to take shape as the blurry parts of my vision cleared, and I could see that I was in a hallway.

"You're alright; take some deep breaths." Tommy said. His voice was still echoing, like we were in a fishbowl. I slowly came to, before I sat up and breathed, propping myself against the cold wall. I could see the double steel door; we must have made it out of the ball room.

"What happened?" I asked groggily, rubbing my eyes.

"You passed out. I had to pull you into the hallway."

"There were so many faces in the dark, and my hearing.
. .it just turned to ringing. Did the moth get me?"

"No," Tommy said coldly. "You wouldn't be here if that thing attacked; you'd be paralyzed, being eaten by its larvae." His hand was outstretched with a glass bottle filled with liquid.

"What's this?"

"Almond water. I don't have much, but you better finish that one. Can't have you passing out again when we're trying to avoid entities."

I took a swig from the bottle, again noticing the familiar taste, before I remembered the bottles in my pocket.

"I found some of that stuff earlier too; here." I said, pulling out the glass bottle and showing it to Tommy.

"Keep it; you'll need it. If you ever feel like that again, make sure to drink." Tommy said, nodding towards the almond water I was holding. "You don't gotta finish the bottle or anything; it's better to just drink it occasionally. Some areas will drain your sanity faster than others though."

"I don't understand; are you saying I just got dehydrated?" I scoffed. Tommy paused, looking at me with a serious face.

"No; you were going *insane*. That will cure it." he said, extending out his hand to help me up. "Now come on; you're either gifted or lucky, but you were right about that door. It looks like it's taking us to a new level."

We began walking down the utility hall, passing under fluorescent lights spread between the square ceiling tiles. It looked completely different from the 1930's hotel we had come from, appearing far more modern, like something from an office or commercial space. I wondered if it would just lead us back to the abandoned office, but the existence of it seemed strange next to the hotel. It made it seem like the hotel was built within some larger modern building, and now we were on the outskirts. Imagine that; a creepy, old hotel, placed miles deep in a building, surrounded on all sides by liminal white tunnels. Who would create such a thing?

"Check it out; another elevator." Tommy said, pointing to another ornately framed set of double doors at the end of the hallway. It stood out against the drab-white, glazed cinder block walls of the hallway.

"Guess I was right. Where do you think it goes?" I asked, as we approached the doors.

"I'm not sure. We're supposed to be looking for a boiler room." Tommy responded, pushing the button on the elevator panel. This caused a mechanical rumbling in the floor, and then shortly after, a loud "ding."

"Boiler room?" I said curiously, as the doors opened. "Why there?"

We stepped into the elevator, which looked eerily similar to one we had come in on, and then Tommy pressed the only button on the panel, causing the doors to close. We began moving down, and that old gramophone music started playing again.

"It's the only reliable link to level 6 from the hotel. Somewhere in there is a completely blacked out maintenance hallway." Tommy explained.

"What then? What's level 6 like?" I asked. "What comes after?"

"Well. . .level 6 is. . ." Tommy hesitated.

"What? What is it?" I demanded.

"It's all pitch black. You can't see anything in there."

"Well, don't you have a flashlight in that backpack?" I said, reaching to unzip his bag.

"Hands off!" he shot, spinning the bag away from me. "Don't go rifling through my stuff; you'll get it all unorganized. And trust me, we *need* it organized." Tommy said seriously, causing me to recoil.

"Sorry." I said sheepishly.

"It's fine; we just can't let our guard down here. And no, flashlights aren't going to help us there. The level extinguishes any light sources."

"It does *what?*" How in the hell are we supposed to find our way out of there then?" I spat, entirely dumbfounded by Tommy's plan.

"Just keep wandering until we reach the flooded house on level 7, thalassophobia" Tommy responded, filling my mind with strange images of an ocean before my attention was grabbed by another loud ding as the elevator then came to a stop. Eager to see where we were, I stepped ahead of Tommy and peered through the growing gap in the doors. All I could see was a dark and dusty room at first, and then felt a pit in my stomach. I glanced over my shoulder at Tommy, who had a disappointed look on his face, and then looked back through the elevator doors. The room was dim and had a haze of dust hanging in the air, but the ornate burgundy carpet and textured walls gave me no question; we were still in the hotel.

"Guess you were wrong." Tommy said, pushing past me into the room. Annoyed, I followed him, and immediately noticed we were at a junction in the hotel. The room was long and rectangular, with couches set across from each other along the walls. Two long hallways stretched into the darkness on both sides of the room, along with a receptionist's desk on the wall across from the elevator. It was barely visible in the darkness, but trimmed with a noticeably worn brass that was colored a brownish-copper tone. The whole space felt murky and claustrophobic, bringing back that familiar feeling of dread.

"Go check out that desk; see if you can find anything helpful." Tommy ordered while staring down one of the hallways. I obeyed, and Tommy's eyes followed me for a brief second as I went over to the desk, before darting back to the hallway.

"Anything helpful?" he said impatiently.

"Not yet," I replied, rummaging through the drawers. There weren't any papers or things that looked like a map, but my fingers found a keyring in the back of one the drawers. It jingled as I pulled it out, drawing Tommy's attention.

"Room keys?" Tommy asked quickly.

"Looks like it. There might be some maintenance ones too."

"Grab 'em' and let's get back in the elevator. Just looks like more guest rooms down here." Tommy ordered, walking backwards towards the elevator with his eyes still locked on the dim hallway. Confused, I followed him to the elevator doors and joined him inside.

"Don't you think we should check it out down here first," I suggested. "There might be some clues as to how to get out of here."

Tommy pressed the elevator button, seeming to ignore

me, but the doors did not move. He mashed it again, then started hitting it repeatedly, but the doors remained open.

"What a sick joke," I said glumly. Tommy glowered at me, punching the button once more before craning his head out of the elevator into the dusty darkness.

"You still got those keys?" Tommy said, slinking out of the elevator.

"Yeah, do you want them?" I said quietly.

"No, but keep them handy." Tommy nodded his head and then the two of us crept into the dim room. His eyes were still locked on the rightward hallway as he led us in the opposite direction. I tested the handle on the first door we reached; it didn't have a room number and looked like it was for staff

"Locked." I said, reaching for the keyring. "Think there's a master key on here?"

The keyring then slipped out of my hands onto the burgundy carpet, landing with a soft clink, and as I bent over to pick them up, I felt Tommy's hand stop me.

"Don't move." he hissed. I glanced up at him and then towards the hallway he was staring down. A dozen doors away, barely visible in the dim, dusty air, there was a figure. It was hunched over, lurking slowly down the hall towards us.

"What. . .is that?" I whispered, slowly standing up.

"Hound. It hasn't noticed us yet." Tommy said quietly.

"It's coming right towards us! What do we do?" I hissed.

"Keep your voice down and stay still!" Tommy snapped. The creature was getting closer, its grotesque features emerging from the darkness. The black, scraggly hair and the bony, arched body; it was the same thing I had seen in the garage. Its face was close to the ground, and it appeared to be sniffing, like a bloodhound. Then something caught its nose; it turned around and headed away from us.

"That's the thing I saw in the garage! How the hell did it get all the way down here?" I exclaimed.

"You better find the key to that room." Tommy said gravely, causing me to quickly crouch over and grab the keyring. I began testing different keys on the handle, but there must have been a hundred on the ring. None of them worked. I desperately fiddled with the lock while glancing over my shoulder every other second. The creature was still following its nose deeper into the hotel, and then between trying keys, I caught a glimpse of its rear end heading into an open room.

"Where'd it go?" I asked quickly, jiggling another failed key out of the lock. Tommy didn't answer, so I nudged him and asked again.

"Find that key!" he snarled. I frantically thumbed through the ring, jamming keys into the lock and failing to turn any of them. Then, out of the corner of my eye, I saw movement, and spun my head over my shoulder to see the creature back in the hallway. Its head was still down, but I froze in fear. My hands were cold, and seeing the creature had caused me to leave a key in the lock. They were trembling, and as I took my eyes away from the hallway, I looked down at the lock to see one of the keys stuck in it. Time slowed as I reached to grab the keyring, and then in a split second, it fell to the floor, making a dampened "clink."

The creature's head shot up from the floor; its empty white eyes leered straight at us.

"Run."

By the time I heard this, Tommy was already sprinting.

I glanced at the keys on the floor, but the first echoing bark of the beast filled me with terror. I forced my legs to move and tore down the hallway, stealing one look behind me at the hound who had already made it to the elevator. Tommy's large figure was barely visible in the gloomy maroon hallway, but I was gaining on him. The gravely cries of the beast filled me with horror, while the carpet felt like molasses.

I was gaining on Tommy, who glanced over his shoulder when my footsteps caught his ears.

"Pick a room!" he shouted, gasping for breath.

"What?!" I yelled back.

"You got luck in here. Pick a room!" he ordered, barely able to finish speaking. I could hear the thudding of the hounds' steps right behind us, and though I doubted we had enough time to get into a room, I knew Tommy couldn't run much longer. I had pulled ahead of him now and was frantically looking side to side for an open door. Old paintings of people on the wall menaced with following eyes and sick grins, and then a propped door appeared. It was cracked open just an inch, with a red light coming from behind it, and as I braced to stop at the door, Tommy raced by me and screamed "Not that one!"

I glanced over my shoulder and saw the dead eyes and face of the hound charging from the darkness, and nearly puked as I hauled my body along to run again. I couldn't even think as I plowed down the hallway, filled with rage. Tommy was still in sight, and I felt hatred burning in my stomach. The barking of the hound was deafening, like death itself. I was again making ground on fat Tommy, who was barely jogging now, gasping for breath. Then I passed him; I would be in the clear once I was far enough ahead. Then another propped door appeared ahead, snapping me out of the red haze. I threw my body into it, crashing down to the room floor. I scrambled to get on my feet and slam the door, when Tommy came flying through. I hurled myself into the door, but the hound had gotten halfway in by the time I reached it.

It thrashed violently, clawing the door and chomping at me with its hideous face. I desperately struggled to crush the beast, forcing my shoulder into the door, but then recoiled in pain as one of its claws ripped through my arm. It fought its way through the door as I furiously kicked its head, rearing its jaws to take off my foot, when Tommy flew in, smashing its head with a crowbar. It recoiled with a scream and continued thrashing before taking two more blows from Tommy. He bludgeoned the bloody, twitching creature a dozen more times before batting it out of the room and slamming the door.

My sleeve was damp with blood, and I pulled it up to reveal three deep gashes along my bicep. Tommy crouched down next to me to investigate the wound, before recoiling with wide eyes.

"Did it bite you?" he said nervously.

I glared up at him, gasping for breath and wincing from the stinging pain in my arm.

"It obviously got me! Get me some bandages or something!" I snapped, still clutching my arm. Tommy's expression turned grim as he stood up and stared at me with his hands on his hips.

"What are you waiting for? Don't you have some gauze or something in there?" I barked, nodding towards his backpack. He didn't budge.

"I asked if it *bit* you," Tommy said seriously.

"I don't know! Just help me!" I cried.

"Try to remember. Did its teeth or its claws do that?" Tommy said, nodding towards my bleeding arm.

I glanced down, noting the lengthy gashes, and then stammered "Claws."

Tommy then slid off his backpack and crouched down next to me before pulling out a bottle of almond water. He then took the cap off and then poured a stream over my wound, causing me to wince in pain. The beige liquid mixed with my blood and trickled down my arm onto the carpet, leaving a cloudy stain. Tommy flushed out my wound with half of the bottle before grabbing a spool of gauze out of his bag, along with some duct tape and began wrapping my arm. The almond water seemed to have numbed the pain, and once Tommy finished wrapping the bandage, my arm mostly just ached.

"That will help prevent infection. Hound wounds turn gnarly if left untreated." he said, packing the supplies back into his bag. He then stood up and reached out his hand. "Come on. We gotta keep moving."

"What? I'm not going back out there! That thing almost killed me! What if there's more?" I spat.

"There *are* more, especially down here. They're attracted to dark areas." Tommy said plainly. "We can't stay here; I can already feel the sanity drain of this room."

"You're crazy. I'm not going back out there." I retorted, pushing myself up off the floor. "I'd rather go crazy than get gored by one of those abominations. Besides, it wouldn't have even gotten me if we had just gone into that first room."

"You obviously didn't see the room number," Tommy said, shaking his head.

"You told me to pick a room and then *left* me!" I snapped, still wincing from the pain of my wound. "What does the room number matter!"

"It was room 666; we definitely do NOT want to go there." Tommy retorted as he shouldered his backpack.

"You're paranoid." I spat, lightly pulling my sleeve over the gauze.

"That's not paranoia; it's common sense. Besides, level 666 is an abandoned mental asylum. Hell if I follow you there." Tommy said with a scoff. I shook my head in disgust; he had nearly gotten me killed. Then, the image of hospital beds left in desolate hallways emerged in my mind; was that really where hotel room 666 went? I tried to convince myself he was lying, but I could distinctly remember the ominous, crimson light coming out from the room's doorway; what if he was right?

By this point, Tommy had begun searching the hotel room. The atmosphere was gloomy and claustrophobic, with a scratchy looking bed positioned in the center of the room between two reddish end tables. The bed was aimed at a dresser that had a blank tv, along with two old paintings set on the wall beside it. Like the others in the hotel, these were dated portraits of people dressed in renaissance era clothing, set on a faded backdrop. They were no less ominous than the others, with eyes that seemed to wander. I felt a growing weariness with each second that passed.

"What are you looking for?" I said, leering at Tommy from the entryway.

"Supplies or another way out," he replied, peering under the bed. "Take a look in that dresser. See if you can find anything. I'm gonna check out the bathroom."

I hesitated for a moment, wary of any more unwelcome surprise, before letting out a big sigh and traipsing over to the dresser. I rummaged around the surface of the dresser and found a remote to the tv, along with some paper coffee cups and an ice bucket. None of these seemed useful, so I reached for the handle on the top drawer. As I started pulling it open, the eyes of the painting seemed to burn down at me. Then the tv turned on to white static. I looked up; the people in the paintings were now grinning at me with wide eyes and wicked teeth. In the background I heard Tommy yelling "Jeff! Get in here!"

I slammed the drawer shut, causing the tv to go black, and the paintings to return to normal. Horribly shaken, I scurried over to Tommy. He was peering behind a shower curtain in the brightly lit bathroom.

"We gotta get out of here," I trembled, looking over my shoulder into the dark room. "You won't believe it, those paintings in there. . ." I stammered.

"We're in luck!" he said, stepping away from the curtain. I looked at him suspiciously, pausing for a moment before walking slowly towards the shower. As I peered behind the curtain, I saw a white tiled hallway that trailed a short way down to a rounded turn, with soft light shining in from the other side. I could hear gently flowing water, too, echoing from down the tunnel.

"Let's go." Tommy said from behind me. I hesitated for a moment and looked over my shoulder at him; a pale face peered at us from a dim corner in the hotel room, vanishing before I could even tell Tommy. He looked at my wide eyes and spun around before looking back at me confused.

"What? What do you see?" he said, shaking his head.

"Nothing; let's just get the hell out of here." I replied, turning to scurry into the tiled hallway. Tommy followed close behind. I never needed to visit The Terror Hotel again.

Chapter 7

The Pool Rooms

As we rounded the corner, the floor dipped down a short ways into a few inches of gently undulating turquoise water, leading off further into the tiled hall. Knowing there was no turning back, I took a careful step down into the water. It was lukewarm, and soaked through my boots, but was actually quite soothing. Our careful steps caused echoing splashes in the water that seemed to reverberate for miles down into what I imagined was a huge complex of corridors. The hallway we were in was wide, and quickly met a junction of interconnected rooms, all made up of the same white tile. The architecture was varied but connected, blending seamlessly into one another as one uniform space.

"Which way?" I said, coming to stop.

"Follow your gut." Tommy answered, waiting patiently for me to make a choice. I looked around at the different rooms that all lead off into well-lit areas and could not help the feeling of Deja-vu. The geometry of the walls and ceiling were like nothing I had ever seen, but the feeling was inescapable. This place looked like the hallway between a locker room and indoor pool, but was so expansive and strangely designed that it had to be out of a dream.

"This way, I guess." I said, nodding towards a room that appeared to have a large opening around the corner. The floor led up out of the water to tiled stairs and brought us to a bridge that ran alongside a small pool. The ceiling here was high and curved down to the water, but I thought this couldn't be the main destination for the level.

"Have you ever seen anything like this before?" I said, as we walked alongside the lightly rippling water.

"Never." Tommy answered in an awed voice. "It's like pools from a dreamscape."

The path along the water led us to another medium sized room that had a large, cylindrical support protruding from a shallow pool in the center that reached up to a tall, arched ceiling. The tiled path bent around it past three frosted, trapezial windows that illuminated the area with a mellow, white light before ending at a dark doorway on the far wall. Curious, I walked over to the windows to peer through to the other side, but they were completely opaque, only letting in the light. There were no silhouettes, shapes, or blotches of color behind them, just a uniform glow of soft light.

"What do you think is back there? Should we try to break through?" I said, looking over at Tommy.

"I wouldn't." he replied, shaking his head. "Let's keep moving; this place is interesting."

I nodded in agreement, and then led us into the next dark doorway. It took us through a narrow tunnel of dimly lit, echoing, rounded hallways, before dipping down into a small, short-ceilinged room. In the center sat a spiral staircase, seamlessly connected to the white tile of the floor. As I walked to the edge to investigate, I noticed that the stairs went down into water, as if they lead to a formerly accessible section that was now flooded.

"Looks like a dead-end." Tommy said. "I'm not interested in going diving."

"Me neither." I replied, growing uneasy as I gazed at the submerged stairs that disappeared into darkness. We followed the tunnel back past the room with the tall cylindrical support and then into a series of interconnected rooms. They were all made up of the same strange, tiled geometry and polygonal pools. Large, crescent indentations in the walls and perfectly symmetrical overhangs in the ceiling made each room feel unique but connected so cohesively that the design appeared intentional. There was no rhyme or reason to any of it, though; support pillars were placed oddly, rooms varied in height, length, and design, with irregular angles of light casting gradients over the architecture. I struggled to find a purpose for any of it; why was this here? Everything was so pristine, too, the tile, turquoise water, and design. Who designed this, and to what end?

The path we had taken was leading us deeper into the level now. We had passed at least a half-dozen more junctions, and I was just following my instincts, mostly mesmerized by the surreal architecture that continued to stir feelings of strange nostalgia and liminal peculiarity. The rooms seemed to grow in complexity as we wandered deeper, too. Circular indentations high up on the walls merged with the dizzying spans of flawless tile. Not one square was out of place. Each tile blended into the warps and curves of the ceilings and walls, as if laser cut and robotically placed. The fact that we had seen a stairwell going down also gave me feelings of uneasy curiosity; how big was the area beneath us, and was it entirely flooded? Was there an upper area too? How big was this place?

Although unnerving, this level gave me far less dread than the ones before. I had no idea if there would be a savage entity around the next corner, but the sound of trickling water and patches of warmth soothed me. It was like an endless bath house of divine architecture and softly illuminated rooms, leading. . .where? Where was the center; the singularity? It really felt like it was taking us *somewhere*; to some large pool or a grand entry to the complex, but the rooms just continued, almost as if they were generated. Perhaps that's what it was; a mathematical equation, with variables that ensure irregularity but always end in perfection. A network of complexly uniform rooms, all eerily fused into one master design that produced an endless journey with no destination.

We had reached the entrance to a particularly unique area when Tommy told me to stop.

"I've never been to a level like this before." Tommy said hesitantly. "I say we find a place to rest."

Ahead of us was a long, rectangular path, leading into a vast expanse of large, ogee arches that touched from ceiling to floor. A foot or so of standing, navy-blue water reached up the feet of the arches, spanning the whole area. The rectangular path stretched further than I could see, with evenly branched paths off of it between each line of parallel arches. This section was dimly lit, obscuring areas further off in the expanse.

"I don't think we can't stop here," I said matter-of-factly. "We might as well keep going until we find somewhere dry."

"Yeah. I'm just tired, and I don't know if it's safe to

sleep in this level." Tommy said, stepping in the room to look around. "I'm also getting low on almond water. Seems like the sanity drain is low here, but we're going to need more soon."

"How do we go about finding more?" I said, wading through the warm water. Tommy was now following close behind, immersed in the repeating architecture.

"Crates, cabinets, lockers; those sorts of things. Haven't seen any here, though." Tommy replied. He was looking side to side at the paths on both sides through the arches that seemed to stretch into oblivion.

"This thing is a labyrinth. Don't get us lost." Tommy warned.

"I figure we just stay on this main path; see where it takes us." I reassured, glancing over my shoulder at the brightly lit doorway we had come in from. I could not see any edges of the room; just endless tiled arches disappearing into the abyss. Perhaps this was the main attraction; a vast, shallow underground pool, like some kind of sensory deprivation tank in the subterranean aquifer of the level. I wondered if we would just hit the perimeter at some point and see this was a dead end, forcing us to backtrack. If there was a perimeter, it was huge; we had already walked a straight half mile down the middle path. The low ceiling, along with the arches and shallow water, made it feel like we were in some sort of subterranean drainage area, like something under a massive bridge or city sewer. It was too immaculate to be a sewer, though; more like an underground spring that was converted to a man-made cave. This was the kind of place you end up after swimming through a secret underground tunnel in a hotel pool.

By now, the light of the entry was long gone; all we could

see in any direction was the evenly submerged architecture and flat ceiling stretching into darkness. The splashes of our steps echoed through the expanse, alongside the gently undulating water; I dreaded what hearing anything other than that meant.

"How far. . .do you think this goes?" I said hesitantly. Tommy didn't reply, so I looked over my shoulder and began to ask again. He wasn't there. I looked in every direction, searching frantically. He was nowhere to be found in the infinite halls.

"Tommy!" My voice echoed far off into the expanse; into areas I had not been. I cried out for him again, desperate for a reply. Nothing; just the sound of my voice, fading into the void. Had I left him behind? Why wouldn't he have said something? I had to find him, so I ran back. My feet thrashed through the water, soaking my pants as I ran through the sprays. It was exhausting, but I pressed on, back towards. . .where? Where was I going? I had lost my direction. I couldn't tell where I had come from; it all looked the same; an endless maze of arches. I fell to my knees; the lukewarm water soaked up my shirt. I was completely lost.

What now? Wait here for Tommy? When had I even lost him? How would I find him? I had already called out to him, over and over, but he was gone. Maybe he had tired out and I just didn't notice. Why here of all places? It wasn't fair; I was completely alone.

"Tommy." I said disparagingly before screaming "What do I do now!"

The unfeeling expanse stood still. It did not warp or change because of my loss, being nothing other than entirely indifferent. It was dead space; a callous surrounding that was completely detached from anything happening to me. It felt darker now; no longer bringing about feelings of sublimity and frightened awe. This was just a desolate, liminal abyss now, cut off from the rest of the world. Home, and my life before, felt so far away. I was unfathomably deep in some kind of wormhole; a transitional space; a purgatory that was unimaginably large. It was the place between "here" and "there" that I wasn't supposed to see. Not just this vast expanse of perfectly tiled pool rooms either; the whole "Back Rooms" felt this way: a series of environments that were familiar, but so expansive and lacking any identifiable purpose that the only explanation was a glitch in reality. It all felt as if I had taken a wrong turn in a department store, hotel, or locker room, and wound up on a path that appeared to lead somewhere, but in fact, went nowhere, only leading further into itself.

But what was "it." I was still trying to figure that out. The only place I had ever been like this was in a dream, where, while inside my house, I tried going to my garage. The familiar path from my bedroom to the garage was different though. Instead of finding the usual white hallway, with family pictures and pieces of furniture, I wound up in a far larger area. It had tall ceilings and strange architecture, but was made up of the same colors and aesthetic of my house. How had I never seen this part of my home, I thought, and where would it take me? This place stretched for forever; how had I never seen this part of my house? Indeed, these "Back Rooms" were the physical manifestation of a dream scape, created solely by the mind expanding on what it has formerly seen.

I knew of spaces in "the real world" that were not so dissimilar to these sorts of uncanny environments; I had worked in them plenty of times. Perhaps it was the human element of these liminal places that gave them such an eerie vibe. They were not alien or supernatural; instead, they were made of all familiar architecture and design that appeared to have been used at some point, but had been long forgotten. Now it stood just as an empty, abandoned space, waiting for. . .what?

I was back walking again at this point, despairing but faced with no other choice but to press on. I still couldn't wrap my head around what was going on. What Tommy had told me about us having wound up in a liminal wormhole seemed irrefutable now. I had no doubt that I was somewhere outside of reality, albeit in a less common way. The Sci-fi movies I had watched never seemed to put the characters in a place like this. It was always some sort of surreal biome, a distant planet, or a fairy land tucked behind a wardrobe, not an endless series of liminal corridors. I mean, maybe in some horror films and purgatorial scenes there were similarities, but those places were never the point of the movie. They were quite literally transitional; relevant to the storyline in some way, but what was the story here? Get out? Was that all this place was; somewhere to be left far behind? And then what would become of it? Would it simply go on existing as this vast, strange, seemingly pointless space, frozen in time?

The thought of leaving it all behind as a distant memory was appealing, but unsettling at the same time. Of course, I desperately wanted out, but this place's very existence was haunting. What would it be like to go on living, knowing all the while that somewhere between the grooves of reality lies a network of bizarre, isolated corridors that wind endlessly through. . .what? What even was "outside?" A large concrete plain with a gargantuan complex built atop it, or just some kind of void? I didn't know if I could even trust a natural setting if I found it; where was the line between "here" and "there?" If there was the sun, trees, and sky, but I was still technically in "The Back Rooms," then how in the hell would I know I was home? Would I ever even trust my surroundings again?

The echoing splashes of my footsteps grew faint as I wandered through the repeating arches. My senses were dulled by the infinite, symmetrical expanse and warm water, which lulled me into trance. I wondered if I might be going insane, but I didn't feel the same as when I had been in the hotel ballroom. I was much more numb and detached, just wandering, unsure if I would ever make it out of here. I suppose this was not the worst way to die; I would eventually just lie down quietly in the water and drift off, forever lost in this subterranean pool. No one would ever find me, and I would never get to know where I truly was.

Just as I had begun to give up hope, a change in the surface of the water caught my attention. It was rippling, glazed with a stream of golden-white light. I followed the light, which took me through an array of arches where, set perfectly in the center of them, a spiral staircase. It led up into the ceiling, illuminated by light shining from above, like a holy beacon. As I approached it, I did not feel the hope or relief I had experienced with the other "exits." I was not anxious or excited. All I felt was a muted apathy. Before I started to climb up, I took one last look out at the liminal aquifer; I was leaving Tommy here, along with a part of me. Something had changed; I wasn't scared anymore. There was only forward; no more trying to get out of this. Maybe Tommy had found a different way out, or maybe he would wander down here forever, but as for me, I had to go.

The staircase led up a half dozen turns, bringing me closer to the bright light. I was curious but hesitant; though I had been alone for what felt like hours, the environment hadn't changed until now. There was a strange comfort in oblivion, and I knew this place was definitely not the boiler room that we were supposed to find in the hotel. I was no closer to the exit; for all I knew, I was still days or weeks away from ever getting out.

The stairs lead me up to a room that was large and rectangular, with a very high ceiling and skywalks, almost like some sort of Olympic pool room. Shallow canals of water branched through walkways in the floor, leading to drainage areas low on the walls, while the skywalk above led to dark openings that caught my attention. I could not help but wonder where they went, but the path to get up there was unclear. The lower level had at least five different routes, but I figured "up" was the only real sense of direction I had. Maybe I could reach the top of the structure and find a way out; what was above this place?

I followed a walkway across the water and then into a round ceilinged hall that I thought might take me up. Instead, it stopped in a medium-sized room with a polygonal pool in the center that occupied most of the floor space. The water gleamed with champagne light from a wide, trapezoid window, centered on the wall next to the pool. It was frosted and completely opaque, and seemed to shine brighter on a small, triangular peninsula of cream-colored tile. The whole floor was almost completely level with the water, where even a small wave would wash over it, but the sublimity of the space was unmistakable, like a summer day by the pool.

Whether it was my declining sanity or exhaustion and

exceptional weariness from wandering for God knows how long, I wanted to lie down. My last "rest" had been in the office, back when I had first met up with Tommy. . . I hadn't even really thought about him being gone yet; the environment had lulled me too much. Him being gone was. . .horrible. I had lost my only companion in this terrible place and couldn't help but feel guilty. He had saved me more times than I could count, and I just left him. The thought of him down there alone, wandering endlessly, abandoned, wondering where his friend went; I couldn't take it. What had I done? He was the only one here who cared about me.

I paced over to the peninsula and sat down, overcome with grief. To be alone here was miserable, and though it had started out like that, having Tommy, only to lose him hours later, made the loneliness that much worse. Going back and looking for him just seemed like a futile way of coping with the reality that he was gone; I knew there was no hope in finding him down there. I had wandered miles trying to find him, and the choice to take the stairs was not out of selfishness, but survival. That said, if he *did* find his way up, I should be visible. That's what I would do, rest at the top of the stairs.

As I stood up to leave the poolside, a scrap of paper slipped out of my pocket down by the water's edge. I looked at it curiously, having no recollection of its presence in my pocket, before swiping it up. It was a note, but not one I had written.

Jeff,

I don't know when or where you'll find this, but I'm guessing when you do, you will want an explanation. After our close encounter with the moth in the hotel, I wrote this note to warn you that there is a chance that The Back Rooms will separate us. While getting lost is always a possibility, being separated by this places' nonlinear physical properties is more likely. There are many unconfirmed links between levels, and I'm guessing one of us found one and ended up no-clipping to a different level.

I didn't tell you about this because I did not want it to scare you. This place feeds on fear, and I knew your sanity would drain quickly with the ever-present threat of being isolated again. Ignorance is bliss, right?

Well, the cold truth is that I am not sure if we will ever meet again. I've heard of a place called "The Hub" that has doors to every level in The Back Rooms. It's a hidden level and looks like an underground car tunnel. As far as getting there, if you see a brown, metal door that looks out of place, no matter which level you are on, take it. I don't know if it will get us any closer to escaping, but it's the only reliable rendezvous point for getting back together.

I hope we make it out, Jeff. I'll wait for you at the hub as long as I can.

Tommy

I stared at the letter in disbelief, and then sighed, looking up at the ceiling. With no clear path out, and levels that now apparently teleported people at random, I could hardly hold on to the hope of getting home. I was quite literally in an unending nightmare, with impossible hurdles at seemingly every turn. Maybe there was no way out of here, and every soul unfortunate enough to come into contact with The Back Rooms was damned. I had nothing anymore; my phone was dead, my partner gone, and my sense of direction completely extinguished. The only thing I had to hold onto was getting to The Hub to see Tommy. I would have to fight total despair to see this thing through; I didn't want to die. I wasn't gonna just be another skeleton in liminal hell; I was going to make it out and tell my story.

These pool rooms were, at the very least, the most mellow place I had been in since I started this whole trip, which brought up the question, where exactly was I when this bad dream started? It had to be somewhere behind that first locked door; somewhere in Caius; the place where the fabric of reality ripped, and I fell in. This couldn't be some kind of outrageous government experiment; it was too vast, horrible, and nonsensical to be of any use to politicians. The reality was far stranger than an evil experiment. It was as if I was in a procedurally generated environment from a haywire computer, lost in space that had no ongoing purpose. A forsaken limbo.

The absence of entity sightings and general calm of this gently illuminated peninsula was a mild antidote to my melancholy; I would rest here for the time being. Drink some almond water, try and get some sleep; anything to keep my mind at ease. Sanity was the currency here. It still felt strange to relax in a place so far away and liminal, but, part of me embraced it; a million miles from nowhere, lounged out next to a shallow pool no one even knows exists. It was like I was embracing being forgotten; committed to the void. Tucked away in this tiled labyrinth, far, far away from any other soul. No reason to fight it; just me and infinity. Mortal impermanence.

***

I wasn't sure how long I slept; it felt like at least six hours, and when I awoke, the sunlight seemed to be coming in through my bedroom window. As I rolled over and opened my eyes, the same, trapezoidal window casting soft, indifferent light across the still water and white tile took shape. The room hadn't changed at all since I fell asleep; I was still in the middle of a surreal expanse of tiled pool rooms with the echoes of gently undulating water radiating through the endless corridors. Sleep had made me feel better; it was the most normal thing I had done in the last three days, and although lying here was preferable to exploring more, I had to keep moving.

Before leaving, I took a long look around the room that had given me my only real rest in the last 3 days. I held onto the feeling, savoring it; making sure I wouldn't forget. I wanted to revisit this place in my mind someday, at a time when the crushing weight of the world and mortality was too much. I could think back to here, where there is nothing; back to a pure, enveloping, void who's inescapably isolating atmosphere was unlike any place I had ever been. It was a break from everything; a nostalgia devoid of subsistence; a dreamlike peculiarity, totally separated from everything else.

My time of respite had given me a subtle appreciation for this experience, even in spite of the overwhelming horror. Whatever this place was, its novelty and strange effects on the human experience were powerfully unique, and aside from just getting home to safety, deep down, I desperately hoped that I would make it out so that I could unpack this whole thing and tell my story. I had never been to a place so bizarre and anomalous.

My plan was to find a way up to the skywalk that lined the perimeter of the tall room I had originally come in on. I traced my way back to that Olympic-pool room, and then took the first path that appeared to go up. It led me through a hall of stilted arches connected to the ceiling, with shallow, warm water reaching up their tiled legs. The hallway then ended at a stainless-steel ladder that I climbed up, taking me into a large chamber that had oval windows high up the left wall. Their grayish-blue light stretched across the tile path towards a large depression in the floor. It dropped at least twenty feet down into a bowl-shaped pool, appearing to have been drained of water. This depression rounded up the wall all the way to the ceiling with a sharp drop off next to the path. There would be no way out if I fell in; the walls were too steep to climb out of.

I stayed along the wall by the windows, wary of getting trapped until someone decided to fill the deep pool again. The walkway led to another room that had a tiled, square staircase leading up, which I followed for a short ways before it plateaued into a corridor that was illuminated by three circular windows. They cast irregular gradients of light along the tiled walls and polygonal pool, giving the room a distinct appearance of being basked in morning sunlight. Then, I noticed a square doorway out onto the skywalk, and immediately scurried past the pool towards it. My stomach churned as I looked down at the three-story drop, but I could see the spiral staircase I had come in from.

The walkway had a rounded, steel railing at waist height, which I kept my hand on while peering down at the floor below. I tried to push out thoughts of falling as I followed the skywalk along the top of the lengthy room, and couldn't help but wonder about where all these hallways led to. The corridors of this place seemed to go on for miles, like a million hotel pools from a dream, winding like a maze that had no end. The image of perfectly geometric, tiled pool rooms stretching off into oblivion brought an overwhelming feeling of minimization, as I was an ant faced with crossing a football field. Getting lost was inevitable, and there was so much around me that I couldn't even perceive.

As I gazed down at the dim, circular opening of the spiral staircase to the aquifer below, I thought of Tommy. Was he still down there, or had he no-clipped to another level? It didn't really matter now; we were separated, and thinking about just how alone I really was brought a familiar, desolate feeling. I paused, staring out at the tiled expanse; one last look before I went. Forgetting this place was impossible; these bizarre halls and pools would go on existing in this weird purgatorial state forever. I might be leaving, but *they* will not be gone; their very existence would remain as an unnerving reminder to me that, somewhere between the threads of reality, there is a place so peculiar and anomalous; a place of unexplained corridors and rooms, all sharing an unmistakable theme of liminality and the feeling that you're not supposed to be there. A kind of modern purgatory; this place was not meant for man to see; not meant to explored. It was to be left as is; a space between reality and heaven; the loading zone for matter.

Chapter 8

Home. . .?

The tiled skywalk led me towards a rectangular doorway into a room with white carpet and a set of stairs across from the entrance. It looked like the basement of a suburban house, painted a soft beige color with two doorways set on either side of the stairwell. One appeared to have a washer and dryer that were illuminated by silvery light from a window that was just out of view, while the other was set in the corner of the room, leading to a dark room. The space felt eerily familiar, like a basement I had been to as a kid and contrasted starkly to the surreal place I had just come from. It seemed so out of place above the expanse of pools; who would build a house above such a place?

I decided to first investigate the laundry room, and quickly found an opaque window high up on the wall that appeared to be letting in sunlight. I considered smashing through it, but figured I should poke around a little bit and see if I could find any supplies. If this was in fact some sort of Back Rooms house, there had to be almond water in the kitchen cupboards or one of the bedroom closets. My gut turned in utter disgust at the thought of wandering through a dark, liminal house though;

I didn't need to investigate anything other than the metal cabinet in this room.

After fiddling with the cabinet's stuck door, I got it to pop open and found a stainless-steel thermos. Curious, I twisted off the cap and saw a reddish-pink liquid inside before bringing the container to my nose and taking a whiff. I instantly recoiled at the acrid, almost alcoholic smell. Whatever it was, I wasn't interested in drinking it, so I screwed the lid back on and looked at the window. With a split second of hesitation, I thought about the possible consequences of breaking a window. What was the worst thing that could possibly happen? Open a portal to an undesirable level? Let in a hoard of entities? Get in trouble for "vandalism" of The Back Rooms? Honestly, I didn't really care; I was rolling the dice no matter what, so I figured I'd go with my gut. The window seemed like the right way, so I raised my arm and then launched the thermos at the glass

I had half expected it to bounce off, but instead, it shattered, causing a shower of glass shards to fall noisily to the floor. The opening high up on the wall appeared just big enough to squeeze through, but I still couldn't see anything behind it. I stood on my tiptoes and wrapped my hand in my sleeve to clear out the remaining shards, but somewhere in the clamor, I heard a door close. My hairs stood on end, freezing me in place. What in the hell made that sound?

"Hello?" I said nervously, before instantly regretting saying anything.

I kept my eyes locked on the doorway leading out into the open carpeted room. I couldn't see the stairwell or the other dark room from where I was standing, so I began to creep towards the door. The glass immediately began cracking loudly beneath my feet, stopping me in place; I didn't need to see what had made that sound. I turned around and crept back towards the window before slowly reaching my hands up to the windowsill, feeling for a place without any shards. The grip was awkward, but with a little jump, I knew I could pull myself through.

I was just about to climb up when I heard a woman's voice say, "help me", causing my head to spin around. I crunched over the glass towards the doorway and then spotted a little girl halfway down the stairs. She was wearing a polka-dot dress with a red bow in her long black hair, taking notice of me as I came around the corner.

"Who are you?" I said curiously, standing in the doorway. She didn't reply and kept walking down the stairs, which caused me to back slowly towards the window. "Are you lost?" I said hesitantly, stealing a look over my shoulder at the broken window. Then she said "help me" again, but her lips did not move.

Horrified, I scrambled towards the window. The girl chased, shouting for help over and over. I leapt towards the window, securing my hands on both sides of the frame and began to pull myself up. I could hear the crunching of her footsteps on the glass. I desperately worked myself through the small opening, and then felt her hand around my ankle. I thrashed my foot violently and eventually pushed off her, sending me through to the other side of the window.

I had fallen on my stomach, and quickly spun around to see if she was climbing up the window. As I looked down into the laundry room, there was no girl, but a large, humanoid creature with white eyes and yellow skin reaching its sucker-ridden arms towards the window. It snarled at me from below and began to climb through, sending me into a panic as I frantically looked for something to block its path. The first thing I saw was a black-cushioned chair. I hauled it towards the window, tormented by the gurgling snarls of the creature behind my back.

The creature was already halfway through the broken window, thrashing about violently as it tried to force its way in. I was too late, so I abandoned the chair and looked around for something to bludgeon the creature with. The only thing I could find in my tunneled vision on the glossy-tiled floor was the thermos I had broken the window with. It seemed like a futile weapon, but with only a few brief seconds to act, I grabbed the thermos and chucked it at the creature that was now shrieking as it battled glass shards.

The thermos exploded with a *WHOOM*, sending up a plume of red smoke as it hit the beast. I heard the sound of its body falling onto the glass into the room below with a loud crash. Motionless, I watched as the red smoke dissipated. The white gloss walls were now spattered with a charred-red color, and bits of burnt debris littered the floor. The blast had blown out the entire window frame, and I could see the lifeless body of the yellow creature lying scorched on the floor below. It was mangled and half melted, but it looked just like the thing I had seen down in the pipe tunnels many levels earlier; a *skin stealer*, as Tommy called it. There was only one way it could shift into a little girl.

Maybe I was just lucky enough to find a thermos with dynamite in it, but who in their right mind would do such a thing? Probably some battle-hardened wanderer that had been stuck here for months. . . I'd have to keep an eye out for any more of that red liquid; explosives would come in super handy here.

I was now in what looked like an entryway to a mall. The ceiling was tall with bright, overhead lighting, and the walls were made up of glossy, marble tiles. Up ahead, I could see that the wide path I had come in turned into a large shopping area, with a wide entrance to a department store on the adjacent wall. It was blocked off by a garage door with horizontal bars and plastic rectangular windows, but I could still see inside. All of the lights were off, and I could make out a series of empty clothing racks and jewelry kiosks. I cupped my hands around my eyes next to the windows to try and see if I could spot an exit that would justify forcing my way in, and got an awful feeling as I saw the silhouette of a humanoid far off in the darkness. I jumped back from the window and tried to shake off the feeling of dread, and then jogged into the main shopping area.

The mall was dead. Every single store was closed with no lights on, and the kiosks down the center walkway were devoid of any merchandise. The place was not in disrepair, though, and there were some faux-leather cushioned chairs and vending machines that gave off the strange impression that people still came here. The main area was well lit and clean, and as I looked up, I noticed an upper level with more retail space beneath a tall ceiling with skylights. I thought I should try to find the way up there; keep ascending, like I had done in the Pool Rooms, which I had nearly forgotten about already. The thought of all those surreal, warping rooms existing under the mall was absurdly weird.

The complete lack of any other human beings,

combined with the mall's quiet, sterile atmosphere, made it feel like I was somewhere I wasn't supposed to be. I couldn't help but wonder if this place had once been bustling with shoppers and merchandise, or if it had always been empty and abandoned? What if it really was a mall from reality? Perhaps it had somehow appeared here in a kind of stasis, as if the whole place was taken from a specific moment in time? Maybe that's what The Back Rooms was; snapshots of liminal spaces from periods of time on earth that have amalgamated together into a deformed maze.

I continued down the main path, peering through glass windows into the dark stores. Booths, shelves, and racks for clothing, jewelry, candles and toys dotted the interiors, but there was no merchandise, just vacant spaces with leftover retail supplies. I figured if I saw something useful in one of them, I would try to break in, but it was at this moment that I noticed the faintest sound of music. It was almost soothing, but so distant that when I tried to listen for it, all I heard was my footsteps against the tile floor. Maybe it was just my mind thinking it heard 2000's pop music because that's what plays in the mall.

I had been lost in thought, looking into stores and chewing on explanations for this place. Now, there was an eerie stillness in the air. The mall was silent; nothing was moving but me. There were faux plants, waste bins, and furniture, but nothing felt alive. It was all artificial and unfeeling. Even the air was cold, like it was air conditioned. I was alone in a place designed for hundreds of people, but there were no shoppers, store owners, security guards, or janitors, just me, isolated in desolation.

A dull whirring caught my ears as I came towards a split in the path, which I discovered the source of as I rounded the corner; a functioning escalator. Baffled, I stared at the milling stairs for a moment before shrugging and riding it up to the second floor. The free movement lulled me into a trance for a few moments before I stepped off into an open area across from another department store. It was vacant but not barred off, and had light from the mall streaming in that revealed rectangular support columns scattered throughout the space. I could also just make out a large kiosk in the center of the store.

I figured I ought to check it out. This was the only open store I had seen so far, and with one bottle of almond water left that was becoming more appealing as the dead mall wore on my psyche, I needed to find some. I sipped it as I approached the entrance to the unlit store, slowly submerging into the darkness. As I searched around the shelves, my eyes kept getting drawn to the distant walls of the store; I couldn't help but gaze past the sea of empty aisles, over the clothing racks and into the empty, shadowy space. It felt strangely familiar, but I couldn't put my finger on why.

I still hadn't found anything by the time I reached the kiosk in the center of the store that I now realized was part of a beauty section. Empty glass display cases built a perimeter around the black tile floor where a pretty attendant was supposed to stand and talk about perfumes. The only woman here, though, was a picture, high up on the wall with heavy mascara. She sat alone in the darkness, looking up at the ceiling of the store. I stood beneath her; everything was still. My peripheral vision wasn't playing any tricks, and there were no disturbing noises from unseen parts of the store; the place was just dead. Nothing really to be afraid of; no critical sensory alerts or grotesque creatures; just a long-forgotten advertisement of a woman left in the void that was meant to be seen by thousands, but now stares eternally into oblivion. I basked, for a second, in the feeling. It was liminal, but purely so. Unsettling, but not dangerous; a kind of limbo that was strangely appealing. It was fleeting, mixed with a creepy sensation that ebbed and flowed with each passing second.

I started searching the display cases and it seemed like I was out of luck until discovering that the case right beneath the picture of the woman had two bottles of almond water, along with a few scraps of paper with writing on them. I considered breaking the glass until I tried the sliding door with a metal lock and it opened right up. I grabbed both bottles, and the notes, and then scurried back towards the golden rays of light on the cream-white tiles streaming in from the mall. I looked over my shoulder at the picture of the woman once I was near the entrance; her fine details had been obscured by the darkness, but I could still see her eyes, staring coldly into the blackness.

"Goodbye, darling."

The notes I had found were long, but I wanted to get away from the empty department store before reading them; avoiding large, open spaces was a rule I had begun to follow here. I started along the upper walk, which had brass railings at waist height with turquoise-glass windows to the floor to block off the large openings to the lower level. The path up here was not straight like the ones below; instead, it curved and bent through the mall, leading me through more areas that I thought might go to the center. The store fronts and mall furniture continued as if the design was intentional, but I wasn't really *going* anywhere, just deeper into the mall.

I figured the exit to the level would probably be in one

of the stores, but I feared just how many levels this one might be connected to. I still had no plan for getting to the "Hub" Tommy wrote about and dreaded the thought of stumbling on another level like the Terror Hotel. I didn't have any sort of guide or rule book for The Back Rooms; just whatever information Tommy had given me. With the growing feeling of being lost, I decided to take a rest at a spot between two faux-palms and three black sofas near a locked outdoor gear store and collectible card store.

I began thumbing through the notes from the department store once I sat down. Two of them had been handwritten, while the third was printed and appeared to have been torn out of a book. It read:

Member Intake #43 - 10/14/2000

Name: Thomas Freid
Entry Date: Unknown
First contact with M.E.G: Level 3 - The Electrical Station
Psychological State upon arrival: Paranoid Delusions
Characteristics; 6'4", ~250lb. Bald. Brown eyes.
Visit notes: After making contact with an expeditionary force on level 3, #43 was taken back to The Hub to be treated for psychosis. He was deployed with members 50 and 52 two days later.

The report ended there, leaving me curious. Who, or whatever M.E.G was, seemed to be some kind of authority in The Back Rooms. Tommy hadn't mentioned the group, but it sounded like The Hub was their headquarters and that they were some sort of authority here. Maybe that's why Tommy was going there; he thought they could help us get out.

I checked out one of the handwritten pages next, but quickly became lost in the writing. The words were all irregularly sized and hardly legible, seemingly scribbled in a panic. Sentences were violently scratched out, while others were underlined excessively, and I couldn't help the feelings of unease it gave me. It looked like the ramblings of someone who went insane, and as I flipped over to the next page and began reading the text that was legible, I realized this was exactly the case.

Day 14,

Unit #43 reporting

I have been separated from my group for over two days now and I am out of almond water. Despite my best efforts to return to the headquarters, I am completely lost. I tried to retrace my steps through the sprawling complex maintenance halls, but I wound up in an entirely different level than I had come from. It appeared similar to a kindergarten classroom, with colorful chairs, tables, and walls. I was overwhelmed with nostalgia and became entranced in the environment. The more I explored, the more spaces from my childhood I discovered. Toy ball pits, play places, school hallways; even old stores that had closed decades ago; the whole place was a big collection of nostalgic environments.

The sanity drain of this level was tremendous, though, and brought on extreme paranoia after what I estimated to be only a day or two in the level. The light faded, and my memories became dark and blurry. Fond memories began distorting into traumatic flashbacks, while evil faces and sinister sounds haunted me from the multiplying shadows. I thought the level may be closing in on itself. Visual anomalies and glitches became more frequent the longer I was in there, wandering through increasingly disturbing childhood places with my dim flashlight.

At the time of writing this, I found what I suspect is level 1, but I fear that if I do not find almond water soon, I will succumb to insanity. I hate the thought of becoming a wretch, but I don't have it in me to kill myself. Hopefully M.E.G finds me soon, but I'm doubtful."

The note was chilling and caused me to gape in fear at the empty mall. I imagined the burned, fleshy, wide-eyed face of a wretch lurking in one of the dark stores, watching me. Whoever had written the note had obviously gone mad, and I was *right* by where they began going crazy. It would weigh on me, no matter how hard I tried to calm myself down, and my only course of action was to put as much distance from me and where I'd found the notes as possible. If that meant going miles deep into an abandoned mall, so be it.

I pressed on, struggling to find a route that felt safe. Going down the center of the path felt too exposed, while staying by the edge near the dark stores was too eerie. No matter where I went, the feelings of isolation and unease were inescapable; even the temperature seemed to be getting colder. Anomalies in the environment also were becoming more frequent, despite the hallways seeming to loop familiarly. Oddly placed support pillars, irregularly shaped storefronts, and decorative fountains appeared as I wandered around the bends in the hallways that I swore led to the same place.

I had come upon a gentle incline in the glossy tile floor that led me between two rectangular planters of green foliage, along with lightly glowing teal streams of wavy designs along the walls. It seemed like the sort of hall you might enter a mall from; long, and a bit narrow with store fronts on either side, but definitely not the "main" area. It felt like a rectangular corridor to nowhere with the cosmic void just on the other side of the walls. Something about the space was inexplicably captivating, with the discomfort seemingly fundamental to the place's strange allure.

New objects began to appear as I walked further. Planted palms, wavy railings, and small staircases in the floor were all things I was certain I hadn't seen yet, despite the feeling that I had already been here. I noticed that the lighting was a bit dimmer too, which drew my eyes up to the skylights spanning the ceiling. It was getting dark outside of the mall, wherever that was, and I truly had no idea how long I'd been in The Back Rooms now. Were days even 24 hours here? I had slept twice, but with no way to track the time, my whole experience had melded into one long bad dream.

The threat of darkness weighed on me. This was the time where most of the shoppers were gone, and the stores began to bring down their metal garage doors. Of course, this mall didn't have any shoppers or stores to close, but nighttime increased the already tormenting feeling of trespassing that had been haunting me since I got here. I tried to calm myself down by thinking back on going to the mall as a teenager; I had been there around closing with friends plenty of times. This was normal; malls close at night. It was just a bunch of retail space that wasn't being used; there was nothing especially wrong with it. As a matter of fact, this whole place was just empty space, not some hellish, alien environment.

I couldn't tell if my mind was just desperately trying to cope, or if I actually believed the things I was thinking. I mean, maybe this place would be easier to comprehend if it was an alien planet; that would make it a lot easier to explain. Instead, The Back Rooms were so eerily similar to many of the places I had already been. It was all human construction; architecture that I knew. Did that mean a human created it, or was it some kind of quantum glitch in reality; a strange adaptation of man-made environments manifested as a desolate compound of anomalous space.

The mall continued to grow darker, barraging me with the unyielding feeling that it was time to leave. I couldn't wander through these winding halls forever, especially with the threat of coming across the wretch who had written those notes. How far did this place go, and what was with all the environmental anomalies popping up? They were unmistakable now, despite the vibe of the entire mall still being cohesive. New objects appeared at every turn. Long, slightly elevated planters, made up of white tile, lined the side of the path I was on, and were dotted with spiky plants that appeared long forgotten. They were overgrown, and some of the mulch from their beds had been strewn on the floor. It struck me as being out of place; this was the first "dirty" thing I had seen here. The mall had been immaculately clean thus far, but as I continued down the path, I began noticing more unkempt things.

The changes were subtle, but most definitely there. Chips in the wall paint, smudged tile, bits of trash on the ground, and damaged retail signs made the mall feel more degraded. It was as if I was deep enough now that I had gone beyond the managed section of the mall. The insides of the stores also appeared to be declining; toppled clothes racks, broken display shelves, and peeling wallpaper all gave the space a more rundown feel. Creepy, but sad, like a fallen dream. This mall wasn't "real" but I couldn't help but see similarities to places I had been to in my past.

The starkest memory I had was CentraPoint mall. My parents brought me there for years on Sundays after church, but the place started declining by the time I was in eighth grade. Most of my favorite storefronts from childhood were replaced with oriental rug shops and niche businesses that changed every few months. The mall was mostly empty storefronts and barren halls by the time I was in my senior year of high school, and I even snuck into at night with a couple bold classmates; one of those exciting, rebellious teenage acts.

Economic factors, along with an increasingly digital world killed the mall, but the owners apparently had trouble getting a demolition permit from the city. This meant that homeless people and urban explorers were the only souls that had passed through the completely abandoned building in the last decade. The ultimate fate of CentraPoint is to be leveled and redeveloped as a strip mall, but until then it just sits, forgotten; left to fall into ruin. I knew why it had ended up that way, but while I stood here, staring into just one of the deserted storefronts in this massive, dead mall, the thought of what the place from my childhood used to be made me feel. . .sort of homesick. I'd never really thought of it that way, even when it closed; I was too busy with college and work, but losing it was a shame. To see a place that I once loved—neglected and left to rot—it was depressing, and this place was a profound catalyst of that feeling.

The atmosphere of abandoned places—with remnants of their past and signs of people that have been gone for so long—is certainly different from those which humans occupy in their day to day lives. A space completely devoid of life and objects that indicate its presence is a form of isolation, but when you introduce the details that show the space *did* have active humans at some point, the vibe becomes stranger. The question of *why* imposes itself again, and even with explanations like the economy and delayed paperwork, the lack of the spaces' immediately identifiable purpose is what seems to bring such an uncanny feeling. It is, quite literally, a space in limbo; a physical manifestation of the in-between; neither here nor there. A transitional space that one was never meant to spend much time in.

This was, perhaps, the best explanation I could find for The Back Rooms; a lengthy in-between, liminal space, that underwent some kind of unplanned mutation which caused the space to be far larger than intended. A wormhole, of sorts; the infinitely divisible distance between two spaces which I had somehow fallen into, filled with anomalies, non-linear halls and strange paths that are inevitable expressions of an environment that was not meant to be accessed. It was not a space to be perceived by humans, and so its anomalous nature might just be my brain trying to make sense of the enigmatic, non-Euclidean space. An illusion.

The skylights overhead were now glossed by a midnight blue sky, dimming the entire mall. The only light now came from white, artificial light bulbs in the sparse can lighting, casting long shadows and patches of darkness along the walls and floor. Some sections were completely dark, as if they had been closed, whilst others were visible in the distance, revealed by patches of fluorescent lighting that touched the abandoned storefronts. The weight of isolation and complete emptiness on my psyche was becoming more apparent by the minute; I could feel my mind slipping into paranoia. Peripheral hallucinations seemed to be starting as well; glimpses of creatures darting into stores and leering at me from the darkness chilled my soul, but I fought to stay calm. My hopes of finding a main exit were gone; I would have to find a way out through one of the stores. The mall was becoming creepier and more dilapidated the further I went, and its drain of my sanity was not sustainable. At this rate, I'd be out of almond water before morning. . .if morning ever came to this place.

Without knowing what to look for, finding an exit inside of one of the stores seemed like it was a gamble. Would I come across another tile hallway in the wall, like the one in the hotel room that led to the Pool Rooms, or would I find some kind of an elevator that would take me back to the office? I had already explored what I estimated to be at least 7 miles of the upper level of the mall, and I figured the store I chose might have some kind of link to the level it led to. I thought of the empty football stadium from my high school as I passed a sporting goods store. Astroturf, bleachers, wide open space and. . .no students. No players or concessions; just a field illuminated by ice-white stadium lights, surrounded by empty viewing platforms and silver bleachers.

The next couple stores were so heavily decayed that I

couldn't make out their signs or what they even sold. The only thing inside them was dirty walls and floors, along with displaced ceiling tiles that had loose wires dangling into the room. Then came a large department store—like a Macy's or Jaycee Penny— and just my luck; it was fully lit. The entrance had a barred garage door that was lowered, but I was able to crawl beneath it and begin exploring. The store was entirely empty, leaving its white walls and shelves exposed to the fluorescent lighting overhead. The brightness was overwhelming, but in the center of the room I saw an out-of-order escalator leading up to the second floor. I scanned the shelves for almond water and supplies as I headed towards the escalator, but there was nothing; just plastic hangers, particle board shelving, chrome clothes racks and empty glass display cases.

I took the escalator up and glanced over my shoulder before stepping off; something had moved in my peripheral. It sent a surge of hot dizziness through my body, spiking my heart rate. I didn't see anything and controlled my breathing to try and calm down. Another convincing hallucination, more than likely; I needed to drink some almond water. I sipped a bottle as I walked through more empty department store space, still unable to find anything leading to an exit. The upper level appeared larger than the lower, but eventually I spotted another large opening leading back to the mall. I had passed a few corridors that looked like they led to bathrooms and offices, but I figured I would try some more stores before exploring hallways that were eerily reminiscent of the ones I had been to in the garage. No way in hell was I going back there.

I was confused when I made it to the department store's exit on the second floor; it opened to more mall space that looked like the base floor. There were no spaces in the floor that looked down to the first or second floor of the mall; just a flat, wide white tile hallway with more abandoned retail space on either side. Was I above that whole previous section of the mall now? The area was well lit and not nearly as dilapidated as the one I had come from, as if I had somehow backtracked or discovered a new section of the mall that was still in good shape. Disconcerted, but not entirely surprised, I trekked into the new space, keeping an eye out for any promising storefronts. I also had a gnawing feeling of being followed in the back of my mind that the almond water hadn't cured. The longer I was in here, the more likely it was I would come across the person, or what *used* to be the person, who had written those notes.

I hadn't gone far when I came across a large bookstore that looked like a Barnes and Noble. It had two stories, and I could see up to the second level from outside with its ceiling to floor windows. It was perhaps the most stocked store I had come across yet, with half-full bookshelves and bits of decoration scattered about. There were also plush, red-leather chairs and soft-yellow lights illuminating the olive toned carpet around the store. The walls were a warm beige color with bits of maroon colored artwork, and I could not help but be lured into the cozy store. It was the most human, familiar, comfortable space I had been to in days, and I even noticed a coffee shop as I walked through the entry. The space was definitely still abandoned, but even with just a few everyday objects, I felt a touch of home.

The coffee shop was the logical first place to check for supplies, or maybe even a *cup* of coffee. Imagine that, sitting back in one of those leather chairs and reading with a hot cup of joe; an absolute luxury. I rarely ever sat down to read a book like that back in the "real world," and with the threat of being followed by a wretch, "relaxing" here would be a long shot. But, reading a book seemed like the most normal thing I could do, and it appealed to my humanity; a bit of normalcy would help my psyche. And, to my luck, hot coffee came out of the large tap behind the counter when I tested its lever, so I filled up a disposable cup and carried it with me as I began browsing for an interesting book.

I didn't recognize any of the titles or authors names, but never having been a big reader, I wasn't surprised. What did it mean if I did find a book I knew, though? How could it have wound up *here*? I wasn't so uncultured that I didn't know of *any* books; I just wasn't up to speed on the latest ones. There had to be at least *one* book I knew, but as I searched the shelves, every title, name, and publisher were completely unfamiliar, despite the covers looking normal. Matte colored backgrounds with knights, dragons, wizards and colorful titles covered the shelves in the fiction section, while lewd covers with hulking men and swooning women were all over romance shelves. There were even some magazines near the registers at the front; a few obviously centered around celebrity drama, while others had pictures of food, clothing, and sports.

The closer I looked, however, the less I recognized. None of the celebrities had familiar faces, and the food was entirely alien. One in particular had a picture of what looked like a fried brown sailboat with seaweed salad and raspberries on the top with a header nearby that read: *The BEST Ethgul Recipes and Cooking with Slarga.* Even the sports magazines were unusual, with a cover picture of what I guessed to be an athlete, dressed in an oddly proportioned football-type uniform leaping towards a flying disc with some sort of glittering club. The title of this one read "*Kyle Louger's Most Dominant Season.*" All the magazines were like this; weird adaptations of traditional covers into distorted pictures of what seemed like an AI's interpretation. That, or these were actually real publications of human culture I'd never heard of, but the magazines being written in English made me think the latter. AI generated stuff was the only thing I had ever seen like this, like when someone plugs in a pizza or restaurant commercial into an artificial intelligence program, and it produces an uncanny, disturbing recreation of that advertisement.

As unsettling as this was, I could not deny my curiosity. The magazine that piqued my interest most looked similar to a nature publication, with a big picture of a dinosaur-looking creature on the front with the title: *Creatures of the Lahgyur Swamps: The Poligostag.*" I grabbed the magazine and carried it over to a leather chair near the back of the store, along with my cup of coffee, before thinking it better to go up to the second floor. I could see out the upper windows into the mall from up there and spot any creatures before they entered the bookstore.

I took the escalator in the middle of the store up to the second level, which was less stocked but still just as inviting. Three plush chairs sat around a coffee table near the window, but before I sat down, I turned one of the chairs so that I could see out the window. I set my coffee down on the table and lazed into cushy leather, but quickly felt a vulnerability leaving the empty store behind me. I stood back up and then positioned the chair so that I sat between the window and store, but I was still unsatisfied. I looked out over the array of wooden shelves and low tables that filled the store, trying to decide if I should go investigate before sitting down. The only section that made me nervous was in the far-right corner of the store; tall bookshelves obscured the area, and I wanted to see if there was a hallway where an entity could sneak in.

I walked by at least a dozen sparsely stocked shelves before passing beneath a low overhang in the ceiling that led to an open, circular area with colorful walls. Stuffed animals, toys, and thin children's books were scattered near the edges of the room on small tables, while a shiny, plastic tree sat in the center. It nearly reached the ceiling, with a yellow slide coming down from the branches and a low tunnel into the trunk. A sense of nostalgia crept into my mind as I looked at the play structure and recalled blurry memories of crawling around a very similar play place at CentraPoint mall as a child. The feeling was alluring, like a desire to get lost in the memory. I was curious, like a child; what treasures—or horrors—lay within the trunk? It was probably foolish, but I wanted to see, so I got down on my hands and knees and craned my neck into the oval-shaped opening in the trunk.

A fairyland, with huge pine trees covered in sparkly teal moss and luminous white moths fluttering through their branches was what I expected to see, but it was just dark. I could feel the scratchy carpet on my knees and the sticky plastic of the tree catching my clothing, and there was no special world; just a hollow in the trunk that's fun was made by the kids who occupied it. I backed out of the tree and stood up, disheartened by the lack of anything special. It was just an empty play place; I didn't know why I expected anything different. A fairyland would have been preferable to an abandoned bookstore, but with The Back Rooms painting every space with unnerving elements, it probably would have been haunting in some accursed way. That said, I had explored the part of the bookstore that I couldn't see from the chair, so now I could go back and rest for a bit. Read that weird book and sip some coffee while I kept an eye on the mall below. A nice respite.

As I passed beneath the overhang in the ceiling, the bookstore looked different.

Chapter 9

The End

The shelves were now completely empty, and the space appeared to have aged. Rectangular support columns around the room were pasted with large, neon *For Sale* signs, and the carpet was now a dingy sage color. I looked towards where I had left my coffee, but the windows out to the mall were gone, replaced by beige walls with grayish outlines of posters and objects that had stained them. Gridded fluorescent white lighting had replaced the warm lights from before, emitting an eerie buzzing sound that I quickly recognized; it sounded just like the lights in the yellow rooms where I had started this whole miserable weekend.

The thing that caught my attention most, however, was pasted on an overhang in the ceiling a hundred or so feet off from where I was. In big letters, it spelled *"THE END."* Confused excitement welled in my bones as I ran around bookshelves towards the sign. It sat above an empty secretary's desk with a cove in the wall behind it that was bordered by tall, empty bookshelves. I did not see any tunnels or signs of an exit, though, so I walked into the cove to inspect the shelves for a clue. I tried pushing them aside, poking at the wood laminate, and stomping on the carpet for a trap door. No luck.

I stared up at the big letters, trying to figure out what puzzle I would have to solve to get out of here. Then a hallway on the left side of the room caught my eye; could it really be that simple? I jogged towards it and soon after began sprinting down the hallway. My mind was spinning; where would I come out of The Back Rooms at? Who would I tell? Would anybody believe me? Would I have to keep it a secret so that whoever created this place wouldn't kill me? Tommy had talked about The Back Rooms like they were a well-known cause of people disappearing, but I'd certainly never heard of them before this. What about Tommy anyway? How long would he wait for me at The Hub, if he ever even made it there? The unfortunate truth was that if I found an exit, I was taking it; he would have to find his own way out. Besides, he was the reason I stuck here in the first place.

The hallway turned and bent around a half dozen corners, keeping the same desolate retail space vibe. I wondered whether it would change into a forest or a city with people. Cars, buildings and shopping, or tall hardwoods reaching up towards a blue sky; I didn't care. Anything that showed I was out. And when I got there, I'd get as far away from where I had exited as possible in case I could somehow get sucked back in. Was it even possible to go back, or would I come through in a portal that would just disappear? Imagine that; appearing in Time Square from some kind of liminal wormhole; hopefully I would come out where someone saw me; that way I wouldn't sound like a crazy person who just hallucinated the whole thing. One thing was for sure, I was NEVER entering Caius again, or any large government building for that matter.

I could see an opening at the end of the hallway and

raced towards it with glee. I had been in here long enough and felt no need to pay homage to the liminal hell before leaving. I would not miss a single thing; my experiences here could live on in a horror tale someday down the road, but I'd need a long vacation before that ever happened. The exit was now just a turn away, and I took a deep breath with a smile before dashing around the corner into an abandoned bookstore. It seemed like a strange place to come out at, but it made sense that liminal spaces in the real world would be the connection to The Back Rooms.

I peered around the store for an exit, out of breath from all the running. I could not see any doors to a parking lot or mall and began rubbing my neck. The gnawing reality ate at me, but I started running again to find another hallway. Empty shelves, beige walls, buzzing lights; I wasn't quite out yet, but I was close. I just had to keep going, and I could see I was almost there by the big letters pasted on an overhang in the ceiling: *"THE END."* I just had to pass under the cove behind the secretary's desk, over the sage carpet and to the hallway on the left.

Just a few more turns, and I'd be out. The light coming from around the corner; that's home. Just a few more steps until I round it and. . . .back to the abandoned bookstore. Of course; I just need to find the hallway now. There's the sign; *The End.* The store must just be really big. One of those massive used bookstores that looks interchangeable, yeah. It made sense why it went out of business; the place was HUGE. Who could afford rent in this big of a store selling books? I just had to keep going; between the shelves and down the halls; the end is near.

A loud, mechanical bang sent a jolt through my body as all of the lights went out. I was somewhere between the hallway and the secretary's desk. The whole place was dark, and I couldn't see where I was anymore. I was lost in the bookshelves, and the library was dead quiet without the buzzing of the lights. Then I heard a staticky voice; it wanted me to come to the secretary's desk. I stayed hidden. I knew I had to be quiet, or *it* would hear me. I could hear shuffling on the carpet on the other side of the shelves. I held my breath, frozen in place.

Another loud bang sent a violent shock through my body. Lights illuminated the store; phosphenes from the abrupt change in light clouded my vision. I instinctively reached for almond water at the visual distortion, guzzling the whole bottle.

Slowly, my mind began to come back. The delusions of escape had cascaded into full blown mania. Still, something was not right here; I had to get out. This was not the end; it was a trap.

I stood up slowly from behind the bookshelves, eyes peeled for anything dangerous. Whatever had been here was gone, at least for now, and I needed to find a place to hide or escape before the lights went out again. I spotted the secretaries desk and the trap hallway on the far end of the room; I needed to search a different part of the library. I passed through a half dozen rows of bookshelves and reached a small seating area with wooden chairs. A neon "For Sale" sign pasted on a rectangular pillar caught my eye. Below the title was a black and white picture of a staticky puppet-esque creature in the middle of the library. It was huge, towering above the bookshelves in the picture with a pentagonal head and black eyes. Its appendages were long and lanky, reaching into four different aisles of shelves, while its body occupied the entirety of the main path.

The text below the picture read:

It offered no explanation for the picture of the freakish creature, but it was definitely a photo of the library. Dread pooled in my stomach, creeping its way up into my chest with a burning sensation; I was in here with whatever *that* was. The memory of hiding behind the shelves was blurry—the voice, muffled steps, and darkness—I couldn't distinguish between what had really happened, and what the fraying threads of my sanity had created. The lights going out had to be real, though, and that meant it could happen again. Darkness would predictably drain my sanity, but I had no idea what to do. I was stuck in this eerie, abandoned library, with the only hallway out just looping me back to the start. There had to be *some* way out; a sliding bookshelf door, a hatch beneath the carpet, or a way up into the venting.

I began frantically searching the bookstore, fighting the feeling of impending doom. Time was not on my side, and if I didn't find a hiding spot when the lights went out again, I feared that creature would find me. The hallway had seemed so promising before, never feeling like I was really going backwards. There were anomalies in there, though; weird rectangular openings low on the walls that had teal light shining from behind them, and distortions in the ceiling and floor. I could even remember a wall of dark windows with something on the other side that I could only describe as an indoor skate park. I could see it in my memory; almost entirely pitch black, concrete half pipes and skate rails disappearing into darkness; it was a horrible memory. The thought of going back into those halls haunted me; into the non-linear corridors and dimly lit paths through hell. My mortality feared the library, while my soul feared staying in the halls too long and phasing eternally into oblivion.

Another reading-nook on the edge of the store caught my eye, pulling my attention away from the impending feeling of doom. One wood chair sat in the middle of the empty space, aimed out at the array of bookshelves, along with a small, uninteresting desk with a pale-white retro box computer a short ways away from it. I could see a small green light on the bottom of the screen; it was on.

I ran to the computer and palmed the bottom of the screen, finding a large power button. When I pressed it, the screen came to life with a high-pitched ring, presenting a black command prompt screen with a blinking green line in the top left corner. I quickly typed "help" before mashing the enter key. A heading then popped up on the screen that read:

LIST OF AVAILABLE COMMANDS.

LEVEL LIST
LEVEL INFO - USE <INFO [LEVEL ID]>
GO TO LEVEL - USE <GOTO [LEVEL ID]>

**USE OF THIS PROGRAM FOR ACCESS TO SUB-LEVELS IS STRICTLY FORBIDDEN. ABUSE WILL RESULT IN SYSTEM LOCK*

I quickly typed in Level List, which brought up an option to display sub-levels. Curious, but not wanting to waste any more time, I typed *NO*. Then the computer froze for a moment, and I thought I had broken it before a flood of lines of text began rapidly scrolling down the screen. I waited anxiously for the list to stop, but the names continued flying by. The words moved faster than I could read, and with an unyielding urgency, I rapidly tapped the desk,

"Come on, come on!" I hissed, when I heard a loud bang overhead. The lights went out, my eyes widened, and I began frantically typing.

<GO TO [The Hub]>

. . .

Unrecognized command

Somewhere off in the bookstore, I heard the faint sound of scuffling carpet. I typed again,

<GOTO [The Hub]>

. . .

"The Hub" is not a valid level ID. Please refer to the ID column for a level's corresponding identifier.

Frantic, I scrolled past dozens of listings before moving the cursor to the scroll bar on the edge screen and dragging it up. Thousands of level listings flashed by on the screen as I moved the bar the slightest bit; there was no way I was going to find The Hub in this mass of listings; there were literally millions, all organized by level number. What do I even pick?

The sound of footsteps grew closer, and I could hear the static voice in my ears.

"I know where you are; I'm coming." it said.

There was no time; I typed in the first code I saw: Level 55, code 1ADDF6EC.

<GOTO [1ADDF6EC]>

Are you sure? [Y / N]
I pressed the "Y" button and smashed enter. The screen froze. I looked over my shoulder. There it was. Red-eyes, evil face covered in staticky black and white; it was huge, reaching over the shelves and headed straight for me. I cranked my head back to the screen.

Loading. . .

A horrible sound of scraping metal, static, and screaming poisoned my ears, echoing like the wails of damned souls off the walls of hell. A claw reached over my shoulder; it was cold, like sharp steel, and I felt it tear into my flesh and pull me. Time seemed to slow as I looked down at where it was holding me, and I could see three large rips in my shirt, but I was not bleeding. My skin was lacerated, but the inside of my cuts was not flesh. There was static inside me, shaking violently, like the screen of a demonic TV. As I turned my head to see the thing again, its mouth was open, revealing a black void surrounded by a head of mummified strands of static. Anguished looking ghosts appeared deep in the void of its mouth while the screams grew louder, and just as its jaws began closing around me, a mighty force began to pull me away from the beast.

The thing thrashed and threw its terrible head in the air, fighting to keep its claw embedded in my shoulder. It shrieked in agony as I grew further and further away, fading into black as the walls of my vision began to close in. Its furious red eyes were the last thing I saw before everything went black. Then purgatory; time lost all meaning. I was in the void for eternity. Then I felt my back thud against the hard ground.

Chapter 10

Mindless Hills

The world was bright, and I could see the blue sky. I felt spiky grass when I pushed my arms out, and when I sat up, I saw yellow houses set on top of round, grassy hills. Something was off about them. There were too many hills; too many houses that all appeared identical. It looked like a suburb, with white picket fences, and I could even see a water tower on a hill off in the distance. This was not home; it was a strange, seemingly infinite landscape of hills and houses, covered by a bright blue sky that had no sun. No clouds either; just a solid sky-blue that stretched over the entire space. The grass didn't feel right, either; it was fake, like a plastic astro-turf, and as I worked my fingers into it, I eventually found a hard base layer of concrete.

The houses were uniform and simple; square bases with pitched roofs starting halfway up on the second story. They had square windows on both floors and were painted a light-yellow color with brown shingle roofs. There was also an asphalt road that ran between the hills closest to me, appearing to lead off further into the level before disappearing into the green valleys. It almost looked like an old windows background, with the vibrantly colored grass and sky, but the part that you didn't see.

I had quite literally teleported myself into what looked like a demented screen saver; to the oblivion that exists beyond the edges of a computer background. The weird hills and houses were not intentionally placed here, rather they were anomalous manifestations in an environment that was not designed for human access. A glitch, like I had walked outside of a virtual boundary.

The horrors of the library felt distant now; I wasn't sure how long I had been asleep on the ground here in that purgatory-like state, but it had seemingly dulled the traumatizing experience. It was starting to come back to me, though, and as I palmed my shoulder where the thing had grabbed me, I felt the frayed strands of my shirt and a soreness that felt like I had been hit with a baseball bat. I had three big scars reaching from my collar bone down to my shoulder blade, but no blood stains on my shirt. I could distinctly recall the pain of the things claws tearing into my flesh, but the lack of blood made me think it had been trying to do something other than just kill me. The screams that came from its throat sounded like the wails of tormented souls; perhaps it brought a fate worse than death. How many people were in there; what was it like?

I couldn't afford to pay mind to it; even the memory of the library wore on my sanity, and with no almond water left, I had to start moving. The logical place to start here was the houses, and so I headed up the grass hill next to me towards the closest one. The sound of chafing astroturf beneath my feet was very muffled, and when I got up to the front door, I paused to see if I could hear any people inside. The place was dead quiet, even more so than the mall. There was *no* sound as I stood still, and when I turned the knob on the door, the creaking of its hinges hardly penetrated the silence. The sound of my footsteps on the vinyl floor inside the house were also muffled, like both of my ears were plugged up, dampening every sound.

The interior of the house was sparsely furnished with a small dining table, wardrobe, and single chair set on the edge of the room. It looked like a prefabricated home, with gray plaster panel walls and a compact design. The main level was probably no bigger than 400 square feet, with the living room, dining area, and kitchen all connected in an L shape.

A short stairwell leading up to the second floor sat to the right of the entry door, and at the top of it, a closed door. I stared up at it from the lower level, picturing a bedroom on the other side. Going up there was. . .undesirable, to say the least. Nothing that I could imagine behind the door felt good; an angry person, grotesque entity, or empty room; the only thing behind that door that I wanted to see was home, and I knew for a fact that home was not there. It would probably just be another empty, liminal room that's presence was generally uncomfortable and unwelcoming.

I was sick of being forced to explore these places that were unrelentingly disturbing with no qualities of comfort, but I literally had no choice; I needed almond water. The Back Rooms was a dice-roll with all bad results; you just hoped to get the least worst. With no guide or useful information, and a completely unintelligible, massive environment with no discernible cause or purpose, it was a damn miracle if a person didn't get lost forever on one level, much less multiple. This was the closest thing to a cursed fate I knew of; explore corridors of ceaseless horror and surprises, or sit still and never get out.

I began to climb up the stairs to the second floor,

following a thin railing with my hand. I stared at the door as I climbed, feeling my heart rate increase with each step, when I suddenly lost my footing and braced off the railing. It tore out of the wall as I fell forward, bringing a large panel of plaster with it that shattered as it hit the stairs. A plume of dust mushroomed into the air that burnt my eyes and lungs, causing me to sputter and curse the idiot who built it. Large holes in the wall now ran along the entire stairwell, revealing a thin layer of cheap plywood; what a joke of a build. I shook my head in disbelief and stood up to begin dusting myself off, when the door at top of the stairs caught my eye; it was open, and a yellow humanoid was standing in the opening.

I recoiled in horror, stumbling down the stairs before falling down the entire flight into the wall of plaster at the bottom. I scrambled to get back on my feet, smashing through more plaster and fighting to run out of the house. I could hear its footsteps thumping down the stairs, but I was already out the front door by the time it reached the main level. I sprinted down the grass hill towards the road, when I heard a human voice yell "Hey! Stop!"

I continued running, thinking it was the voice of another shapeshifter. It was chasing me and yelling, but I had already put at least a hundred feet between us. I planned to disappear into another house once I got out of their line of sight. A bend in the road ahead led between two grassy hills and appeared to be the perfect breakaway point, but as I rounded the corner, I ran full boar into a milk truck parked directly in the middle of the road, knocking me flat on my back. I wheezed as I tried to catch my breath, struggling to get back on my feet but crippled by pain. I could hear the footsteps of the shapeshifter getting closer, and with no time to run, I turned to fight.

"I'll tear your heart out!" I screamed, throwing my arms in the air. To my surprise, the shapeshifter stopped. It looked completely different from the girl in the basement; this one was wearing a full yellow hazmat suit with a black mask covering its head, and a biohazard symbol on its chest. I wondered if I had scared it, but then it reached into its pocket and pulled out a gun with a flat rectangular top and a green bar spanning the muzzle. I recoiled as it pulled the trigger, which sent a ray of green lasers towards me, spanning from my head down to my feet. The gun let out a series of beeps, causing the shapeshifter to inspect the top of it before holstering the gun.

"You aren't even close to transformation; what the hell is wrong with you?" it said angrily.

"You. . .can't trick me. I know you're gonna change into one of those gruesome skin-stealers any second." I answered shakily.

"Hah, I s'pose you don't have an entity scanner. Fair." they said light-heartedly. "What's your name, bud?"

"I. . .I'm Jeff. Who are you?"

"Vata. M.E.G number 44891. I was collecting data on this level when I heard you. Thought you were an entity at first, but when you started running, I figured you were either lost or close to wretch transformation." he answered. Excitement began to well inside me.

"Vata, nice to meet you! I've been lost here for at least four days now. I've been trying to get to The Hub; my friend Tommy is supposed to meet me there. Do you know the way?" I asked excitedly.

"Yeah, of course; that's where the main M.E.G base

is. It's a ways from here, probably a day's or so journey. Do you want me to take you there?" he replied, filling me with joy.

"God, yes! I lost contact with Tommy 4 or 5 levels ago in this level filled with pools and tiled architecture. Super weird."

"Level 37; the Pool Rooms. One of the better levels to get lost in. How in the heck did you end up here?" Vata said before reaching into his pocket and pulling out a bottle of almond water. "Here, take this. Your sanity clocked in around 25 percent. Best to stay on top of it."

I took the bottle from Vata and thanked him before guzzling down half of it. He then motioned to follow him, and so we started down the asphalt road into the expanse of green hills.

"Well, after the Pool Rooms I ended up in a suburban basement looking place," I started. "Then this little girl came down the stairs and turned into a skin stealer, so I climbed through a window in a laundry room and ended up in a dead mall. I wandered through there for what felt like days before finding a bookstore that took me to an abandoned library." Vata glanced over at me from behind his mask.

"The End?" he said curiously.

"Yeah, I saw that pasted on the ceiling. I thought I was almost out, but the hallways just kept taking me back to the store. Then this giant abomination started hunting me and nearly killed me before the computer teleported me here." I concluded before pulling down the collar of my shirt to reveal the scars on my shoulder. "See, that's where it got me."

"The librarian; you're damn lucky to be alive! Most people don't make it out of there." he exclaimed. "That thing will tear your soul right from your body."

"That was the worst thing I've seen yet, and that's saying something in here." I said solemnly. "Speaking of in *here*, Tommy told me this is The *Back Rooms*. Is that true? And what's M.E.G?"

Houses on hills littered the landscape covered by the uniform blue sky. If this wasn't The Back Rooms, wherever we were was certainly sinister and strange.

"Unfortunately, yes, you are in The Back Rooms." Vata said sympathetically. "M.E.G is the largest group here. We have bases on multiple levels and try to help wanderers where we can. And I already know what you're going to ask; no, we don't currently know how to get out. Most of our operations are dedicated to helping people escape and avoid dangerous levels. That and research about them."

My heart sank upon hearing this; another person who couldn't help me get home. At least he could bring me to some semblance of civilization, whatever that meant in this place.

"So, if you guys help people out and study The Back Rooms, are you also trying to find an exit?" I asked quickly.

"We have expeditionary groups of explorers that try to chart paths through the deeper levels, but those groups regularly lose members." Vata explained. "As I am sure you are well aware by now, many levels are confusing and riddled with entities. That, combined with The Back Rooms' non-linear properties and sanity-draining effects, makes these expeditions very dangerous. Entire groups of M.E.G members have gone missing on some levels, and with them goes their research and documentations of those levels."

"I see; damn. I'm still trying to figure out what this place even *is*. Sounds like you guys are too." I said, shaking my head.

We had now walked at least a mile down the winding road that had periodic traffic signs with curved arrows and yield symbols. The level was still starkly quiet, and I wondered where exactly it was we were heading. Various objects of interest had appeared on the horizon, like water and cell towers, while we passed by road signs and fire hydrants, but Vata paid no mind to them; he was just following the road.

"We're still developing theories on it. I can bring you to the archives and show you some of the latest studies, but with so much of this place still unexplored, we don't have a fully developed theory yet." Vata explained. "Some think it's a simulation, while others are convinced it's some sort of wormhole, but most of our research is aimed at specific levels and their properties to keep our members safe."

"Do you know anybody who *has* made it back?" I asked curiously.

"That's just it; we have no way of contacting the outer world. If one of our expeditionary teams goes missing, we have no idea if they made it out or got lost." he replied. "Look, there's where we are headed." Vaya pointed to a large, semi-translucent object on the horizon that looked like it was floating.

"That's still pretty far, isn't it?" I said with a twinge of concern.

"Sort of." Vata turned his head towards me. "You scared of getting lost again?"

"Well yeah! I'll be right back at square one if I lose you." I retorted.

"Just stay close. Barring anything unusual, the way back is static." Vata reassured me.

We continued on through the expanse of rolling hills

of fake grass, following the road towards that big thing in the sky. The quiet was almost deafening, with no sound of the wind or birds. No sunshine to make me squint, and no clouds to decorate the sky; just a vast suburb-like environment illuminated by something unknown. I felt lightheaded after some time, which I staved off with almond water, but wondered about how Vata was doing.

"How do you drink with that suit on?" I asked. "What's it even for anyway?"

"There's an internal bladder of almond water," he replied. "Certain levels have various biohazards, too, so M.E.G members wear them as a precaution."

I nodded and then the object in the sky caught my eye again. It was close enough now that I could make out some details; it was in the shape of a large castle, colored a light-pinkish blue, with towers on all four corners that had rectangular crenel-merlon crowns. The bricks were lustrous, emitting a hazy light that gave the entire building a glowing aura, and though it still appeared translucent against the sky, the interior wasn't visible. This was the most "magical" thing I had seen in The Back Rooms yet, and I couldn't help but wonder what was inside.

"How are we going to get up there?" I asked, staring at the floating castle.

"You'll see." Vata replied.

We followed the road around a dozen or so bends before heading off it towards the castle. Green hills dotted with houses stretched off in every direction, like something out of a 1930's stop motion film. By the time we had reached the base of the castle, the sky was getting darker, and I noticed that Vata had pulled out a polaroid camera and was now taking pictures of the landscape. He waited for a moment as the photo printed, and then inspected it before scoffing.

"It's things like this that make charting levels so difficult. Here, have a look." he said, holding the photo out. As I looked closely, I noticed that the picture appeared grainy and completely devoid of the shadows cast by the dwindling light. It just looked like blurry green mounds with yellow rectangles on a blue background.

"Weird. Is the camera working right?" I asked.

"Works just fine; some levels mess with photos, usually highly anomalous ones." Vata replied, tucking away the photo. "Alright, it should be around here somewhere. There's a rope that takes us up."

Vata began to search the square shadow cast by the overhead castle, and quickly found a jute rope coiled on the ground that stretched up into the castle. I scurried over to him as he started to climb, and then grabbed the rope to hoist myself up. It was rough and scratchy, and I instantly felt the fatigue of days of wandering in my bones. The castle appeared to be a hundred or more feet up, and once I was a ways off the ground, my arms began to cramp, causing me to let out a pained gasp.

"You alright down there?" Vata said, continuing to climb.

"I don't know. My arms are dead." I replied, clutching the rope.

"Well," Vata huffed. "Not to alarm you, but the entities come out at night. Nothing I can do if you fall."

I stared at the ground with wide eyes, imaging myself running from hordes of terrible beasts through the infinite hills. This was enough to keep me moving up the rope, despite the relentless aching in my arms and back. My periodic glances out at the landscape were met with a darkness that grew by the minute. Distant houses had faded into hazy outlines, and the sky was now colored with a gradient of charcoal and gray. I wondered about what might be out there— trapdoors into underground bunkers, hidden treasures in the water towers, portals to different levels in the houses—how deep would someone have to go to find them? Better yet, where was the edge of this place, and what was even there? It was so open and seemingly traversable; surely it couldn't go on forever?

We were now just a few more pulls to the top, and the ground was blanketed in complete blackness; falling meant certain death into the abyss. I could see that Vata had reached the bottom of the castle and was now climbing through a square hole in the bottom, and as I neared the opening, I felt the rope shake from below. This sent a chill up my spine, causing me to yank myself up through the trap door. I threw my body onto the floor and worked to catch my breath, watching Vata as he stood with his hands on his hips, breathing heavily from behind his mask.

"I wasn't sure if you were going to make it." he exclaimed.

"Something," I gasped. "moved the rope."

"I told you there's entities down there. Take a second to catch your breath and drink some almond water. We've just got a little longer to the hub. You can rest up there." he said, filling my mind with the image of a warm bed and dinner. I hadn't eaten in days, and though I had no idea what the food situation would be like, any place that I could call safe for a few hours would be extremely welcome.

The room we had come into had blue and yellow tile floors and matte-pink and dark green striped walls. It was reminiscent of a carnival funhouse, like we were in the basement or service area of it. Overhead HVAC tubing and plumbing stretched down the walls, intermittently lit by exposed lightbulb sockets that cast shadows in between the piping. Characteristically unnerving; I had fooled myself into thinking I was going to a fairy land again.

"Another damn creepy place." I groaned. "Where to?"

"This way." Vata said, nodding towards an amber-colored metal door down the hall.

The door opened to a room with a ceiling that had nearly tripled in height, and appeared to be some sort of large gymnasium. Spans of bright fluorescent lights covered the ceiling, shining down on an array of children's recreational equipment. The first thing that caught my eye was a huge, yellow inflatable bounce house. It had a large slide that led down into a rainbow-colored ball pit that was surrounded by a large play place structure, like the kid's area in a fast food chain. The structure had square tunnels that were surrounded by black netting, along with purple foam covered supports and plastic climbing platforms.

"I woulda loved this place as a kid." I said, causing Vata to scoff.

"Me too. Don't touch anything, though; especially anything that looks familiar." Vata warned as we navigated around the ball pit.

"At this point I should know better than to ask, but why not?" I said curiously

"Nostalgia traps. This is another area we're studying,

but in some instances, The Back Rooms will create objects that are from your childhood." Vata explained. "Things like a toy car or doll. When you see it, you'll experience a flood of nostalgia, followed by a longing for that thing. If you touch it, you'll be instantly sent to level 18."

"Freaky." I said, gawking at the play place. "You know, that level sounds familiar for some reason."

"That whole place is one big nostalgia trip. The environment morphs into places unique to your childhood. Play places, children's libraries, school hallways, kindergarten classrooms, even entire neighborhoods had been reported on that level." Vata said, shaking his head.

"Kindergarten. . .that's it! I found this note back in the mall." I exclaimed, pulling out the scraps of paper from my cargo pocket. "Looks like this guy ended up on that level and went mad."

Vata took the note and inspected it for a moment before letting out a mournful sigh.

"What? Did you know him?" I asked quickly.

"Don't think so; it's just always sad finding notes from fallen comrades" he replied before turning to the next page. "Was this with the note as well?"

"Yeah, I found it all in a pile in a department store of the mall." I replied.

"Why would he have torn out an intake document?" Vata muttered. "Hmm, this is an old report, too. I wasn't even in The Back Rooms back then. Thanks for this; M.E.G will be able to close this case now." Vata then packed away the papers and then continued on.

We passed by more sports equipment and colorful toys

as we headed towards the end of the room, but I was careful to keep my eyes off anything specific, heeding Vata's warning about traps. I was far too close to take any chances now. A set of double, steel gymnasium doors led us to an area that looked like a food court, with rows of empty blue-and-white-colored booths spanning across a black and white tile floor. There was also a central buffet area with teal-tinted glass awnings that were trimmed with brass rods, hovering over empty, stainless steel serving dishes. It reminded me of the breakfast part of a hotel after hours—void of any food, dishware or servers—just an empty space waiting for people. It was classically liminal, yet so far from ever being used. Was there ever a time where people had gathered here to eat?

Two tall doors sat on opposite sides of the buffet, and as Vata led us towards the one on the right, I asked him where the other one went.

"The food court keeps on going that way; this is just the buffet area."

"Have you been over there before?" I asked, looking over at the other doorway. The area appeared much larger, like a mall food court, and I could even see some abandoned storefronts. "It looks a lot like the mall."

"I have. It's actually a bridge to that level." Vata replied. "One way though."

"Eesh, how do you get back then? How big is the food court anyway?" I asked, following Vata through the doorway.

"It's pretty big. . .ten square miles or so." Vata chuckled. "Bit of wanderlust, huh?"

I shook my head in denial; I had no interest in going anywhere other than The Hub.

"No, I still just have so many questions." I said, before noticing a large bridge perpendicular to our path. It was pearly white with ornate railings along the sides, and led over a large pool of cerulean water. "Is that where we are going?"

"After intake, you'll do a debrief with the commander. She'll be able to answer more of your questions." Vata said before turning towards the bridge. "That is the bridge to the Dream Palace. Unfortunately, we aren't going there."

"Well damn, of course we aren't! Why?" I yelled. "Wait, lemme guess: horrible entities, psychological hazards, and an infinite labyrinth of desolate, castle halls?"

"Hah, pessimism and wander lust; you'll be in good company here." Vata teased. "It's actually quite the opposite. Here, take a look at this." Vata led us over to the start of the bridge and pointed at a jeweled plaque.

Indulge at The Dream Palace

Enjoy diamond-colored rooms that shine with brilliant opalescence. Swim in the fountains made of pearl beneath our lovely rose-quartz chandeliers. Basque in the beauty of the architecture, wandering through ornate doors decorated with jewels. Breathe in the luxurious air from our choice selection of tropical plants while you get lost in the streams of glimmering light that stretch through the tall arched ceilings of our majestic corridors. Whatever your heart desires, be it young maids in black and white with silver platters of desserts, or ravishing men in tuxedos that reveal their best parts, the honey gushes in The Dream Palace.

I stared at the plague in disbelief before turning to Vata.

"It's all a lie then, huh?" I said gloomily.

"No, it's all true. Our headquarters was founded around it; The Hub is right around the corner." Vata said, nodding towards the doorway at the end of the path. "With how horrible The Back Rooms is, you can understand why a place like this would be desirable."

"Well. . .what's the catch then?" I said, staring at the bridge that stretched out over the water into a light fog.

"Everything you could want is in there. Food, sex, drugs, luxury; why in the hell would you want to return to The Back Rooms?" Vata said, before removing his mask. He was young, with long brown hair and a narrow face, and stared at me with an intensity that was unsettling. "You go in there, and you'll never want to come out. The bliss will be intoxicating, but empty. You'll never escape."

I stared back at Vata in silence, and then out at the bridge. I could see the faint glimmer of stars in the fog, like a cosmic aura, and imagined myself in the palace, basking in ecstasy. I considered what I would return to if I did manage to escape The Back Rooms; the dead-end HVAC job, my 30 year mortgage, going home alone to my couch to watch TV every night. The news, wars, and culture that I loathed. The death, the violence; why should I go back? It wasn't even easy to get there; I would have to fight my way through liminal hell to return to. . .what? I couldn't think of a single person that would care even if I did return home, other than my boss. The only reason not to cross the bridge seemed like some sort of philosophical virtue; losing myself in another world forever felt wrong in principle, but who cares? If there's happiness on the other side, what does it matter if it's "real?"

"You know, Vata," I said, turning towards him. "There's not much for me if I ever do make it out of here. Honestly, despite all the terrible things that had happened since I got here, it's been refreshing to actually feel something." Vata stared at me with a scowl, and then looked over his shoulder towards the doorway.

"The Hub is right over there. You can either come with me and work to get out, or you can end this whole thing and walk down that bridge."

I looked over at the doorway, and then back at Vata, who now wore a neutral expression and appeared to be growing impatient.

"Is there really no turning back if I go in there?" I asked.

"You can leave anytime you want, but you won't want to. It's like a drug; once you come down, the world is just as cold and unfeeling as when you went in. Why face it?" Vata shrugged. "That's why I've never gone in."

I took another long look out at the bridge, and then paused for a moment before saying "I'll think on it." A smirk grew on Vata's face and then he motioned for me to follow as we headed towards the doorway to The Hub.

Chapter 11

The Hub

Vata led us down a flight of stairs that bottomed out on a concrete floor, before opening a gray steel door to what looked like a subterranean car underpass. The tunnel was round and made entirely of concrete, with a tall ceiling that was covered in dim amber lighting and stretched as far as I could see in both directions. The walls disappeared into blackness, dotted with evenly spaced doors, each with a black number painted on it. The center of the tunnel had a black-asphalt road with yellow lines and was bordered by a thin sidewalk on each side.

"Is this. . .it?" I said quietly. "I expected a stronghold or something."

"Right here," Vata said, walking over to a keypad on a nearby door. He punched in a sequence of 8 numbers, causing the door to swing open to a laboratory. Along the left wall was a large window that had a control panel of buttons and levers in front of it. Four empty desk chairs were positioned in front of the controls, and on the other side of the glass was a network of yellow rooms with fluorescent overhead lighting. It looked just like the place I had climbed into from the office, and as I walked over to gawk through the window, Vata removed his hazmat suit and hung it up with the others on the wall of the lab.

"Look familiar?" Vata said, walking over to my side.

"Yeah, just like the basement of Caius. How in the hell did we get back here?" I said, perplexed. Vata then patted my shoulder and said "if only it were that simple." I stared at him in confusion before a door on the far end of the laboratory opened, grabbing my attention. In the opening stood a tall woman wearing black boots and a military uniform. She had pinned black hair and a stern face, along with a large gold symbol on her chest in the shape of an eagle.

"Vata! Good to see you back. How did your survey on level 55 go?" she said, before noticing me. "And who's this?"

"I brought back some samples for analysis, but I wasn't able to find the bunker." Vata replied. "This is Jeff. I found him on level 55. He's been lost for a few days now."

The woman smiled and walked over to me, the sounds of her heels clicking on the floor.

"Commander Vex; nice to meet you." she said, extending out her hand. I shook it and nodded. "You must be pretty tired, but I'll need to get some information from you before letting you into the headquarters. Vata, why don't you drop off that sample and then let intake know we have another wanderer."

"Yes ma'am." Vata said before turning to me. "I'll see you in a bit."

"Follow me." Vex said, and then led us to a door that opened to an office that had a large steel desk and filing cabinets along the wall. She sat in a chair behind the desk across from me and then pulled out some papers from the drawer, along with a notepad and pen.

"So, Jeff," she said, still shuffling papers. "when did you

realize you were in The Back Rooms?"

"Um, not until I met up with Tommy. He's the one who told me about them."

"And, how did you meet Tommy?" she said, now scribbling on her notepad.

"I was sleeping in a cubicle on level 4. One of those wretches woke me up and Tommy scared it off." I said, readjusting in my seat.

"Lucky you! And where is Tommy now?"

"We got separated in the Pool Rooms," I said before my voice cracked. I felt tears welling behind my eyes. I took a deep breath, trying to keep my composure and then pulled his note out of my pocket.

"He left me this." I said, placing the note on the desk before wiping a small tear from my eye. "He said if we got separated, I should go to The Hub and meet him here."

The commander inspected the note and then looked up at me from her glasses. "I'm sorry, we haven't had any new intakes in the last couple days." she said with a canted frown, causing me to sigh and look down at the desk.

"I figured it was probably a long shot; I was lucky enough to find Vata."

"Incredibly lucky." she said, leaning back in her chair. "We might have a file on Tommy, though. I could try to see what expeditionary team he's a part of and begin a search and rescue."

"I don't think he was a part of your group. He didn't mention anything about it, just that The Hub was a good place for us to meet up." I explained.

"Hm, maybe he stumbled across one of our documents

from The Hub somewhere. Hopefully he finds his way here. Got some questions for him as well." she said, packing away some papers in her desk drawer before shutting it with a thud. "Did Vata tell you about our organization?"

"Just a bit. He said you guys research The Back Rooms and help people who get lost here." I replied.

"That's correct. We were founded nearly 30 years ago by a small group of wanderers who were trying to survive. The organization expanded as new members brought new skills and labor, eventually growing into the largest group in the Back Rooms." Vex said proudly.

"Are there other groups of people here too?" I asked curiously.

"Only a few. Most are just small groups of roaming traders but there are a few hostile organizations on the deeper levels. Encounters with them are extremely rare, though."

"Seems like coming across *anyone* here is rare." I said, causing her to purse her lips and nod. "So, how do people. . .end up here?"

"Well, where were you when you noticed things got strange?" she said, looking at me over her glasses.

"I'm not sure. I was doing HVAC work in a basement when I lost the key. My boss sent me in deeper to find a different way out."

"You probably no-clipped somewhere in that basement. You know, one of those liminal wormholes." she said, scribbling on her notepad. "What did you say the building was called?"

"Caius; it's a government building." I replied. "What is *no-clipping?*"

"The best explanation we have for how people end up

in The Back Rooms." she said matter-of-factly. "Have you ever played any video games, like Minecraft or stuff like that? Or maybe your kids have?"

"I don't have any kids, and no, not really." I said confusedly.

"Me neither, but it's the analogy a lot of our members like to use." she said, pushing a sheet of paper towards me. She read it aloud from memory as I read it.

"No-clipping is the act of traversing through a game environment with collisions disabled, giving the player the ability to pass through solid walls, objects, etc."

"I'm not sure I understand." I said, rereading the sentence. "Walking through walls, like a ghost or something? Wouldn't that just take you into another room?" I said, unsatisfied with the half-baked explanation.

"That's exactly what I said, and it is apparently true for the majority of game environments," Vex said, shrugging her shoulders. "But I'm told that certain areas of the game are not meant to be accessed, and so entering them produces a variety of visual and auditory anomalies."

"That's the leading theory on how people end up here?" I said in disbelief.

"It's just an analogy. The full theory is far more complex." Vex said with a shrug before pushing back her chair. "I'm sure some of our headier members would be happy to go into more detail with you. And, there's a lot more information in the archives on the topic of no-clipping and the environments where it is possible." She then stood up and extended her hand out towards me. "Welcome to The Hub, Jeff. They should have a bed made up for you by now. Go introduce yourself to the other members and get some rest."

"Thank you." I said, standing up to shake her hand. She smiled and nodded, and then I headed towards the door. I was halfway out when I stopped, turning to look back at her

"Ms. Vex?" I said, holding onto the interior of the door. "Has anyone ever been intentionally sent to The Back Rooms?"

Her brow furrowed as she looked at me from above the glasses on the brim of her nose. "As in, by another person?"

"Yeah." I said hesitantly.

"No, none of our members that have gone through intake ever reported such a thing." she replied, looking at me with a squint. "Why do you ask?"

"Well," I started, pacing halfway into the room. "This whole thing started when I got locked in Caius's basement. I tried calling my boss to get me out, but instead of having a janitor or first responder come, he sent Tommy."

"Hmph" she muttered. "Why would he do that?"

"He told me it was to save face with the building owner; didn't want me messing up the company's contract with them. Bad optics, I guess." I said. "Anyway, Tommy called me and told me to give him my phone info so that he could track me while I made my way to the first level of the building. I got lost on the way there, so I tried calling 9-1-1, but Tommy intercepted my call and told me to keep going."

A skeptical look appeared on the commander's face as she put her hands on her hips. "Phones don't work in The Back Rooms, so either you weren't quite in yet, or you hallucinated the phone call." she said sternly. "When was the last successful call you had?"

I thought for a moment before remembering the call

with my boss. "A stairwell in the parking garage; I talked to my boss." I replied, causing a disappointed look to appear on the commander's face. She then pulled her desk drawer back open and slapped a pile of papers back on the surface, seemingly irritated.

"Then you no-clipped shortly after." she asserted with a twinge of irritation in her voice. "Or you were in sooner and hallucinated the call. That's all I got for you, Jeff."

I looked at the ground with a sigh, unsatisfied with the explanation. Noticing this, she walked over and put her hand on my back.

"Another person's sinister intent might be easier to accept than the reality of the situation." she said sympathetically. "The mind is desperate for any explanation on what exactly "this" is, but I would be doing you a disservice if I told you anything other than the truth."

I looked over at her with weary eyes. She was nodding with pursed lips, like some kind of parent explaining to their child why they can't eat ice cream all day. Her reasoning felt condescending, like I couldn't handle the reality of the situation and that I had made my story up. I wasn't going to make any progress with her.

"Thanks." I said, concealing my frustration.

"Happy to help." she replied, lightly pushing me towards the door. "Now go get some rest. It will help you come to terms with things better."

Anger bubbled beneath my skin as I fought the urge to curse her and insist on telling more of my story. She shut the door behind me as I left the room, and then I saw Vata waiting for me in the laboratory.

"All set?" he said with a smile.

"Yeah, I guess. Where to now?" I replied, suppressing my anger.

"Through here," Vata nodded towards another door in the lab, which led into a huge concrete room. The ceiling must have been 50 ft tall with dim amber lighting, while the walls of the expanse stretched out so far that they disappeared into a fog. Square structures of concrete with rectangular openings covered the floor, like some sort of large-scale population center for natural disasters. I could see a few people gathered around the house-like structures, most of which looked rough, with overgrown hair, dirty complexions, and tattered clothes. It looked desolate and impoverished, but the few souls present gave the space a slight semblance of humanity.

"This is it, huh?" I said, looking around at the unfeeling, concrete gymnasium-esque place.

"Yep," Vata replied dimly. "See why people want to go to the Dream Palace?"

"No doubt. . .Is this everybody?" I said, counting less than a dozen people.

"Not quite, most of our other members are on expeditions. These guys are just getting back." Vata said, nodding at the tired looking group of four gathered around the nearest concrete house. "We have a few small bases on other levels too, but this is an average day in The Hub."

"This isn't really the bustling community I was expecting." I said, scratching my head. "How, uh, big is this place? Where am I staying?"

"Your shelter number is C-4. The rows work like a spreadsheet and each building is labeled." Vata said, pointing to a painted red number on the nearest house. "The next available space was way down on H-42. You should be happy I got you something so close to the entrance." Vata said, bumping me with his elbow. "Come on, let's go meet Theta Team. They just got back from level 0.01."

Vata led us over to the group of four wanders outside of the concrete hut who were sitting on straw bales. There were three men and one woman, each wearing black cargo pants and tan collared shirts that appeared to be made of a thick cotton and had an eagle emblem, like the one on Vata's hazmat suit.

"This is the new intake I was telling you guys about." Vata said as I hung behind him, walking towards the group. "Came all the way from level 0. Linear progress up through level 5, too." Vata said, seemingly praising me. "Matter of fact, he found a new link between the Terror Hotel and The Pool Rooms."

Unsure of how to respond and a bit bashful, I just smiled and stayed silent, but then noticed the group of people who were now staring like they expected me to say something.

"Uh, my name is Jeff. Nice to meet you all." I said, faking a smile.

"Welcome, Jeff." said the man seated furthest from me. He was lanky and crouched with his arms over his knees, wearing a tired expression beneath messy black hair and a distinct red and black neck tattoo in the shape of a dragon. "I'm Shiloh, this is Ivan, Jonesy, and Catarina." he said, nodding towards the members as he named them. Ivan looked older, with long white hair and a medium beard, along with a wide face that's age lines gave him perpetual scowl. He wore gold reading glasses and appeared immersed in a book, hardly noticing my introduction.

Jonesy was black with short hair, bearing a large scar on the left side of his jaw. He dwarfed Catarina with his size, who was seated next to him drinking a bottle of almond water. She had short blonde hair, a soft round face, and a meek stature that contrasted her dirty uniform and weary expression.

"Vata said you found a note from a fallen wanderer on Level 33." Shiloh said, glancing up at me as I nodded. "Guess you'll just have to take their place then."

Confused, I shook my head, causing Shiloh to scoff and smirk at Vata.

"What? You didn't tell him?" Shiloh sneered.

"It's his first day, give him a break." Jonesy interjected. I glanced over at Vata in confusion, causing him to return a sympathetic expression.

"Better to just get it over with." Shiloh said, exhaling as he stood up and walked towards Vata and I. He stood in front of me and stared intently before saying "If you want to stay here, you must become a part of a group. It's how you pay for the safety and supplies from M.E.G."

"I have to go. . .back out there? Are you kidding me?" I said in disbelief.

"Go to that dream palace if you aren't game." Shiloh replied. He then gave Vata a dirty look before heading towards the concrete house the team was seated around. This caused Catarina and Jonesy to stand up and head towards another house, leaving me unsettled and confused. Ivan was the only person left now, and he was still reading, seemingly oblivious to what had just happened. I turned to Vata who was looking at the ground and rubbing his head. His eyes then looked up at me and he sighed.

"Sorry man, I shoulda told you sooner. Exploration is pretty much mandatory. That's why there's not a lot of people here."

"How long before I have to go back out?" I said resignedly.

"Vex usually gives new intakes a day or so before basic training." Vata replied. "You'll be assigned to a group and then given a mission timeline after that."

"Only a *day!*" I spat. "How long does a mission take? And what about when I get back? *If* I get back, that is." I said, trying to come to terms with the dreary reality of the situation.

"Mission duration depends on the assignment and the level's hazard rating. Because you're new, you'll be assigned to easier levels; probably just a mapping job. Once you're done, you'll get a couple days to go through debrief and rest before your group is redeployed." Vata said, patting me on the back. "Some more experienced members can be temporarily reassigned to Archives to document their findings, but that only happens after you've surveyed at least two dozen levels or discovered a new one."

Vata looked at me with a pained, sympathetic smile before patting me on the back. He then nodded towards a concrete house a few rows down on the left. "My place is right here. If you need anything, feel free to stop by. I'll let you know before I'm deployed again. You should have everything you need in your house. It's C-4, in case you forgot." Vata concluded.

I nodded at him and said a half-hearted thanks. He patted my back again and said "You'll get used to it" before heading off towards his house. I then took a bearing of the house numbers, and spotted C-row a short ways down. Downtrodden and exhausted, I shuffled towards my cubicle before I noticed Ivan look up at me from his book.

"You found a way into the Pool Rooms from level 5?" he said curiously.

"Yeah. In one of the hotel bathrooms." I replied.

"Where exactly?" he pressed.

"I don't quite remember. It was a dark part of the hotel. Really dusty air, entities too."

Ivan looked at me skeptically for a moment, and then closed his book. "And how about leading up to the hotel?"

"Well, I took an elevator there from an office building. I was lost in there for God knows how long." I replied.

"Hm. How did you manage the entity hoards on level 3?" he said with raised eyebrows.

"Level 3; pipe tunnels, right? One of those skin-stealers chased me, but I found an elevator to the office." I replied, shuttering at the memory of that horrible creature in the halls; the picture of its silhouette looming in the darkness.

"Level 3 is a hundred-square mile network of red-iron barred hallways and industrial corridors," he said ominously. "Does that ring a bell?"

I thought for a moment about his description, but then shook my head. "No, nothing like that." A smirk grew on his face, and he stood up and peered at me through his glasses.

"There's been rumors of a link between level 2 and 4; looks like you found it. That's two new bridges between levels you've discovered; incredibly lucky. Keep it up and you'll get a day to work in debrief." Ivan said with a nod. I looked at him with a reluctant smile, and then he grabbed his book before pointing towards the left end of the concrete expanse.

"I'm over at A14. If you happen across anything else strange, stop by and let me know. I'm one of the Archivists here; Theta Team was giving me their debrief when you and Vata showed up." he said. "Nice to meet you, Jeff. I'm off to bed now. You should do the same."

I nodded in agreement with a smile, silently pleased with the fact that he wasn't a part of that group that had just given me the cold shoulder. I needed all the friends I could get here, and I thought I might talk to him more about my entry, but now wasn't the right time. He seemed like he would actually listen to my story, unlike Vex, and I planned to catch up with him more tomorrow. I needed rest now, though.

I passed by a few square concrete houses that were evenly spaced a short ways apart until coming to the one marked with a large C4 in red paint. It had no door, just like all the others, and was nothing more than a 150 square foot concrete room with a straw bed, metal toilet, mini fridge plugged into one outlet on the wall, and white porcelain sink. It looked like a prison cell, with no windows or decorations, but it was the only place I had been to in days that felt truly safe. My weary bones ached, and my body felt like it was experiencing double gravity, and though the straw bed was pokey and scratchy, laying down felt sublime. I positioned my body so that I could see the doorway into my cell, and eventually drifted off, staring at the amber lighting that crept halfway into the room along the cold floor.

***

I awoke from a nightmare of being chased down a long,

gray hallway by a giant black spider with a white face. It had dropped down from the ceiling and I hid in a hotel room when I saw it; the thumping of its massive legs sounding on the carpet on the other side of the door. My eyes shot open; the concrete cell I was sleeping in hadn't changed at all. There was no shift in lighting or sound of birds; just the same, unfeeling space. I tried to breathe slowly to calm my rapid heart rate from the dream, and while I did feel a bit better physically, my mind was still a mess. Nothing felt right. I woke from a nightmare into a nightmare, with grim prospects and a sense of hopelessness. The only easy way out was the palace, and this was a horrible thing to wake up and think about; quite literally giving up. I had to get out of bed and go see some people or do something; laying here was just growing a knot of anxiety in my chest.

My legs ached as they hit the floor, and my mouth felt dry and sticky. There was no sink or water source in the room, but the humming mini fridge in the room was stocked full of almond water. I cracked a bottle and enjoyed the refreshing and subtly sweet flavor, splashing my face with some and drinking until I was quenched. I felt human, despite the completely inhumane environment, and realized that I was in the absolute best place I could be in The Back Rooms. It was safe, there was sustenance, and everybody here was dedicated to getting out; I just had to pull my weight.

Right when I stepped outside my cell, I saw commander Vex standing with two members I didn't recognize. One was an average looking guy with a curly-blonde afro, and the other was a girl with a silky, brown ponytail. Vex was holding a clothes hanger with a tan uniform draped from it that the others were wearing, and once she spotted me, she smiled and said: "Jeff, good morning! Hope you're well rested; you overslept! Go put this uniform on and then follow me to the classroom."

Shaken up by the abrupt event and still groggy from sleep, I traipsed over to the commander and grabbed the uniform before returning to my cell to get dressed. The uniform was a full jumpsuit made of a thick, cotton canvas-like material, and had a large image of an eagle on the right chest in a metallic bronze color. It thankfully fit a little loose, giving me a bit of flexibility in the rigid material.

As I exited the house in uniform, the commander ordered me and the other conscripts to follow. She led us through the entrance to the lab past the large window to the yellow rooms, and then back into the car tunnel. There was another door a short ways from there that opened to a baby-blue walled room with bright overhead lighting and desks pointed towards a fabric projector screen at the front.

"Have a seat," she said, before dimming the lights and turning on a projector at the back of the room. The screen then lit up to a glitchy blue color with a white 0:00 timestamp and large *PLAY* text at the top left corner, like a VHS tape. A staticky audio then began to play, alongside a strobing lo-fi-esque music, like the sounds they might use for space in old movies. An outdated voice that sounded like a man over the radio during WW2 then began to narrate.

Welcome to the M.E.G. Introductory Training Course. This class will provide you with the basic safety protocol for The Back Rooms. There are four principal hazards that an individual will face during an expedition.

The scene changed to a seemingly infinite, white-walled hallway with brown doors along both sides. The camera then zoomed in on a section on the wall that appeared grainy.

The image of a black moth displayed on the screen. It was clinging to a burgundy-red wall, like the wallpaper of the hotel.

I shuddered at the thought of this terrible fate, recalling the moth I had seen with Tommy. The scene changed to what looked like the interior of a closet, with black and green walls that had strands of purple goo webbed across the room, along with a large pile of squirming white maggots in the center. A huge moth clung to the back wall; the gray and black skull and bones pattern of its wings was captured by the camera.

the event that a smiler is encountered, members are encouraged to abandon their light source and leave it illuminated before finding a light area.

A pale-skinned bony creature bent over on all fours then displayed on the screen. It
had scraggly black hair and dead-white eyes, just like the creature I had seen in the parking garage.

Hounds - Commonly encountered in lower levels of The Back Rooms, hounds are one the most dangerous entities new wanderers will face. Alongside razor sharp teeth and claws, hounds are incredibly fast and can infect wanders with a virus similar to rabies by biting them. The onset of this virus is characterized by effects such as vomiting, cramps, mange, and migraine-like symptoms that will result in transformation of the afflicted wanderer into a hound within the first 30 minutes of being bitten. Any M.E.G. member that has been bitten is to be terminated at the first signs of disease.

Wretches - A "wretch" is the term used to describe a wanderer who has succumbed to the effects of sanity drain. The transformation process begins with psychological effects such as psychosis and aggression, progressing into extreme tactical sensitivity and skin rashing. Although almond water can be administered at this point, the wanderer will suffer from scarring and deformities as a result. Beyond this stage, a wretch's skin will become reddish brown and the individual will undergo additional deformities, such as disjointed limbs, emaciated features, and a perpetual wide grin.

I stared at the screen, frozen in disbelief. These were some of the most horrible
descriptions of creatures I had ever heard of. Each one sounded like hell spawn, and the thought of going back to the place where they resided was a death-sentence. Knowing more about them made my past encounters that much more horrifying, and their existence begged that same old question: what the fuck are they, and why are they here?

Level specific entities, such as the 9ft tall, shadow humanoid "Kitty" on level 974, or the Assault Gorillas in the caves of level 8, are also present in The Back Rooms. These vary greatly in their danger level and characteristics. It is the expeditionary group's responsibility to inform their members of all the entities present on their assigned levels prior to deployment.

A comprehensive list of known entities is available in the entity database of the archives, however, be aware that new entities are regularly discovered. As such, members should exercise caution, particularly when exploring new and not-well documented levels. Report all findings of new entities to an archivist and remember: if you see something, tell someone.

The image of a staircase appeared on the screen as the cameraman climbed up it. At every landing, there was a door that was open to a different environment. One was a dark forest, another a suburban neighborhood at night. I recognized the third one as the green hills, and then the next was an abandoned arcade.

Section 3: Environmental Hazards - Different levels pose varying threats to a wanderer. Most common are the psychological hazards, with some levels having a drastic drain on an individual's sanity. Additionally, certain biological hazards, such as the presence of harmful bacteria or poor air quality are possible. A company issued Haz-mat suit should be utilized when exploring levels with these sorts of risks but be advised that these suits do not protect from all known environmental hazards. Once again, it is the expeditionary group's responsibility to familiarize themselves with the risks present on a particular level.

The screen transitioned to an image of a grainy-textured person standing in the yellow rooms. They were holding a glass bottle, and then the room began to darken. The sound of static and voices began to play, and then the person drank the bottle, causing the room to turn bright again.

Section 4: Psychological Hazards - This effect is ever-present in The Backrooms. Liminal environments, anomalous objects, and the overall isolation of The Back Rooms all contribute towards degraded sanity. Every member of an expeditionary group is required to bring at least 3 liters of almond water with them at the start of each mission. Though the possibility of running out is real, particularly on levels with high-sanity drain, this quantity has been established as the most practical amount to carry to ensure all members of a group return safely.

We are in the process of developing a highly concentrated almond-water solution, but for the time being, the consumption requirement for high risk levels has been a major challenge for deeper exploration.

The screen went black before the image of a shield emblem appeared with an eagle in the center.

Levels are classified between one and five for their hazard level. This metric accounts for the risks of no-clipping, entity count, environmental and psychological hazards, along with any other risks to members. Under certain circumstances, levels may be assigned additional identifiers based on their anomalous properties, environmental consistency, and degree of documentation. Information on these identifiers can be found in the archives.

Always remember: Stay safe, stay sane, stay together.
This concludes the M.E.G introductory training course.

Commander Vex turned off the projector, and the lights came on, revealing the blue-walled classroom. She then walked to the front of the room, and as I looked over at the other members, I could see the dread in their faces.

"That is what we are up against." Vex said seriously. "And this was only the tip of the iceberg. We have documented over 1,000 levels now, along with dozens of entities and unique objects, yet there is still a tremendous amount that's unknown. Everything from undocumented entities, levels, and anomalies, to links between levels, like Jeff here discovered." Vex said, nodding at me, causing the other two students to look over at me. "Information is the most valuable thing we have here, and you will be rewarded for gathering it."

Vex then pulled on the bottom of the projector screen, causing it to fly upwards in a roll, revealing a wooden board pasted with two dozen sheets of paper. Each one had large text at the top, along with a body of text with pictures spread throughout.

"This is our list of current open investigations." she said, tapping the board with a telescoping pointing stick. "Each sheet is a different assignment with the corresponding level and details about the mission. They are also marked at the bottom with the presumed hazard levels between 1 and 5. Because you are all beginners, you will be barred from going on any missions beyond level 2 hazard." Vex turned from the board with her hands behind her back, holding a perfect posture. "Once you've decided on an assignment, your group will go to the archives and collect as much information on the assignment as you can before coming to me for approval. If I sign off on the mission, I will assign you a timeline and then mark the posting as under investigation. This will prevent other groups from taking the mission. If you do not return in the assigned time frame, a recovery group will be dispatched when available."

I stared at the board of assignments, wondering what sorts of things we were going to be investigating. Despite my stark aversion to going back in, I was curious.

"Any questions?" Vex said, looking for a moment at each of us. My mind was still spinning from the video, but then the girl next to me raised their hand.

"So, what do these missions have to do with getting out? Are they all for finding an exit?" she said accusingly, causing Vex to glare at her.

"We all want to get out of here, Hazel, but the theorized

exit levels are deep and behind dangerous levels. Only our most experienced groups are permitted to explore them, and even then, many members have failed to return." Vex replied.

"Well maybe they found the exit. It seems like a waste of time to send people to explore levels that don't lead out." the male conscript interjected, causing Vex to walk over to his desk and place her hands on it.

"If you think you know the way out and want to go running into a level that's crawling with bloodthirsty entities and maddening darkness, be my guest, but you're not taking any other M.E.G. members or resources." Vex snapped, causing the student to lean back with wide eyes. "If you want to stay here, you play by our rules. We keep people safe and are all working together to try and get people home." Vex stood up from the desk and returned to the front of the room. The room remained uncomfortably quiet for a minute before I reservedly asked: "What kind of rewards do we get for completing missions?"

"Good question," Vex replied with a smile. "Every mission has a bounty posted at the top. You will need to complete the requested task in order to get the full bounty. Any supplemental discoveries will pay extra, and pay is determined by the difficulty of the mission and significance of discoveries." Vex paused for a moment, leering at the male conscript who she had just shaken up. "Bounty is used to buy time off and various objects from the store. Specialty foods, like moth jelly, cashew water, energy bars, along with helpful items for missions like super-battery life flashlights, liquid-pain grenades, and weapons are available. Other items for your living space also come in from time to time, like wool blankets, ultra-bright lanterns, and mold grow kits."

Every conscript in the room seemed to be in disbelief as Vex described the things they could buy with bounty. It was stupefyingly strange—to buy novelty objects—in a place as disheartening as this.

"Where does. . .all this stuff come from?" Hazel said, perplexed by the commander's monologue.

"From different levels and entities. Our members bring them back, along with roaming groups of traders that buy and sell at The Hub. They are typically the ones that bring the strange and unusual objects that are highly sought after by M.E.G. members." Vex replied.

"You said we can use bounty credits to buy time off. What happens if we run out of credits?" the male student said, seeming to irritate Vex.

"You will be assigned a mission instead of being able to pick one. If you refuse to go on it, you will be asked to leave The Hub." Vex said seriously, looking at each of us one by one with a cold expression. "Now, if there's no more questions, I'd like you to get acquainted with one another and select a mission from the board. Welcome to M.E.G, Zeta Group."

I looked over at the other two conscripts, realizing now that we were teammates. I had hoped to get on a team with Vata, or at least someone who had more experience; not total beginners.

"You have until tomorrow morning to present me with a mission for your group." Vex said as she headed towards the door. "Oh, and your group will be starting with 100 credits thanks to Jeff's early discoveries. I'd encourage you to wait to spend any until I get you outfitted with the gear for your mission. No point in buying something that you'll have on loan." Vex concluded before shutting the door, leaving the three of us alone in the quiet room.

The male conscript sauntered up to the board "What do you guys think, tier 2 hazard? These are gonna pay the best."

"Let's start with something easier. I had enough jump-scares on my way in here already." Hazel said earnestly.

"The sooner we get to the higher tiers, the closer we are to getting home." the male said confidently. "I say we try and rank up our group as quickly as possible."

Hazel scoffed, causing him to leer at her before turning his head towards me. He then shuffled over to my desk and extended out his hand.

"I'm Rich, by the way. Good to meet you." he said proudly. I reluctantly shook his hand. "Vex said you already have a bunch of discoveries; I bet you wanna go high hazard, too, huh?"

"Why don't we just see what info they have on the assignments before we pick one," I replied before standing up and walking towards the board. Hazel's eyes followed me up to the front, where I skimmed the postings for a minute before looking back over my shoulder at Rich.

"We should start with a safe one; at least get our feet wet. The pay is not all that less, either." I said, glancing at Hazel, who now seemed a bit less tense.

"I'm just trying to get out of here as quickly as possible. Why should we waste our time on pointless missions?" Rich said, shaking his head.

"They aren't pointless, Rich. They still earn us credits." Hazel exclaimed, fed up with his reckless attitude.

"Fine. Just pick one then, Jeff." Rich said, folding his

arms across his chest. I looked over at the array of papers posted on the board, scanning for ones with a low hazard level. Most were rated in the 3 to 4 tier, with warnings about unidentified entities and high no-clip risks, but one with a low hazard rating caught my eye.

"Here's one," I said, taking the paper down, before reading aloud the description. "Level 40. Investigate an abandoned video store. Collect and return any working VHS tapes and CDs to The Hub. Document any entity sightings and strange objects and determine the levels suitability for a settlement."

"That sounds boring as hell." Rich said, before tearing a different sheet off the wall. "What about this one?" he said, shoving the paper into my hands.

"Level 90; the *fun* rooms. An infinite network of claustrophobic rooms styled as if for a child's birthday party. Unsafe, unsecure with severe mental hazards. Mission is to investigate the source of piano music and child's voices that are present throughout the level. Prepare for the darkening event. Multiple confirmed entity sightings." I said aloud, lowering the paper to glare at Rich. "Are you insane?"

"Hey, it's only a level 2 hazard. I bet we could do it." he said with a taunting grin.

"*That's* level 2 hazard? What could be worse than that?" Hazel exclaimed. "Let's do the video store one."

"I vote for the video store too. Besides, the paper says it's a few levels away from the closest link at The Hub, so we'll have to do some research on how to get there." I said, pinning the fun rooms paper back up on the wall.

"Whatever." Rich scoffed. "Let's go to the archives

then and get this over with."

I followed Hazel and Rich out of the classroom back into the amber-lit car tunnel. Rich led the group past the entrance to the laboratory and living quarters to a door that was etched with the image of a book. It opened into a large room with tall bookshelves covering the perimeter, and Ivan was sitting at a desk near the front. He looked up at us from his glasses once we entered.

"Ah, our newest group. Got a mission picked out then?" Ivan said cheerfully.

"We're going to level 40 cause these two are too scared to sign on to something harder." Rich said boastfully, shooting a dirty look back at me. Ivan raised his eyebrows and then pushed back in his chair before heading towards a nearby bookshelf. He skimmed over the book spines with his fingers before removing one and bringing it back to the desk.

"Here's what we have on levels 20 to 200. If I remember correctly, the route there is moderately complex with minimal entity counts. You'll have to go through a couple other levels to get there, but this is a good mission to start out with. Barring anything extreme, you should all return in one piece." Ivan said with a smile, handing the book to Rich. He flipped through it quickly before pushing it towards Hazel, who fumbled and dropped it to the ground with a thud.

"Be careful with that!" Ivan snapped, lurching up from his seat.

"I. . .I'm sorry!" Hazel apologized, scrambling to pick up the book. I glared at Rich who was shrugging, seeming to hold back a smile from the event.

"Bah, off with ya! The study section is over there." Ivan

said, pointing towards an arrangement of desks on the far end of the room. He then plopped back down into his chair and resumed intently reading from a large book propped open on his desk. The three of us sat down at a gray table and Hazel opened the book to the front page, quickly finding level 40 listed in the contents. She flipped to the section and began to read.

"The abandoned video store was first identified in 2004 by group Alpha 1 during their search for a link between level 11 and level 176. Although other routes to level 40 are more than likely to exist, the only confirmed one at this time is through level 31." Hazel read before stopping and looking up at us. "I've been to level 31. It's a giant 90's roller-skating rink." I looked at her curiously, wondering what her journey here had been like. She then resumed reading. "The entrance to level 40 was found approximately 8 miles deep in level 31 through a set of revolving doors. Despite the long distance, the time to reach these doors can be reduced by renting a pair of. .. roller skates from the sales booth."

"What?" Rich sneered. "*Roller skates?* You've gotta be kidding me."

"That's what it says." Hazel retorted before continuing to read. "Be aware that using skates on areas other than the roller rink brings the risk of no-clipping to other levels. These may include but are not limited to: Level 18, 0, 31.1, and -25."

"18. That's the nostalgia level." I said quietly.

"You been there?" Rich said, looking at me with wide eyes.

"No, but I read the note from a guy who did. He turned into a wretch after." I replied, causing Rich to leer at me as if I was lying. I held his stare, causing him to lift his head with a smug grin.

"Freaky shit, huh? I fought off a couple of those things on my way in. Suckers are fast." Rich boasted. "So what? We gotta go to level 31 now? Sounds like a piece of cake, especially if *you* made it through there." Rich mocked, craning his head towards Hazel who shot him back a dirty look before peering back down at the book.

"*Well,* we have to get to the roller rink first, don't we?" Hazel snapped. "And it says here that the safest way is through level 25." Hazel flipped past a dozen pages to the section on level 25, which had a large, printed image of an arcade. The top of the page had, in bold text: *Safe, Secure,* giving me a sense of relief.

"So. . .we need to find a hallway that leads from the arcade to the roller rink; shouldn't be too bad." Hazel said, still skimming the page.

"But. . .how do we get to the arcade then?" I said hesitantly.

"Uhm, a few ways. One of the doors here in The Hub will bring us to The Art Gallery, which is. . ." Hazel stopped.

"What? What does it say?" Rich pressed, leaning over to read the page.

"A *hundred* square miles?" Rich yelled. "How in the HELL are we going to find anything in there?"

"What are the other ways?" I interjected.

"There's just one more that The Hub directly links to. Level 197." Hazel said, flipping pages until nearly reaching the end of the book. "The closing grocery store. Perpetually dark, moderate hostile entity presence, with some environmental complexity. It says the exit to the arcade is only a short ways in, though. We'll have to find an automatic sliding glass door that leads to a colorfully carpeted area." Hazel concluded before looking up at us from the book with an apprehensive expression. Rich clapped his hands and shouted "Boom, let's do it! Easy peasy. Time to go find some video tapes or whatever."

I looked at Hazel and gave her a little smile before saying "It's probably our best bet. Seems like we would get lost in the art gallery." She stared at me for a moment before nodding, and then her attention was taken off me by Ivan, who had appeared next to the table.

"Ay!" Rich yelled, recoiling. "When did you get here?"

"I came to see what all the commotion was about. I'm guessing you guys have a route planned out now." Ivan said before placing a packet of stapled papers on the desk in front of us. "Now you're going to fill these out and bring them to Vex to sign off on. Do it well; this will be your guide for the mission. Fill out all the entrance and exit information for the levels and keep a strict schedule. If you haven't reached one of your checkpoints in the allotted time, turn around and resupply. It's not worth one—or *all* of you—running out of almond water and turning into wretches. Understood?" Ivan warned, looking at each of us intently.

Despite Rich's brash arrogance, he seemed a bit shaken by Ivan's warning, remaining silent during the encounter. I nodded at Ivan in agreement as he stared at me, before a smile appeared on his face.
"Good." Ivan said, seemingly satisfied with our response. "I look forward to seeing what you guys find."

Chapter 12

The Mission

We spent nearly 3 hours in the library, filling out the packet and going over mission details. The work paid off, though, as Vex signed off without a fuss. Then we were set to deploy the following morning. Vex would gather our supplies for the mission and wait for us in the amber car tunnel by the door to Level 197, but I had a little bit of time before leaving to talk to Ivan. He was the only person that I thought might have a clue about being intentionally sent to the Back Rooms, so I stopped by his concrete cell after parting with Hazel and Rich. He was out front, seated on a bale of straw next to a lantern, reading as usual.

"Jeff," he greeted me happily. "Excited for the big day?"

"Not exactly. I wouldn't go if I didn't have to." I replied glumly.

"Ah, you'll get over it. Try to stay curious and hopeful, and before you know it, you'll be back with me in the archives doing a debrief." he rebutted, causing me to blow air out my nose.

"Not sure I'll ever be *curious* and *hopeful* about getting sent into hell." I said wryly. "I did have a bit of a strange question for you, though."

"Everything's strange here. Sit; I'll see if I can help." he said, motioning towards another strawbale across from where he was seated. It was poky and uncomfortable, but felt strangely comforting, reminding me of a hayride.

"I talked to Vex about this, but she didn't seem all that interested. It has to do with how I got here." I said, half-regretting my words. Going behind her back seemed like it might come back to bite me.

"Ah yes, the whole no-clip explanation. It's a weak analogy, I don't blame you for having more questions." Ivan said, shutting his book. "What do you want to know?"

"Not about that. I mean, I do have questions about that, but I was wondering if you'd ever heard of someone being sent here on purpose." I said reluctantly, causing Ivan's white eyebrows to raise.

"Hm, that's a new one. You think someone *tried* to send you here?" he said curiously.

"I mean, maybe. I know people get paranoid and hallucinate here, and I sort of got stuck here by my own doing, but the whole thing just doesn't add up for me."

"I've already reviewed some of Vex's intake info on you. Matter of fact I have it right inside." Ivan said before standing up and scurrying into his cubicle. He returned with a clipboard and papers and began to read. "So, you didn't get the master key to Caius and then your boss sent you in deeper to find a person to. . . break you out? Then you no-clipped somewhere in the basement."

"Yeah, that's all correct. He sent a guy named Tommy who called me and said he had moved my work van out of the parking lot. I gave him some info off my phone so he could track me."

"Oh, I see now; it was a government building." Ivan continued, flipping the paper. "Your phone got disconnected from emergency services, and Tommy. . .found you?" Ivan stopped. "Where did he find you?"

"Level 4, or perhaps a sublevel of it? I had fallen asleep in a cubicle. A wretch woke me up, but Tommy was there and scared it off." I replied. Ivan's brow furrowed as he flipped the papers and then looked at me.

"This is critical information. Why didn't you tell this to Vex?" Ivan asked sharply.

"She wasn't buying it. Seemed to think I had been hallucinating." I said, causing Ivan to scowl and continue thumbing through his papers.

"So, your exact no-clip point is unconfirmed. It says you may have hallucinated a call in the parking garage." Ivan paused. He seemed perplexed "What do you remember? Walk me through *exactly* what happened."

"Well, after I lost the key, I climbed through a trap door beneath a desk in the room I was doing HVAC work on. Then I went through a bunch of weird yellow rooms until I found the parking garage." I explained before Ivan interrupted me.

"Those yellow rooms; what were they like? White fluorescents, mushy carpet, same unnerving vibe as the later levels you went to?" he interrogated. "Did they look like the ones on the other side of the window in the lab?"

"Yeah, exactly. And my phone wasn't working very well. I had a map of the area, but most of it wouldn't load." I replied.

"Did you have any phone calls after that? Any you can

remember distinctly?"

"Yeah, absolutely. Tommy called me in a place he called the "manila room" and told me to look for a secret lever. Then I talked to my boss in a stairwell of the parking garage, just like the report says." I replied, furrowing my brow as I looked at Ivan who was now staring at me with a strange expression.

"And this Tommy character; how did he say he found you?"

"I. . .don't think he did? He just said he'd been trying to catch up to me for a while and that he was deeper in The Back Rooms then he ever had been before." I said, before scratching my head and looking at the ground. "That doesn't really make sense now that I say it. How would he have found me, especially if he didn't even know the way out?" Ivan shook his head and then began to scribble on the clipboard.

"No, none of this makes sense. He would have no way of tracking you in here, even with your phone's information. The magnetic distortions disrupt all forms of GPS; that's why your phone map wasn't working on level 0. Not to mention he somehow entered The Back Rooms after you." Ivan said, still furiously scribbling.

"Level 0?" I said, confused.

"The yellow rooms, that's level 0. It's the first level; everybody starts there. Your phone would have absolutely no contact with the outside world at that point." Ivan said quickly. "Did Tommy say anything else? Like where he was taking you or why he was sent?"

"He said he was lost too, and that he was just following the boss's orders. He knew quite a bit about The Back Rooms, though. Told me about wretches and hounds, the Terror Hotel;

he even knew about The Hub. I went looking for it when we got separated." I replied. Ivan scribbled without saying a word for another few minutes before lowering the clipboard.

"None of this is adding up, Jeff, and I don't believe you hallucinated all of it. I'm going to look into this tomorrow morning. Stay safe on your mission, and I'll hopefully have some more answers for you once you've gotten back." Ivan said seriously. I sighed a big breath of relief, and then stood up, looking at him with a smile.

"Thank you so much. It means a lot." I said. "Vex made me feel like I was going crazy."

"No problem; we'll get to the bottom of it. Now you should get some rest and take your mind off it; I'll handle it from here. You'll need all your strength for tomorrow." Ivan said. I nodded in agreement before thanking him again, and then headed off towards my cell. It was still just as uninviting and cold as before, but I knew that I would miss it tomorrow.

Our mission detail was thorough and relatively safe, but I still had no faith that I would make it back. It seemed anything could happen here, and that most of MEG's research was little more than a helpless grasp at understanding the enigma that was The Back Rooms. It felt like I was in the same position I had been in for the last five days; forced to explore with little hope of escape, and doomed to wander this liminal hell forever. At least Ivan was looking into the strange circumstances surrounding my entry.

I had trouble sleeping, staring at the amber light streaming into the room for what felt like hours. Besides the mystery of what I would be facing in the morning, I couldn't get my mind off Ivan's and I's conversation. That, and Tommy;

where was he? Better yet, how the hell did he get *sent* here by my boss? How did he find me if he was lost, and why did he already know so much about The Back Rooms? His story didn't make sense now—getting sent in to rescue me and becoming lost—but what other explanation was there? I was the one that had lost the key and lied to my boss about my whereabouts, but Tommy was the reason I was *still* in here. He was the one who cut my phone off from 911. Why?

***

By the time I was heading to meet Vex for deployment, I had only gotten what felt like 4 hours of actual sleep. Rich was late to the meeting, putting Vex in an irritable mood for the duration of our encounter. She had equipped each of us with almond water, a flashlight and a small watch. Then we headed down the car-tunnel towards the door to level 197.

Vex stopped and looked at us intensely once we reached the door, causing Rich's jabbering to stop.

"You will return in no less than 72 hours. Document what you can and be sure to stay together." Vex ordered. The group nodded in agreement, and then Vex opened the door, revealing a hallway that stretched into darkness. I shuddered as cold air rushed through the doorway that made the group hesitate. Vex remained silent, seemingly unbothered by our fear, before she motioned towards the hall with an open palm.

"Time's started." Vex said, as if to make us "get on with it." Rich sauntered into the hallway, then Hazel, and finally me, taking a look over my shoulder one last time to see the amber light of the car tunnel as it disappeared from the doorway. Vex

204

closed the steel door with a bang that echoed through the hall. I lingered for a moment, staring at the door.

"Let's go Jeff. Time to move." Rich ordered. I exhaled softly, and then caught up with the two of them, pressing on into the darkness.

"We're looking for a stainless-steel door. That will take us to the freezer section of the grocery store." Hazel said, clicking on her flashlight as we wandered further from the light at the entrance. We had only gone a short ways when the beam of Rich's flashlight shined on an object down the hallway, causing him to announce that he had found it. The door had a large latch handle, which stuck for a moment as Rich pulled on it before it gave way with a loud creak. Then we walked into a rectangular, gray room with a series of refrigerator windows on the right wall. The sound of humming fans filled my ears as we walked past tall racks of milk, eggs, and cheeses that sat in front of the windows and obstructed the view of the rest of the grocery store.

"Think we can eat any of this stuff?" Rich said, shining his flashlight on the goods as walked by them.

"I wouldn't." Hazel said, leering at the food as she walked past. The refrigerator area continued on for a ways before dead ending at a set of glass sliding doors that appeared to open to a parking lot.

"This can't be it." I said loudly as Rich approached the doors. "That looks nothing like the arcade."

"There's no other way." Rich snapped back, before his eyes were drawn to Hazel who was moving a rack out of the way of one of the refrigerator doors. She then propped the door open before looking back at us with a smug expression.

"You two coming?" she said with a grin, causing Rich to scoff. We followed her through the refrigerator door into the dark grocery store. The floor was made up of glossy, white, square tiles that appeared waxed, and although dimly lit, the store appeared to have been recently in use. We stood at the end of the aisle that was sparsely stocked with bags of chips and canned goods, but the sparse lighting that dotting the ceiling took all my attention; an unmistakable, eerie darkness hung in the air over the entire building.

"Look at this stuff," Rich said, removing a red bag of chips from the shelf. "It looks just like Doritos, but it's some sort of off brand kind. Crimson Crisps; wonder if they have anything on brand?"

"I don't think so. There was stuff like that on the mall level too. None of the brands were real." I said, looking over the array of strange but familiar packaging on the shelves.

"Would you two stop looking at chips and stay focused!" Hazel hissed. "It's creepy in here."

"Oh what, you're scared already? Give me a break." Rich retorted.

"She's right, this is the most dangerous part of our mission. We should keep moving. What's next, Hazel?" I said, peering down the long aisle we were standing next to. I could not see to the end of it, and now noticed aisles all around us that stretched off into the store as far as I could see; there were no visible edges of the building.

"There wasn't really a set direction in the book. All it said is to find an automatic door that leads to a carpeted area." she replied, reading from a notebook.

"Let's just get moving then." I said as I started to walk

down the aisle. "Keep an eye out for any movement."

We passed by an array of more strange products on the half-stocked shelves, all with big letters advertising ingredients I'd never heard of. There were also glass jars of what looked like alien vegetables next to colorful containers of spices and boxed cereals with disturbing mascots pasted on them. We eventually made it to a path that ran perpendicular to the aisles, and it was here that that same old disturbing feeling of trespassing in a desolate expanse came back. The open path stretched off further than anyone could see and revealed that we were quite literally in the middle of a dark, labyrinthian grocery store.

"Well," I said hesitantly. "which way?"

Rich strutted out past me into the endless path before holding his hand over his eyebrows and squinting towards the blackness. He scanned the store for a moment and then said "There," pointing his finger at an aisle a ways down. "There's a sign that says produce; we'll be able to see more of the store there."

"You can see that far?" Hazel challenged.

"I got good night vision; better than *both* of you it looks like. Come on, follow me." Rich boasted. I considered protesting as Hazel and I followed him, but as the produce sign came into view, I couldn't really argue with his plan.

The path took us past box displays and multiple segmented aisles that appeared to lead to entirely different sections of the store. The layout was jumbled, seemingly designed with no attention paid to making the space cohesive. I already felt like we were getting lost, but then we then came upon a large, unlit area dotted with half-visible, low display cases that were unmistakably for fruits and vegetables.

"I don't like this very much." Hazel said as we reached the start of the produce area. "I feel like we're being watched."

"Are you gonna do this every time we go to a new place?" Rich teased.

"Didn't you pay attention to the lesson? Entities are in dark areas, and we can't even see how big this place is!" Hazel shot back.

"Well then you can stay here while Jeff and I look around." Rich said, sticking his nose up as he headed towards the produce. He then froze in place, staring into the black. "Wha. . .what is that!" he shouted, raising a trembling finger.

Hazel jumped towards me; my eyes frantically searched the darkness for what he had seen before I spotted a humanoid figure. My mind raced as I thought about where to run; could we make it all the way back to The Hub, or would we get lost and end up on some other horrible level? Then I heard a snicker, and saw Rich turn around with a sick smile on his face.

"I got you guys so good! It's just a mannequin, relax." Rich bragged.

"Why would you do that!" Hazel spat. "You're an idiot!"

"Calm down. It's not my fault you're such a scaredy cat. Come on, let's go see what's around it." Rich said, heading towards the mannequin. Hazel looked at me in disbelief. I didn't even know what to say, causing her to fold her arms and say "asshole" under her breath.

By the time Hazel and I had caught up with Rich, we were past the produce section and now in a completely different part of the store. Clothes racks and mannequins filled the large, half-lit area, reminding me of the abandoned department store in the mall. Clearance tags and big "SALE" signs covered the racks, giving the unmistakable impression that the store was going out of business.

"Check this out," Rich announced. He was holding up a yellow collared shirt in front of his chest. "Limited edition Back Rooms shirt; I'm taking this one back," he said, pulling the shirt over his head.

"You look like an idiot." Hazel said, causing Rich to shake his head.

"Just admit it, you think I'm sexy!" Rich retorted, rubbing his hands down the shirt. "There's a security tag too? What the hell for?"

"Quit fucking around and let's go!" I shouted, causing Rich's eyes to widen.

"Fine, but I'm keeping the shirt," he replied.

"Are we even on the right track?" I said, looking at Hazel. "This doesn't look like a grocery store anymore."

"It mentioned other stuff might be in here. I guess it's more of a hyper-mart." she replied, scanning her notebook. It didn't seem right, but I could see an area up ahead was better lit than the grocery aisles, so I led the three of us towards the light. Then we started passing all sorts of home goods. Washing machines and dryers, dishwasher displays, plates, and even some mattresses were scattered around the room. It was beginning to feel more and more like a department store in the mall, and the fear of wandering too far in and ending up back *in* the mall festered in the back of my mind. I dreaded what it would take to return to The Hub; somehow find the bookstore miles in and then face that horrible thing in the abandoned library again? No way in hell was I going back there.

"I'm not sure guys, this doesn't seem right. The book

specifically said grocery store; I think we should turn back." I said, glancing back at the dark area we had come from.

"I think it's the same level, Jeff. Here, let's look at the notes." Hazel said, handing me the journal. I was just about to sit down to read when I felt Rich's hands grab my shirt and throw me to the ground. Enraged, I jumped to my feet and saw Rich standing with a scared look and his hands up.

"What was that for!" I barked, ready to punch him in the face.

"You're a fool is why." He replied sharply, filling me with more anger. I was just about to hit him when he looked over my shoulder at Hazel.

"You don't know either? Gah, got paired up with a couple of newbies." he mocked.

"What are you talking about!" I demanded.

"You really don't know? Look behind you," he said, pointing to the mattress I was going to sit on. I shook my head, shrugging as I glared at him in disgust.

"Wild! I would have told you guys if I had known. Mattresses can no-clip you to level 900." Rich said before pausing, looking at us as if we were supposed to realize something. "The infinite mattress store. . .50 miles to the exit and if you lay down you get sent back to the beginning. . .the horned goat that stands on two legs and plays the lullaby. . .you guys don't know about this?" he said, seemingly in disbelief.

"Bullshit." I said, glancing at Hazel to see if she knew something I didn't.

"How do you even know about that?" Hazel interrogated. "That level is way beyond our assignment."

"I did a bit of extra reading, you know, to keep us safe."

Rich said, before holding his hands up. "A little thanks would be nice."

I stared at Rich for a moment, skeptical of his story, before sighing and looking at my watch. "We're already over an hour in. We need to find this arcade." I said, trying to brush off my anger towards Rich. "Try to think, where would an arcade be in a department store?"

"By the toys." Hazel replied, pointing towards an aisle with games and action figures beyond the pillows and mattresses. Everyone seemed to agree.

As we walked into the first section of stuffed animals, I noticed that they were distorted. Oddly placed and sized eyes, deformed appendages, and disconcerting smiles seemed to plague every animal, giving them an incredibly off putting and creepy appearance. Rich and I had made it to the board games and when I turned back and saw Hazel still standing in the stuffed animal aisle, staring at one high up on the shelf. She appeared enamored with it, and was just starting to reach out and grab it when I sprinted towards her.

"No!" I shouted, causing her head to spin to the side, looking at me in confused anger.

"Oh what, he gets to take a shirt and I can't have a stuffed animal?" she snapped.

"That's not it! They're nostalgia traps." I replied, half out of breath from running.

She stopped, glancing up at the stuffed animal on the shelf, before looking back at me. I stared at her with worried eyes, still breathing heavily, and then noticed the detail in her brown eyes. They were flecked with a bit of gold, but the fear behind them softened me. She saw my worry and returned it with silent gratitude that helped me catch my breath. I don't know how long I looked into her eyes, but then Rich yelled from afar:

"What happened!"

Her eyes worried as I looked back at her, stopping me right before answering Rich. I thought for a moment, and then gave her a little smile before leading us back to Rich. He was standing at the end of the aisle with his hands on his hips, wearing a look of annoyed confusion.

"The hell happened?" he asked.

"I thought she found a nostalgia trap." I said, shrugging my shoulders.

"Traps everywhere in this damn level, I don't blame ya." Rich said, shaking his head. "Check this out, though."

Rich led us around the corner of the toy aisle to a series of cash registers that were sitting in front of a large window, along with a set of sliding glass doors to a carpeted area beside it.

"You found it!" Hazel cheered.

"Sure did, but look out the window." Rich said, nodding towards the glass. As I walked over to the window, I saw that we were high up above an enormous concrete plain. In the distance, I could see an abandoned, rectangular storefront with rainbow paint around the entry doors. The top of the store had the faint outline of letters that were once pasted up there, and it almost felt like I was looking out the window of an airport.

"Weird, huh? Just a giant store in the middle of concrete nothingness." Rich wondered aloud.

"It looks like some sort of old toy store or something." Hazel replied.

"That's what I thought, like an old Toys-R-Us. I wonder if we could get in there?" Rich said, staring out the window. "I bet you it has some stuff M.E.G would be interested in; stuff we would be rewarded nicely for."

"Come on, we gotta stay on track," I said, nudging Rich. "We can report the discovery and check it out on another mission. Plus, I don't even see a way down there."

"Mmm, you're scared too, huh?" he said with a scoff, before walking backwards towards the sliding doors to the carpeted area. "You guys are no fun, but fine, we'll just stick to the mission." The doors opened automatically as he neared the entrance, and then right as he walked through, a loud alarm started blaring.

"What is that!" Hazel cried. The alarm seemed to have only mildly bothered Rich, who was now lingering behind the open doors with a confused look on his face.

"Y'all comin' or what?" he said. "It's just an alarm; we all know this place doesn't want us here."

Hazel glanced over at me as if I was meant to do something. I could see the panic in her eyes, but I tried to remain calm to console her. The alarm had spiked my heart rate, like a warning for something terrible that was about to happen, but I met Hazel's gaze with a nod towards the door that seemed to reassure her. There had been nothing in the notes about alarms, but surprises were to be expected here.

Hazel followed me towards Rich, who led us down the carpeted floor away from the loud alarm that was now beginning to sound familiar, like that of a theft detection system at a mall. The hallway we had entered was dim with dark red walls and black carpet that had neon-yellow and green stars and squiggle patterns. It reminded me of the kind of hallway that led into a movie theater from the main lobby, turning and bending before eventually coming to another glass sliding door that opened to an arcade. The doors opened automatically, dulling the sound of the alarm as they closed behind us.

We were now standing in a large room with black walls that had countless rows of glowing, neon-colored game machines. Some of their screens were lit up with digital menus and 80's themed designs, while the rest of the machines appeared to be turned off.

"This looks like a laser-tag arena I went to as a kid," Rich said, gawking at the arcade. "What kind of games do you think they have?"

"Have you ever been diagnosed with A.D.D?" Hazel said snidely. Rich didn't reply, still enamored with the environment. His care-free, curious attitude was wearing on both our patience, and with our mission destination still far off, the burden was on Hazel and I to keep the group on track.

"What are we looking for now?" I said, joining Hazel's side as she pulled out her notebook and began to read.

"There's a revolving door somewhere in the arcade. Follow the space-themed decor. That's all I have." she said, looking up from the notebook at a planet decoration that was hanging from the ceiling. A trail of glow in the dark stars was also pasted up there, leading off deeper into the arcade, and so we followed iit, navigating between the beaming arcade machines. The whole place appeared to have an outer-space theme; games like asteroid blaster, Martian invasion, and planet spinner were most notable, while the entire carpet appeared illuminated by a blacklight that bolded its neon star and planet patterns. The out-of-order ambience was still very apparent, however, as the place appeared dated and forgotten, with the decor reminiscent of 80's space themes and old technology.

I had to keep hollering at Rich to keep up, as he would regularly fall behind, seemingly enchanted by the arcade. He was experiencing the greatest bit of nostalgia in the group, but I felt the effects as well. So much of this arcade looked like the sorts of places I had been to in my teens and brought up hazy memories from my past of spending hours in front of the machines— drinking sodas, eating pizza and then skating home—not a care in the world. The arcade was from an entirely different era that was now a piece of history, phased out by new technology and a changing world. The feeling was not so different from what I had felt in the mall; a subtle burden of inescapable sorrow mixed with a rose-tinted view of the past that these sorts of environments seemed to cultivate.

The starry trail stretched on for what seemed like miles, bringing us through different parts of the arcade. Some sections were more rundown than others, with torn carpet, dusty surfaces, and broken machines that had exposed wires, while others appeared perfectly maintained. The outer space theme was consistent throughout the level; designs of stars and planets glowed on the walls and black carpet despite having no identifiable light source. We had also come across other sections of the arcade, including a large cafeteria area and indoor play place that reminded me of Chuck E. Cheese. Restrooms and "Employee Only" doors had been popping up during our venture, and despite being curious about the sorts of places they might lead, I knew it was better to just follow the overhead stars and find the revolving door as quickly as possible. The level did not seem especially dangerous psychologically, but the nostalgia effect was bringing about strange emotions that were distracting from the objective.

We were about an hour into the arcade when I began to hear the mellow tones of classic 80's pop music.

"Do you guys hear that?" I said, looking back at Rich, who appeared travel weary and half awake.

"The music? You're just noticing it now?" Rich said, looking up at me tiredly.

"When did *you* start noticing it?" Hazel said quickly, glancing over at Rich.

"I don't know, a while ago? Can we take a break? I'm exhausted." he replied.

"You fought off hordes of wretches and you're tired after just *walking?*" Hazel teased. "It's a miracle you made this far."

"We can stop once we get to the roller rink," I said, turning around to lead the group again. "Drink some almond water, Rich; it'll make you feel better."

"How much further anyway? I don't like this level." he said, uncapping a bottle of almond water.

"You were so into it when we got here," Hazel jeered. "What, now you're scared?"

"No!" Rich snapped back. "It's just unsettling; reminds me too much of my childhood. The music, too; feels like I'm 13 again with my brothers back playing laser tag. Where's that music coming from anyway?"

"It sounds like it's getting closer." Hazel said, trotting up beside me before whispering "I think he's losing it a bit."

I looked down at her with a curious expression before

something at the end of a row of arcade machines caught my eye. Her head jolted to the side, and then we stopped, staring down the aisle at the shadowy figure

"What is it?" Rich puffed, bending over with his hands on his knees as he joined us, before lifting his head to see down the aisle. "Is that a person?" Rich said loudly, causing the figure to bolt into the darkness out of view. My heart thumped rapidly, while my mind spun with countless possibilities of what it could be.

"Great job, now it knows where we are!" Hazel spat, glaring at Rich.

"We should probably get out of here." I said quietly, trying to conceal the panic in my voice. I started fast walking with Hazel by my side, and as the creeping feeling of being watched seemed to haunt each of us in the back of my head, our jog quickly turned into a full sprint. We were still following the stars, darting into and out of rows of machines and open areas with prize booths and tables. Rich wheezed for air as he tried to keep up, but there was no time to rest; whatever had seen us had moved so unnaturally, seemingly blinking out of view. Its shape had been humanoid, but the edges of its silhouette were spiky and glitched, like some sort of apparition that moved so fast it left a light-trail. I didn't know for a fact that it was chasing us, but getting as far from it as possible was absolutely the move. I was used to sprinting from horrible things by now, and though Hazel had no trouble keeping up, Rich was falling behind. Then I heard a subtle tearing sound, like a bullet cutting through air, and caught a glimpse of the shadowy creature in my peripheral vision. I cranked my head to the side to see a long row of arcade machines, but there was nothing at the far end.

"Jeff!" Hazel shouted, drawing my eyes from the row of machines. "Look!" she said, pointing to a revolving door that appeared to lead into a large movie theater lobby.

"Where's Rich?" I yelled, looking behind Hazel at the empty aisle of machines. I froze at the junction of the arcade and lobby, staring into the darkness and wondering if it had gotten him. Seconds felt like hours as I waited, debating on whether to turn back and find Rich or get to the doors. Then I saw him come sprinting around the corner with a look of horror on his face.

"Go!" I shouted, pushing Hazel towards the lobby as Rich closed the gap between us. We then sprinted out of the carpeted arcade into the movie theater lobby; the sound of our footsteps clapped against the tiled floor. I followed Hazel as she darted around the concession booth in the center of the room, and then into the revolving door on the other wall, followed shortly after by Rich. The doors slowly rotated us, filling me with panic as I stared back at the empty lobby, ready for the apparition to come charging out of the arcade. After leaping from the door, the three of us immediately spun around to stare out the glass, anxious to see if it had followed us.

"What in the hell was that?" Rich said, gasping for air. "I thought that level was supposed to be safe!"

"It didn't look like any entity from the M.E.G. video." I replied, still staring out the glass. "We should file a report once we're back."

"*If* we make it back!" Rich exclaimed.

I kept my eyes peeled on the entrance to the dark arcade across the movie theater lobby. There were no more signs of the apparition, but everyone seemed content to rest for a minute, and I couldn't help but stare at the quiet lobby. It looked like it had been pulled right out of the early 2000's. Logos of fireworks and neon-lights decorated the tall, beige walls, along with a large crescent window above a line of glass doors. It appeared perfectly liminal, and gave me a kind of strange satisfaction that seemed to flutter in my lower intestine. We had transitioned through a transitional space, which, despite being redundant, was exactly how these spaces were *supposed* to be experienced; quickly, and without much thought, almost like a loading screen. The lobby appeared cold, lonely, and forgotten, like a place that was grieving from being once loved and cherished, but now sat uninhabited and forsaken.

Hazel had been quiet since the three of us had come flying through the revolving door, seemingly enamored with the place it had led us. The area was expansive, with red and yellow fluorescents on the big ceiling overhead that cast a hue of color over the large, concrete oval in the center of the room that stretched off further than I could see. A knee-high wall of burgundy carpet connected to the floor, along with a metal railing that separated the concrete oval from the rest of the room. It led along the left side of what I now realized was the roller rink, while the back wall had geometric designs running the span of the rink. The 90's era ambiance was unmistakable, accentuated by pop music that was playing from speakers overhead.

"I can't believe I'm actually going back in here." Hazel said drearily. Rich and I remained silent, causing her to look back at us with a sullen expression. "I was here for *three* days trying to find a way out. It's huge, and the rink goes on forever."

"Let's see if we can find the rental booth. Skates will make our trip here much faster." I said, attempting to reassure

Hazel. She still seemed unnerved by the fact that she was going back to a level she had already escaped, and I couldn't blame her; returning here probably felt like a huge step backwards.

The area around the rink was carpeted and had a series of booths that ran alongside the rinks' wall, along with some vending machines and blacked out windows on the adjacent wall. All the lighting in the area came from the overhead fluorescents and strands of neon lights that were dimmed by the dark colors of the walls and floor, giving the space a disco-type ambiance. Despite the playful lighting and decor, the place felt lonely without any people. That, along with the large open sections and eerie darkness made my hair stand on end. I felt exposed, like a kid who had trespassed at his favorite skate spot after dark.

We quickly found the skate rental booth, which was a small room indented in the wall that had an opening where an attendant would usually be. A sign pasted on the edge of the opening had large red lettering that read "NO SKATING ON THE CARPET." This was exactly what the book had warned us about, and after looking over the shelves of skates, I climbed over the counter and began searching for my size.

"Give me a 9," Rich said, leaning on the counter. I quickly found his pair, and handed them over before searching again for the 12's that I needed.

"What about you, Hazel?" I said, still unable to find my size.

"6 if they have women's." she said. Once again, I found the size easily, but still couldn't find mine.

"What are you waiting for, Jeff?" Rich said, loosening the laces on his skates.

"I don't see mine," I replied, before noticing a door on

the backend of the rental room. "Hang on, let me see if they have some back here."

Fear immediately crept over me as I headed towards the door, seemingly out of nowhere. My mind raced with thoughts of what might be back there; a hound jumping on top of me, one of those skin stealers lurking in the shadows, a gaggle of wretches, or maybe opening it would no-clip me away from Rich and Hazel; that was probably the worst thing that could happen; lost and alone again. It seemed to be an ever-present threat, and perhaps the most dreadful thing about The Back Rooms. The creatures and the risk of death were one thing, but being all alone and completely lost in this seemingly infinite maze of liminal rooms; nothing was as bad as that.

Just do it; tear off the band aid and open the door. I yanked on the knob, opening the door to a big gray room that was mostly empty. It was dimly lit, with a few objects propped up against the walls that gave me the impression that it was a storage room. Stuff from the rink, like floor wax, yellow caution signs, janitor supplies, and broken skates sat next to old advertisements for brands of beverages, skate equipment, and party dates. I could also see folded up cafeteria tables and what looked like workout equipment on the far end of the room that was almost entirely dark.

"Find some?" Rich said loudly, causing me to shut the door to the uncomfortable space and join him and Hazel back at the counter.

"No. I guess we'll have to find a different booth." I said with a sigh.

"You said you're a 12? What about those right there?" Hazel said, pointing to a pair of pink and blue skates on the bottom shelf. They were out of position, placed next to rows of much smaller pairs, but as I inspected the tag, I found that they were exactly my size.

"Good eye!" I said, happily grabbing the skates as Hazel let out a little giggle. I jumped back over the counter and then headed towards the rink with Hazel and Rich. The three of us sat on the carpeted edge of the divider in the rink and began putting on the skates.

"Have you guys ever skated before?" Hazel said as she stood up and began gliding around the floor before Rich and I even had them fully on.

"It's been a while," I replied, staggering as I stood up. Rich was still fumbling with his skates, while I began to push myself along the floor. The movement felt natural, almost as if the wheels were partially magnetized to the floor, helping me keep balance and comfortable movement. By the time Rich was on his feet, Hazel and I were coasting effortlessly around the rink, enjoying the feeling of smooth speed.

"This is easy!" Rich shouted, racing past us on his skates out into the rink.

"We better keep up with him," I said, smiling at Hazel. Then I saw the glimmer of neon lights in her eyes. I paused, adoring her delicate cheeks and soft skin before she smirked and dashed off, leaving me standing half-dazed for a moment before racing after her. Her body danced in and out of the beams of colorful light, standing alone against the endless expanse of the gray rink ahead. Skating felt effortless, like a euphoric glide in the clouds, but I could not take my eyes off Hazel. Her motion was gentle and natural, lulling me with every stride. Here we were, sailing into oblivion, yet she had found bliss, unbothered by the tragedy of the situation. Watching her was the first thing that had truly taken my mind off of this place, and for a moment, I didn't care that I was horribly doomed. She was here, and the dream of spending forever with her was enough to take all my attention.

"You're a natural at this." I said, praising Hazel as she had slowed down enough for me to join her side.

"I told you; I was here for three days." she replied, spinning as she skated around me. "Those look *great* on you." she said, giggling as she pointed towards my gaudy skates.

"Hah, the only ones in my size. How do you figure that?" I said, shaking my head. She raised her eyebrows at me before gliding to my side and looking out at the vast stretch of illuminated rink ahead.

"Do you think we'll ever make it out of here?" she said in a subdued tone.

"I sure hope so. . .How did you wind up here anyway?" I said, glancing down at her as we continued skating. Rich was still a ways ahead, periodically looking over his shoulder to make sure we were keeping up.

Hazel looked at me with a frown before letting out a sigh and gazing back off into the rink.

"I was picking up my little sister at school after seeing a play she was in. She got stage fright and ran off halfway through, so I went looking for her." Hazel explained, before her voice cracked. She paused for a moment, letting out a melancholy sigh before continuing. "I couldn't find the way backstage to where she had run off to, and ended up wandering to an entirely different section of the school. I mean, I went to school there too, so it's not like I was entirely lost, but it was after regular hours, so all of the lights were off in the hallways and classrooms. I thought I was getting close when I made it to the gymnasium, but after that, everything started getting strange. There were far too many classrooms that could fit in that building, and the hallways became longer and creepier. I'd thought I'd recognize a room, but then it would be too large or oddly laid out. I went through dozens of music classrooms, art studios, dark gymnasiums, and teacher offices before eventually coming upon those yellow rooms everybody talks about." Hazel concluded.

"That sounds. . .horrible." I said, picturing her story in my mind. "God, imagine that; getting lost in your old school at night and ending up in an infinite, liminal one."

She looked at me with a grimace, causing me to shrug and quickly apologize.

"It was. . .what about you? I'm guessing it wasn't at a school." she said shortly.

"No, it wasn't. I, uh," I stammered. "I do HVAC for a living; got locked in an office during one of my jobs. I tried to find a way out and ended up in those same yellow rooms like you." I replied, thinking it was unnecessary to burden her with the more sinister parts of my story. Her description had relieved a bit of my paranoia about being sent here intentionally, as no part of it included suspicious details; it just sounded unlucky. I mean, that *was* the leading theory on how people end up here—being unfortunate enough to stumble across a temporary liminal wormhole—but again, why had I never heard of this before? Why was it not getting mainstream attention?

"Vex told me the yellow rooms are where everybody starts out," Hazel said, now looking past me at the carpeted region outside of the rink. "Why do you think that is?"

"Couldn't say; I thought I was still in the building I was working on for a long time. It was only once Tommy found me that I learned I was in The Back Rooms." I replied, following Hazel's gaze outside the rink. "What do you see?"

"Thought I saw something move; probably just the lighting playing tricks on my eyes." she said, looking back at me with a smile. "Who's Tommy?"

I paused for a moment, unsure of how much to tell her, causing a scowl to appear on her pretty face. "What? Is he your *boyfriend*?"

"No!" I shot back quickly. "They sent him in to come get me."

"Come get you?" Hazel said, perplexed. She slowed to a halt on her skates, looking at me suspiciously. Rich seemed to notice as this happened, and began skating back towards us.

"Yeah, my boss sent him. He was supposed to get me out." I said sheepishly.

"That doesn't make any sense. How would he get *in* here? And your boss; he *knew* about this place?" Hazel snapped, now with a growing looking of anger on her face. "Why didn't you tell us any of this?"

"Tell us what!" Rich shouted as he neared our spot. "What are you guys waiting around for?"

"Jeff says that his boss sent someone in here to save him." Hazel said, crossing her arms.

"What?" Rich howled. "How would he send someone here?"

"I don't know," I retorted. "That's just what he told me when I got locked in the office. He found me a while later, but said we were too deep now, and he didn't know the way out anymore."

The group remained silent, staring at me with skeptical expressions.

"You must be losing it. Drink some almond water." Rich ordered, reaching for my pocket. I swatted his hand away, shooting him an angry look.

"I'm fine." I retorted. "I'm telling you, that's what happened. You don't have to believe me; the commander didn't either, but it's the truth." I said firmly. Rich and Hazel continued glaring at me. Then their eyes grew wide, staring at something behind me. Confused, I shook my head.

"What? What are you looking at?" I asked angrily before turning around to see what they were looking at. I couldn't believe my eyes; it was Tommy, badly beaten, wearing the same blue mechanics suit that was now filled with rips and splotches of blood.

Chapter 13

Tommy

"Well you're a sight for sore eyes!" Tommy exclaimed, limping towards me. "Got any almond water?"

Rich and Hazel were frozen in place, but I quickly pulled out a bottle from my pocket and handed it over to him. He let out a blissful sigh of relief before chugging the entire bottle. After wiping his mouth with his sleeve, his eyes shifted away from me towards the other group members.

"Who are they?" he said, nodding towards them before he noticed our uniforms and a look of glee grew on his face. "Are they from The Hub? You guys know the way back there then; I can't believe it!"

"Who the hell are *you*?" Rich spat, glaring at Tommy.

"I'm Tommy; Jeff told you about me, didn't he?" Tommy said before glancing towards me with a confused look.

"I was just telling them when you showed up. They, uh, have some questions." I said sheepishly.

"Sure, yeah; I'll answer whatever you guys want. Can we go back to The Hub first though please? I haven't slept in days." Tommy begged. The group remained silent, and my mouth hung open while I tried to find the words to explain what was going on. "What? What is it?" Tommy said, his face plagued with confusion.

"We, uh, are trying to get to the next level; we're investigating it for our mission." I explained, looking over at Rich and Hazel for support.

"Mission? Is that what the people at The Hub do?" Tommy said, laughing uncomfortably. "I'm sure they will understand you guys coming back to rescue me."

"Let's take him back, guys. I'll deal with Vex." I said, hoping they would have some sympathy.

"We came all this way and now we're gonna turn back? Just have him come along." Rich said wryly.

"The skate rental is at least 2 miles back. Why don't we just call it a day?" I pleaded. The group remained silent. "I can just take him back if you guys want to go on. He obviously needs help; might not even make it back as is." I said, shrugging my shoulders.

"No!" Hazel shouted, before her eyes darted around in embarrassment. "We're not supposed to split up."

There was another long silence while the four of us stood beneath the chandeliers of red and yellow neon lights. I could a fork in the rink ahead, stretching off further into the building.

"Why don't we take a vote? Tommy doesn't get one." Rich said, raising his hand. "All in favor of finishing the mission, say I."

Hazel looked over at me, and then at Rich, who after lingering with his hand in the air for a moment, had a look of disgust come over his face. "Oh come on! We're not going to make anything for all of this then! We'll just have to go right back out! It's going to look terrible for our first mission!" Rich cried.

"I guess it's settled then," I said, turning back the way we came.

"Just hold on a minute!" Hazel shouted, drawing the group's attention. "Tommy has some explaining to do before we go any further."

One by one, each member's eyes locked on Tommy, who remained silent for a moment before letting out a sigh and looking at the ground. "I figured I'd have some explaining to do if Jeff made it to The Hub. Go ahead, I'll answer what I can."

Hazel's arms were crossed as she nodded at me like I was supposed to ask the first question, while Rich continued fuming about the mission.

"There's a lot that doesn't make sense, Tommy. You being sent here to save me, somehow miraculously finding me on level 4, and the phone calls too. The commander seems to think I hallucinated the whole thing. I don't get it; either you lied to me, or this whole thing is one big setup." I said, sighing as I shook my head. "Our Archivist is back at The Hub looking into all of this, and you're going to have a lot of explaining to do once we get back."

The questions had drawn intense focus from both Rich and Hazel, who were staring at Tommy. He had been rubbing his neck and gritting his teeth through all of my questions, and after staring at the ground for a while after I had finished talking, he finally looked up at me in remorse.

"It was never meant to go like this." he said, looking guiltily off into the distance. "I mean, look at this place; it's hell. No one should ever have to go through this." I stared at Tommy in confusion while rage bubbled beneath my skin; what in the hell was he talking about?

"You did this to him?" Hazel shouted, sending Rich into fury. He stormed over to Tommy and grabbed him by his collar.

"Start talking! What did you do! How do we get out here!" Rich screamed. Tommy met his anger with a neutral expression, unphased by the event.

"Get off him!" I barked, yanking Rich away.

Tommy appeared unbothered by Rich's abrupt violence, holding his chin high with a nonchalant expression on his face.

"I don't know anything about you two," Tommy spat, glaring at Rich and Hazel. "My assignment was Jeff, and you're damn lucky to have him in your group. Guys' a born survivor." Tommy's praise had no effect on me, and while I didn't agree with Rich's actions, I thought I might do the same thing. If Tommy really sent me here on purpose, and he knew the people responsible, I might actually kill him.

"Yeah, you were a study, Jeff. The boss sent you here to confirm a no-clip zone in that building." Tommy said, infuriatingly unemotional about what he had just said. "My job was to make sure you went in."

"You're a monster!" Hazel said in disbelief.

"No sweetheart, my boss is a monster. He's the one who wanted the no-clip zone in Jeff's building investigated." Tommy retorted, shooting Hazel a smug look.

"So everything you told me was a lie. You were never lost; you just led me deeper and then abandoned me when you saw fit." I said, despondent and overwhelmed by the absolutely twisted reality of the situation.

"No, none of that's true." Tommy exclaimed. "You were sent in to investigate a theorized entrance to The Back Rooms, but you were never meant to make it beyond the parking garage. That's where I came in; I was supposed to find you and lead you out."

"Bullshit!" Rich spat. "We've all been to that level; it's huge, and there's no confirmed exits on any of the levels below 100. M.E.G has documented and explored them extensively."

Tommy shook his head. "Well then M.E.G is wrong. There is an exit on that level; I've been through it a half dozen times. Jeff could have been out days ago if he just stayed put in that garage, but here we are." Tommy said.

"How did you even get in then?" Hazel demanded.

"It's my *job* to get in," Tommy said condescendingly. "The boss has a couple of old commercial buildings, you know, part of his "HVAC" business. Inside one of them is a no-clip zone that, unlike many others, has a static presence. The one Jeff was sent into was the only other static one the boss had heard of, hence why he wanted it investigated."

"You make it sound like this is just some everyday occurrence, sending people into liminal hell. It's evil is what is it!" Hazel accused.

"I'm not disagreeing with you, but there's not a lot of people that are all that interested in signing up to see what it's like." Tommy said with a shrug. "Jeff has no wife, no kids, little to no contact with his family, and a mountain of debt that he will never pay off with his deadened HVAC job. So, the collateral damage from sending him here was minimal, and while I'm not saying it's right that he was sent here, he was never meant to go this deep. It was just supposed to be a quick and in-out mission."

"So that's it then?" I said, half in shock. "My life seemed sad enough that the boss saw fit to use me as a test subject, and then when it came time to get me out, you failed." I glowered at Tommy, filled with grief and rage.

"I tried to *save* you, Jeff. The boss told me to leave you once he saw you were beyond the ramp, but I went back in after you." Tommy pleaded.

"*SAVE* me? You are the reason I am here!" I spat, turning my back to Tommy as I walked towards Rich and Hazel's with a sullen grimace on my face.

"Hold on," Hazel said, looking suspiciously at Tommy. "How would you have known where he was? How would your boss know?"

"Jeff's phone; he gave me his IMEI number on our first call." Tommy explained.

"That doesn't make any sense; phones don't work in The Back Rooms." Hazel argued.

"They *mostly* don't work." Tommy retorted. "With that information, my boss can track the level someone is on, but that's it. When he saw Jeff had made it to the ramp, he sent me in to find him."

"That can't be true either because you called me in the manila room, and I *distinctly* remember the phone call with the boss in the stairwell of the parking ramp." I argued. "You're full of lies!"

"Those weren't real calls, Jeff." Tommy said ominously. "That was AI trained with my voice and the bosses to talk to you. Its job was to make you *think* you were just in an abandoned part of the building and to wait in the parking ramp for me to come find you. I bugged your phone with it after you gave me your IMEI. That was your last real call; behind the locked door in that office."

I stared at Tommy in disbelief, still trying to wrap my head around what exactly was going on.

"You expect me to believe that you're guiltless in all of this? That somehow I'm supposed to be *grateful* for what you did?" I clamored, causing Tommy to shake his head with pursed lips.

"I left The Back Rooms to see what happened when I couldn't find you in the parking ramp. The boss showed me that you were already on level 4 and said you were a lost cause. Told me that going after you at that depth was a suicide mission, but I went in anyway. I tried to help you, Jeff." Tommy said sincerely, resting his palm on my shoulder. I looked at him bleakly, confused and overwhelmed by despair.

"Why? Why would he do this?" I said, almost in tears.

"You're not buying that crap, are you Jeff?" Rich interjected, drawing an angry look from Tommy. "Everything we've learned in M.E.G is contrary to what this guy is saying. Either they are all lying, or he's lying, and I'm inclined to believe the people that have been here for decades. What if he's just crazy? He looks like he's been lost here forever."

"He has a point, Jeff." Hazel said, causing me to look at her skeptically before glaring back at Tommy.

"What else do you know? Who is your boss? Why did he do this? What does he know about The Back Rooms?" I said, firing questions at Tommy faster than he could respond.

"I know that you are not the first person who he has used to test one of these no-clip zones, and you won't be the last. He pays me well for my job—getting people in and out—

but I'm not allowed to talk about it with anyone on the outside." Tommy said calmly. "I only know about M.E.G and The Hub from the notes I have found on the lower levels during my missions; my boss never mentioned anything about the group. Beyond that, I'm guessing you guys probably know more about The Back Rooms now than I do." Tommy said, raising his hands as if to indicate he was innocent.

"But what would be the point of it? Sending people in here? Did your boss create this horrible place?" Hazel said, still perplexed by Tommy's answers.

"I don't know who, or what, created this place, but it wasn't him," Tommy said, shaking his head. "That's what I've been trying to get across to you guys, I don't know much more than you do. If I did, I wouldn't be stuck here, covered in blood and going on three days without sleep."

I looked at Rich and Hazel, who appeared skeptical but not unbelieving of Tommy's story. His account had answered some of my questions, but also opened many new ones. At the very least, I knew now that my suspicion of foul play was true. So much of what Tommy had said would be groundbreaking for M.E.G, and now the most important thing was getting him back to tell his side of the story. What we had now was far better than any anomalous discoveries in an abandoned VHS store; we had someone who had confirmation of entrances and exits to The Back Rooms, and who had been through them multiple times. If Tommy could lead M.E.G to the exit in the parking ramp, everyone could go home. We would be heroes.

"So what, you're lost here because you went in too deep trying to find Jeff? Why wouldn't your boss just come get you if he can see what level you're on?" Rich said, still skeptical of

Tommys' story.

"You got the wrong idea, Rich. If Tommy *is* telling the truth, then his boss doesn't actually have any control over this place." Hazel said matter-of-factly. "It sounds to me like he's just sending people in to get more data on this place. It's evil, and wildly unethical, but unless he is masterminding the whole thing, he's nothing more than a greedy CEO trying to see if he can make money here."

I stared at Hazel, astounded by what she was saying. If that was true, then this place was even more terrifying; what the hell was it if he didn't make it?

"Exactly," Tommy said gratefully. "Like I said, my boss didn't want me going in any deeper because he knew as well as I that there was no turning back beyond the parking ramp."

"But you do know the way out on that level?" I said, looking at Tommy intently.

"Well yeah, I just don't know how to get back there. That's why I'm trying to get you guys to take me back to The Hub; I'm sure M.E.G knows the way." Tommy replied, drawing excited looks from all the group members.

"What are we waiting for then? Let's get the hell out of here!" Rich cheered.

Everybody was in agreement, overjoyed by the thought of returning home. I knew there was still some work to do, as we had to go back through the arcade and department store, and then coordinate the best way to the parking ramp with the commander, but there was a light at the end of the tunnel. For the first time in as long as I could remember, I had hope. Real hope, not delusional, self-soothing ideas about being lucky enough to stumble upon an exit. There was a way out now, and though it was Tommy's actions that had gotten me stuck here, I could forgive him if he got me out. I would never forget the hell of this place, and perhaps it would haunt me in nightmares for years to come, but at least I would be out; free once again.

Our pace was slowed by Tommy's injuries and lack of skates, giving me plenty of time to gawk at the liminal roller rink that I knew now I would never come back to. There were plenty of places in reality that looked just like this—forgotten spaces with objects and decor from the past—and I could not help but wonder why it had ended up here? What was it about these sorts of uncanny places that The Back Rooms decided to include it in its mass of levels? Each place in here seemed to be an extension of psychologically uncomfortable places I had been to, but how did this place know to display these sorts of environments? Maybe whoever created it wanted to study the effects of liminal spaces on the human psyche, but it felt like this was just my mind grasping at an explanation again. This place was far too expansive and anomalous to serve a purpose, and the only explanation that made any real sense was that it was a limbo between reality and the other side. These were the kinds of places an insane mind creates, like one plagued by the effects of dementia or schizophrenia; places that look familiar, but are strange and isolating, like being lost in an infinite labyrinth of a distorted version of a world that was once ordinary, but now appeared desolate and disturbing. It was as if a mind had run haywire, creating an abyss of spaces from a perverse interpretation of the experiences that formed it.

The more I tried to explain it, the cloudier my reasoning got. It was a paradox; the closer I looked, the further away it got, like trying to reach for keys in between the car seats. One thing was for certain though; once all these people made it out and shared their stories, there would be a massive study. Perhaps The Back Rooms really was one big government experiment, and this place was created by a demented mind that was hooked up to a sentient AI computer that had the power to build environments. The story would not be over once we escaped, and perhaps the accounts of the people who had been stuck here would change history as we know it. The long-term effects that this place would have on the people who were unfortunate enough to visit it were anyone's guess, and though getting home safe was the thing I wanted most, the thought of going back alone was disheartening. I mean, maybe I would have some interviews with my group on the news, but then what? The very *existence* of this place was haunting; would we really all just return to our lives and carry the burden of our experiences here alone? I didn't even know where any of these people lived, much less if we would have contact after the fact, and this brought up a burning question that weighed heavily on my heart; would there be anything with Hazel and I after? Perhaps it was too soon to think about that.

As the exit to the roller rink that led into the movie theater lobby came into view, I remembered the shadow apparition that had chased us out only a short time ago.

"Is this it?" Tommy said, stepping off the rink.

"There's an entrance to an arcade up ahead," I replied, beginning to unlace my skates, when panic filled my chest as I saw Hazel skating towards the carpet, seemingly day dreaming.

"Careful!" I yelled, reaching my hands out in front of her.

"What?" Hazel murmured, hardly noticing my warning.

"Oh, duh." she said, looking at me nonchalantly before casually stopping and untying her skates. I glanced over my shoulder at Rich, who was halfway into a lunge with wide eyes. He had seen the same thing I did—Hazel gliding off the rink with her skates on—she would have no-clipped through the floor. My heart thumped as I watched her gingerly remove each skate, and after the panic of losing her subsided, I could not help but admire her body and wonder what had distracted her so much.

"We're not out yet," I warned, looking at Hazel. "Can't have you getting separated now."

She muttered something inaudible before stepping off the rink, seemingly unbothered by the fact that she had almost just no-clipped.

"How big is the arcade?" Tommy said, looking over his shoulder as Rich and I stepped off the rink. Hazel had gone ahead and was already waiting at the revolving door.

"Not too big, but there was an entity in there." I replied, joining Tommy's side.

"Fast son of a bitch too," Rich said, shaking his head. "You're toast if you can't keep up."

I glared at Rich who shrugged with a smug expression, and then the four us headed out the revolving door into the lobby. It was disturbingly quiet, and as I looked up at the ceiling, I saw tall, cylindrical pillars of beige stone supporting it, along with potted palms trees reaching towards the skylights. The entrance to the arcade was dark and had beams of green, blue, and pink light streaming from the game machine. We headed towards it, but I stopped at the concession stand when I noticed that the popcorn and slushie machines were running. I wasn't sure if I had seen them on before, but the fact that they were on at all was incredibly disconcerting; how long had they been left running here in the middle of nowhere, and what was the point? Who in the hell was coming *here* for a movie? Were there hallways to theaters somewhere in here, and what kinds of movies were even playing in them? Guess I'd never know.

Going back into the arcade with the apparition was unnerving, to say the least, but the four of us just resolved to follow the trail of glowing stars and keep our eyes peeled for entities. The sense that we were being followed festered in the back of my mind, but I sipped from my bottle of almond water to stave off the paranoia. The group's morale seemed to be high with a clear way back to The Hub, and as we pushed further into the arcade, the thought of getting home became more real. Barring any more strange events, home was just on the horizon; all we had to do was have M.E.G take everybody to the parking ramp and then Tommy would lead us out. This did bring up the question of what to do if someone did get separated, though. . .Tommy **had** to get back safely for our plan to work, but what if Rich wandered through a no-clip zone? It would be a tragedy, but going in after him would be suicide. Unfortunately, it was every man for himself at this point, especially with the possibility that the M.E.G headquarters would be abandoned after they found the exit. God; imagine no-clipping away from the group and fighting all the way back to The Hub, only to discover that everyone was gone. Nothing was more liminal than that.

The sliding glass doors back into the department store appeared like a gift from heaven, bringing excited smiles to everybody's faces. One more level and we would be back.

"How much further?" Tommy said, wearing a pained grimace on his face as he fought to catch his breath.

"Home stretch," Rich replied, strutting towards the doors. As he passed through, the alarm blared again, sending a jolt of panic through my body.

"The hell! This place just doesn't like me, huh!" Rich said, glaring up at the alarm speaker above the door. "Tough luck, we're getting out of here whether you like it or not!" he shouted, shaking his fist at the alarm. Hazel rolled her eyes and walked past Tommy, who was still lingering in the arcade with a concerned look on his face.

"It went off when we came in too," I said, trying to reassure Tommy.

"You know as well as I that entities are attracted to sound," Tommy warned, before his eyes were drawn to Rich up ahead. "Hey, what's that on your shirt?"

"Me?" Rich said, spinning around to look back at Tommy. "Oh, security tag. Crazy, right? Who's trying to keep people from stealing in a place like this?"

"That's probably what set off the alarm." Hazel said, glaring at Rich. He scoffed out a chuckle before taking off the shirt and throwing it to the ground.

"There, happy?" he jeered.

"It doesn't matter now you idiot," Hazel snapped. "It's already going off."

"We're almost there, let's just go!" Rich hollered before turning to run into the store. Hazel and I started after him, followed by Tommy. We jogged through the toy aisle and past the appliances, but the blaring of the alarm echoed through the entire store. Tommy was having trouble keeping up, and I kept having to stop at the aisle junctions to make sure he knew which way to go.

"Wait up!" I yelled at Rich, who had nearly gotten out of view. Hazel was a little ways ahead of me, but stopped when she heard my voice. Her eyes were wide with panic as she looked back at me.

"Jeff!" she shrieked, pointing her finger behind me. I spun around and saw Tommy limping through the aisle of mattresses. There was a fast-approaching shadow behind him.

"Tommy!" I screamed. "Behind you!"

A look of horror filled his face as he tried desperately to flee from the apparition. It was too late, though; the entity was in arms reach. The creature lunged towards Tommy, and then in a split-second decision, I yelled "The mattress! Jump!"

Tommy obeyed without thinking, leaping onto a nearby bed as the shadowy claw of the entity grazed his body. He disappeared into the white mattress, distracting the entity for a split second. I sprinted towards Hazel and saw Rich up ahead, trembling on the edge of the dark produce section. He started running once he saw us.

Evil whispers and the sound of staticky tearing hissed in my ears as we ran through the darkness, while visions of the shadowy apparition blinked in and out of the aisles in my peripherals. We chased Rich back into the grocery section, rushing between the aisles of alien goods until the door to the refrigerator section appeared at the end of one of them. He tore it open and Hazel and I leapt through before fumbling the door shut behind us. Seconds later, the glass frosted over, followed by the sound of nails on a chalkboard and claw marks dragging through the frost on the glass door.

The three of us charged towards the heavy steel door on the edge of the refrigerator room and pulled it open before piling into the dark hallway. I threw my shoulder against the door to force it closed, heaving for breath. Rich was laid flat out on the ground, while Hazel sat hunkered over on the wall, breathing heavily.

"What. . .happened?" Rich said, gasping in between words.

"He's gone," I said despondently. "I can't believe it."

"It killed him then?" Rich said grimly. "I knew he had no chance moving that slow."

"No," Hazel interjected, still gasping for air. "Jeff told him to jump on one of the mattresses. He would have been dead otherwise."

"You did WHAT!" Rich barked, raising his head to look at me with wide eyes.

"I had no choice. The thing was right behind him. I wouldn't have thought of it if you hadn't told me about it earlier." I replied, laying my forehead on the cold steel door.

"You're one sick bastard, Jeff." Rich accused, shaking his head. "That might be one the worst levels someone could end up on. I'd rather be dead."

"You and that stupid shirt are the reason why we got chased in the first place!" Hazel snapped, leering at Rich.

"I didn't know the alarm would go off," Rich shot back, pushing himself up onto his butt.

"None of us did," I said wryly, turning from the door. "But you were reckless that entire mission, and this place is littered with dangerous surprises. Your actions brought them right to us, and now look what happened; we lost our way out!" I yelled, infuriated by Rich's insolence.

"I was just trying to have some fun, Jeff; we're all in the

same boat here. The least we can do is try to find some novelty in the tragedy of this whole thing." Rich replied, dusting himself off as he stood up. "God, sucks for Tommy though; wandering endlessly through the foggy aisles of mattresses. If he wasn't insane before, the goat-headed entity will get him there."

"Just shut-up, Rich." Hazel said, walking over to my side. I stared at the ground bleakly, coming to terms with the sudden death of my dream of getting home.

"Come on, Jeff, let's go tell the commander what happened." Hazel said, resting her palm on my back. I looked at her with sorrowful eyes, filled with grief about what had happened, but knew deep down that it would have been worse if it had been her. Leaving her here to wander alone forever while I sat at home safe would have been unbearable, and though we might never see Tommy again, we did have a clue to the way out. He hadn't told us exactly where to go, but we knew which level to investigate, so even with losing him, our mission hadn't changed; organize an expedition to the parking ramp and find the exit.

"Are you guys ready or what?" Rich said loudly. "Let's get this debrief over with so I can go get some sleep before our next trip into hell."

"Yeah, we'll be right behind you," Hazel said, causing Rich to shrug and start heading down the hall back towards The Hub. Once he was out of ear shot, Hazel leaned towards me and said gently "Are you okay? I know he was your friend."

I sighed, staring down the hall. I was still in disbelief, but as I looked back at Hazel—into her sympathetic, loving eyes—I thanked God that it hadn't been her.

"I'll be alright. He made his own choice to come in

here." I said, trying to be logical about the situation.

"It's noble that he tried to save you, but do you believe everything he said?" Hazel asked carefully.

"I don't know, I'm still trying to put the pieces together." I replied. "At least we have an idea of a level to check for an exit now. "

"Right," Hazel replied before her brow furrowed and she let out a little sigh. She turned from me to head back towards The Hub and said, "We better get going then."

"Hazel," I said, placing my hand gently on her arm to stop her. She turned around and looked at me with teary eyes before hugging me tight. I wrapped my arms around her, feeling her soft body pressed against mine, there, in the empty hallway. I didn't know what happened, but it felt right, like we were there to fill the void in each other and quell the sorrow and tragedy of the many days spent alone in this hell. There were no words, but I knew it was love when I looked into her darling eyes that said they needed me. To have her was enough, and though the risk of losing her had already been weighing heavily on me, I knew now that I would not think twice about sacrificing myself for her. Neither of us may ever make it out of here, but giving her a chance at freedom was more important than anything.

"If we ever *do* make it out," I said quietly, ready to ask her what would become of us if we did, but before I could say the rest, Hazel put her finger on my lips and whispered "I don't know, Jeff. All we have is now."
I looked at her longingly, desperate for a life together after, but her eyes told me that now was not the time. I loved her too much to force the issue and nodded in acceptance. My heart longed to know why, but she held me tight again and made

everything feel okay. Then we walked together, hand in hand, back to The Hub.

Chapter 14

Debrief

As Hazel and I exited into the amber-lit car tunnel, I saw that Rich was already talking with the commander by the door. She was nodding slowly with a skeptical expression on her face as Rich babbled about our mission, and then as she noticed Hazel and I, she marched towards us, leaving Rich with a perturbed look on his face.

"Rich tells me you didn't complete the mission objective," Vex said critically. "You'd better have a good reason for turning back that far in."

"We do," Hazel replied quickly. "We made contact with one of Jeff's friends who said he knew of a way out."

Vex raised one eyebrow, looking at Hazel suspiciously for a moment. "Well, where *is* he?"

"He nearly got picked off by a shadow entity. Jeff ordered him into a no-clip zone at the last second to save his life." Hazel explained.

"That's. . .quite a story," Vex said condescendingly, as if she thought we were lying. "Let's head back to my office so we can get some of these details straight. Rich shared some other information that I want to clear up."

As Vex began leading us back towards her office, Hazel and I scurried over to Rich and whispered, "What did you tell her?"

"That we abandoned the mission after we came across a guy named Tommy who was lost and said he knew the way out." Rich replied, shaking his head. "What? Was I not supposed to tell her that?"

"She just asked us why we turned around," Hazel hissed. "Was she trying to see if you were lying or something?"

"I don't know, but she doesn't seem happy about it. I told you guys we should have kept going." Rich said, before the commander glanced over her shoulder and noticed the three of us whispering together.

"This way, come on now." she said, holding the open the door to the laboratory. I looked at Hazel with concern before taking the lead through the door. Vex leered at each of us as we walked through, and then let the door shut with a metallic thud. The three of us then filed through the laboratory into her office and sat down one by one in a line of chairs behind her desk. Vex entered the room after us, and then after walking slowly over to her desk, plopped down a bundle of papers in front of us. She stood with her hands on her hips, staring at us in uncomfortable silence for a moment before smiling and sitting down in her seat.

"So, Rich tells me that you turned back because you found a guy named Tommy who said he knew the way out, but now he's gone. Is that right?" Vex interrogated. "And that he was nearly killed by an entity on a well-documented level, but that Jeff here had him go into a no-clip zone to save him."

"I tried to tell them not to turn back," Rich interrupted, causing Vex to raise her eyebrows. "But they insisted because

Tommy knew the way out. I never believed any of it. He was already in rough shape when he found him; probably had been hallucinating."

Hazel scoffed in disgust, while I glared at Rich with my mouth hung open. He was throwing us under the bus to try and save his own skin.

"Be that as it may, your group failed to complete the mission and wasted valuable resources in the process." Vex said disapprovingly. "Understand that this reflects poorly on this group, especially for its first mission. Credits will be deducted for this."

"Hold on," I said quickly. "Tommy told us he entered and exited The Back Rooms from the parking ramp level. We came back as fast as we could to tell you."

Vex chuckled before looking at me with a smug expression. "Ohhh, so now this Tommy character can enter *and* exit The Back Rooms" Vex said patronizingly. "Why does his name sound familiar; isn't this the person you told me about when you first went through intake?"

"He's telling the truth," Hazel defended. "Tommy told us that his job was to get people in and out of the lower levels. That's why Jeff told you about him; Tommy is the reason he ended up here in the first place."

Vex leaned back in her chair, looking at Hazel suspiciously, and then seeming to notice my admiration for Hazel, let out a frustrated sigh.

"Jeff, I already told you; no one sent you here. Now you got Hazel believing this lie." Vex shook her head, looking down at the desk. "I'm gonna have to reassign you two."

"What!" I cried, lunging out of my seat. "You can't do

that!!”

Vex crossed her arms, staring at me with raised eyebrows. “One mission and you two are already deluding ourselves about a way out.” Vex said sternly. “I can’t have emotions disrupting my group’s progress. If you two are so smitten, go to The Dream Palace together. Missions are not the time for romance.”

I collapsed back into my chair in disbelief, horribly defeated by Vex’s cold heartedness.

“I swear he wasn’t hallucinating,” I exclaimed, desperate to change her mind. Vex appeared unphased, and as Rich shook his head at me disapprovingly, rage bubbled beneath my skin. “Rich is full of it; He was careless the entire mission and is just trying to save face with you now.” I said accusingly. There was nothing to preserve with him now.

“Now’s not the time to start pointing fingers, Jeff.” Vex said, shaking her head. “This is just giving me more reasons to break the three of you up.”

“Can you please just look into it?” I pleaded. “Hell, send me; I’ll go investigate the ramp myself.”

“No!” Hazel blurted before sinking back into her chair, seemingly ashamed.

“You two have been gross from the very beginning,” Rich mocked, causing Hazel to shoot him a dirty look.

“Enough!” Vex said loudly, slamming her palms on the desk as she sprang to her feet. “I won’t have this infighting in my office! You three are lucky I don’t deport all of you!” Vex shouted, before taking a deep breath and shutting her eyes. She canted her head to the side, and then stared at me intensely.

“What do you want me to do, Jeff? Send out a bunch of groups to investigate a supposed exit on a level that is over a dozen levels away from The Hub?" Vex shook her head. "That level has been documented extensively, and you're convinced solely by the word of this Tommy guy that it's the way out. How do you know he wasn't lying? What if he was just leading all of you into a trap? Why wouldn't he just leave if he knew how to get in and out?"

I glared back at her in frustrated silence, not believing a word of her accusations, but then my ears perked up as Hazel started talking.

"He had a full account of Jeff's entry," Hazel said earnestly. "Phone calls, level progress; it all matched up. He told us that he got lost trying to save Jeff going beyond the levels he was familiar with."

Vex stared at Hazel skeptically, before shifting her eyes back to me. She did not appear disappointed or frustrated anymore; now she looked ambivalent, like we had pushed her over the edge and she didn't care anymore.

"I see what's going on now," Vex said grimly, packing the papers on the desk back into the drawer. "I should have known from the beginning."

"What do you mean?" I said cautiously, unnerved by her sudden change of tone.

"It's okay, Jeff. It's completely normal, even for people that have been here for many years." Vex said, backing away from the desk. She then brought her hand up quickly to the radio on her collarbone and pressed a button before hissing into it: "Code 7 in my office. Units' 779 and 751."

"What's she doing?" Hazel said confusedly, glancing at me. I shook my head; I didn't know, and then the door to the office blasted open. I saw them take Hazel first; two large men in black jumpsuits, and then I thrashed violently as I felt heavy hands grab onto me. They pulled me out of the chair as I fought desperately to get loose. I could hear Hazel screaming as they dragged her out of the office, and as I tried to turn my head to see where they were taking her, my face was bashed back towards the office by a gloved hand. I saw Vex standing there; pursed lips, holding her arms behind her back, and Rich, wearing a face of confused terror. I was dragged through the laboratory out into the amber car tunnel, and then the world went dark as a coarse blindfold was forced over my eyes. The sounds of Hazel's screams echoed through the concrete, growing more distant with every cry. I fought desperately to escape my kidnappers, and then I was thrown onto a hard surface before feeling straps tighten across my body. Then I felt movement, like I was on some kind of vehicle, and after a long darkness, I heard the sound of a closing door.

I had been put in a quiet room, and after a few minutes of lying there, blind and strapped down, the blindfold was removed, and I saw the black mask of a person in a yellow hazmat suit.

"What is going on!" I screamed, thrashing to try and free my body from the straps. The person remained silent while taking notes on a clipboard before they motioned towards a window that sat high up on a wall of the room. I could see three other people in hazmat suits behind the window, and as I snapped my head back towards the person that was next to me, I saw them leaving the room. Then a hissing sound began, and the room filled with a beige tinted mist.

"I don't want to die!" I cried, trying desperately to break the straps. It was no use, and as the mist reached my eyes and nose, they began watering and burning like they had been exposed to chlorine from a pool. My body weakened with each breath, and my mind slowed. I was groggy and barely able to maintain consciousness, but then the hissing stopped. The mist in the room began to dissipate, and then I was left lying there in silence, drugged and unable to move. A dull pain in my arm caused me to drowsily look over and see a person in hazmat suit putting a needle in me and drawing blood, next to two others taking notes on clipboards.

"What are you doing?" I mumbled, hardly able to move. They ignored my questions and continued with their work, syringing my blood into a small machine that began humming as they powered it on. Then a bright green light filled a bulb on the top of the device, causing them to look at each other as if surprised. The two people with clipboards then left the room, and as I groggily leered at black mask of the remaining person, they lifted it, and then I recognized them. It was Vata.

"You?" I snarled dizzily.

"Calm down, Jeff. It's just a safety protocol." Vata said, squinting at me as if I was a science experiment.

"Protocol; what are you, Joseph Mengele?" I spat, slumping my head backwards. My stomach churned and my head spun as if I was drunk.

"We do this to anybody who exhibits signs of transformation when returning from a mission," Vata said. "The mold's effects will wear off soon."

"*MOLD?*" I cried. "You drugged me with MOLD?"

"Claviceps Liminus; it's an anesthetic and sedative species of mold found on carpet in The Back Rooms," Vata replied.

"What the hell did you sedate me for?" I demanded.

"Like I said, we do it for people who are suspected of being in the early stages of wretch transformation." Vata explained as he started loosening my straps. "Your blood didn't have any traces of the pathogen."

"*THIS* is your protocol? Abducting people and throwing them in a gas chamber?" I said in disbelief. Vata stopped undoing my straps and stared at me intently.

"You obviously aren't familiar with the horrors of wretches. One getting loose in The Hub would be catastrophic"

"Someone could have at least told me! And where's Hazel? Is she getting gassed too?" I asked angrily.

"I haven't gotten her blood results yet, but yes, she was also examined." Vata said.

I was now untied and seated upright, rubbing my arms where the straps had been tightly cinched, but then it dawned on me that my office visit might be the last time I'd see Hazel.

"Where is she? Can I go see her?" I said, jumping off the seat before stumbling from the effects of the mold. Vata quickly caught me and tried to sit me back down.

"Not until you're fully recovered. She's going to need some time too, assuming her blood work checks out." Vata said coldly, causing me to fight off his hands and try to stand back up.

"She's not a wretch! The only reason she was taken was because of me." I snapped, pushing past Vata. "Now *where* is she!"

"You need to calm down, Jeff. She's gonna be fine. And if her bloodwork doesn't pass, there's nothing you can do anyway."

I leered at Vata with drowsy eyes, still determined to find out where she was. Walking was nauseating and laborious though, and after struggling a few steps from the bed, I let out a frustrated sigh and turned back around.

"Fine. Just please let me know when she's out." I said defeatedly. "Can we just get out of here? I just want to go back to my cell and sleep."

Vata looked at me skeptically, as if he was trying to decide whether I was going to run once we got out of the room. His scowl eventually softened, and then he glanced up at the glass window on the wall before walking over to me.

"Here," he said, slyly pulling a vial of purple gel from his pocket and handing it to me. "Take this; it's moth jelly. It will curb the effects, but don't tell anyone I gave it to you."

I gawked at the vial suspiciously, wondering if I was being drugged again, but then, noticing the slight compassion in Vata's eyes, I snatched the vial and quickly dumped it into my mouth. Vata glanced over his shoulder as the strange flavor coated my tastebuds. It was sweet and succulent, like blueberries mixed with honey, and within seconds, I felt my strength and lucidity return.

"*Wow!*" I hissed, bringing a small smirk to Vata's face.

"I know, it's good stuff," he whispered. "Now listen, you gotta report to the archivist before heading back to your cell. Give him your mission details and any anomalies your group discovered."

I perked up as he said this, remembering everything I had told Ivan; I had so much more to tell him now. I could only imagine what he might say about Tommy's story, and I wondered if his word might have more sway with Vex. Perhaps he could convince her to actually look into the theorized exit on the parking ramp.

"Wait," I said as Vata headed towards the door into the room with the examination window. He glanced back at me and just as I was about to tell him about the exit on level 1, the door to the examination room opened, causing his head to snap back to where a person in a yellow hazmat suit now stood.

"Unit 751 passed. Vex is requesting additional interrogation on the two of them though." the masked person said in a muffled voice.

"That can't be right." Vata said firmly. "He hasn't met any of the criteria."

"It's what she's requesting." the masked person replied, before leaning in and whispering something to Vata that caused his brow to furrow.

"I'll have a talk with her." Vata said before glancing back at me. "What were you saying, Jeff?"

I paused for a moment, suspicious of what this other person meant by interrogation.

"Uh, just wondering how to get back to the archives." I replied.

"Take a right when you come out of here; I'll have someone come get you if we have more questions." Vata said, nodding towards the door.

"What about Hazel?" I said impatiently.

"She's fine, Jeff. She'll be back this evening."

I stared at Vata, trying to decide if he was telling the truth, before reluctantly opening the door back out into the car tunnel. The section I had entered did not appear any different than the area back by the commander's office, with lines of infinite, evenly spaced doors down the smooth concrete walls. I took a right like Vata directed, but I had no idea how far I was supposed to go, or which door led back to the archive area. The space was still empty and desolate, devoid of any M.E.G members or unique details. It felt just like any other level; liminal and unsettling, and I wondered just how far down the tunnel went. Would it dead end, loop me back, or just go on forever—an amber-lit, half-ellipse, concrete subterranean stretch into oblivion—this was the most disturbing possibility, that, if you just kept walking, you could be miles from the M.E.G headquarters, far-off in some remote area. At that point, the only option would be to check doors until one was unlocked, and then pray the level it leads to wasn't terrible. This did bring up a lot of questions, though: How far had M.E.G gone down this tunnel to investigate? Were there assignments that required groups to enter a door miles away from the headquarters? How many doors had they investigated, and what was behind the locked doors? I had much bigger fish to fry now, especially with everything I was going to tell Ivan, but I couldn't help the discomfort brought on by so much of this place still being unexplained.

The numbers on the doors were not sequential, but I soon discovered the one with an etched image of the book on it. I let out a sigh of relief, and began to wonder where I was even going to start with Ivan? Would I tell him how Tommy knew the way out, but then got attacked by a shadow entity at the last minute and no-clipped? Or how Vex did not believe the story and then had Hazel and I abducted? The discoveries from our actual mission seemed entirely irrelevant compared to Tommy's story, so that's where I planned to start; tell him everything Tommy told me.

As I entered the door, I recognized the tall ceiling to floor bookshelves and desk where Ivan had given us our first mission book. He wasn't there, though, so I rang the bell on the desk and ogled at the shelves while I waited. There were literally thousands of books, and as I walked over to skim the titles, I was astonished at the fact that they all were Back Rooms specific. *Hounds 101 - Staying Alive, Anomalies on level 147: The Endless Foggy Pier, Fundamentals of No-Clipping, Liquid Pain - Dangers and Benefits, Backrooms Trading Manual, Thalassophobia - Levels to Avoid, Theories on Entity Emergence.* All bizarre titles with hundreds of pages, but the one that piqued my interest most was *Theories on The Psychological Effects of Liminality.* As I pulled it down from the shelf, a voice sounded behind me.

"Are you checking that one out?" the stranger said as I spun around with the book in hand.

"Oh, no, I was just taking a look." I stuttered, startled by the fact that it wasn't Ivan. This guy was much younger, with ginger hair and a narrow, pink face.

"Is there anything else I can help you find?" he said, seeming to be annoyed by the fact that I had helped myself to a book.

"I. . .uh. . .am looking for Ivan? He's usually here. Are you, his assistant?" I said, glancing around for any signs of Ivan.

"Uhm, *no.* I'm Kris; I'm the new archivist here. Ivan was deployed yesterday."

"*What?*" I exclaimed, looking at him with wide eyes. "*Deployed?*"

"Well yeah, he couldn't stay in the cozy archives forever. Vex thought it would be a good idea to change up his schedule a bit." Kris said with a shrug. "Sounded like he was getting a bit of cabin fever."

I became short of breath on hearing this and had to lean on a nearby bookshelf. My mind spun with ideas of what this meant. Vex had "deployed" him because of me. She was evil, stopping anyone who tried to escape.

"Are you okay?" Kris stammered, looking at me with wide eyes.

"I. . .just need a second." I stuttered back.

"Wait, aren't you Jeff? Your friend Rich was just here for debrief." Kris said with a smile, while I struggled to stay on my feet. I breathed rapidly while the library spun around me, and then I slumped to the ground. Kris scurried over to my side, nudging my shoulder to try and wake me up before pulling out a walkie. He said something garbled into it before the world went dark.

***

"Jeff? Are you awake? Can you hear me?"

The voice sounded familiar. It was soothing, and as I opened my eyes to a bleary room, I saw a person next to me. Their facial features began to reveal themselves, and then I recognized Hazel.

"What happened?" I muttered.

"You passed out in the archives. They said you left treatment too soon." Hazel said gently.

"Treatment. . .That's right." I said with a grimace. "They did it to you too."

"Yeah, I was stuck in that chamber all night. That gas

261

was awful." Hazel said, shaking her head.

"Did they tell you why they did it?" I asked, looking at her intently.

"They said it was a safety protocol for signs of wretch transformation. Seems a bit extreme, but I guess they don't want to take any chances."

"Hazel," I said, sitting up and grabbing her arm. "Something is not right here. They are trying to keep us from getting out."

Hazel frowned at me before brushing my arm away.

"Jeff, that's the kind of talk that got us put in that gas chamber. You're gonna end up right back in there if you go around saying that kind of thing." Hazel warned.

"Please, you have to listen to me." I begged, drawing a perturbed look from Hazel. "Vex got rid of Ivan while we were gone. He was the only one other than her who I told about Tommy. She's hiding something."

"Ivan. . .the archivist? Why would she get rid of him?" Hazel asked.

"Before we left, I told him everything. He said that none of it was adding up and that he would look into it." I exclaimed. "And now she has us abducted and gassed for telling her about an exit? She's trying to keep us here!"

My eyes shot to the doorway as I noticed a person appear in the amber light of my cell. It was Vex.

"Oh good, he's awake!" Vex said, sauntering over to my bedside. She then looked down at me with a smile that chilled my soul. "Hazel's been here all-night waiting for you to wake up. She wouldn't stop asking about you after treatment."

I faked a smile at Vex and then glanced at Hazel who

appeared to be fighting a look of surprise from what I had just told her.

"I figured it was only right for her to have some time with you before her deployment." Vex said, causing me to lurch up.

"What!" I cried. "You're still breaking up the group!"

"Woah, calm down," Vex chastised. "She's gonna be in a group with some *very* experienced members. They'll keep her safe."

I shook my head in utter grief, ruined by the thought of her going in without me. My despair coupled with fury, and all I wanted to do was strangle Vex.

"It's for the best, Jeff. They are highly skilled in The Back Rooms and will keep her safer than you ever could." Vex said with a slow nod, as if to torment me. "I'll leave you two to have some time together." Vex patted me on the shoulder before turning to head towards the door. She then stopped in the doorway and looked at Hazel. "Shiloh's group will be returning from their mission soon to debrief at the archives. Make sure to introduce yourself." Vex said, nodding at Hazel with a smile before leaving the doorway.

I looked at Hazel in despair while she glared at the empty doorway. She stared despondently for a minute before squinting her eyes shut and turning back towards me, looking at me in a way I had never seen before.

"What do we do then, Jeff? Run away and try to find the exit ourselves?" she said with an exasperated sigh. "Besides, Tommy's gone. Without him, we have no idea where the exit is in the parking ramp, and you know as well as I that that place is enormous."

"That sounds better than going on these hellish missions and dealing with the menace that is Vex. We could try to find some info on how to get back to the ramp in the archives and see if there's any hints at an exit." I said hopefully, trying to stoke Hazel's enthusiasm. She looked at me skeptically for a moment before her eyes looked up and then she lightly bobbed her head from side to side; she was considering it.

"I'll see what I can find when I meet with my group at the archives. It won't raise any red flags that way." Hazel said reservedly. "If they really are trying to keep us in here, we have to tread carefully."

"Yeah, and how many of these M.E.G members know that people are being kept here intentionally?" I said curiously. "It can't just be Vex."

Hazel crossed her arms and let out a huff.

"It still doesn't add up that Vex, or anyone for that matter, would try to keep people here at all." she replied. "I'm not saying you're wrong or that Tommy was lying, but it's still a leap to decide that this is one big conspiracy."

"That's the thing I'm most confused about, Hazel." I said seriously, pushing myself up off the bed. "If M.E.G—or whoever they are working with—created The Back Rooms, then why fight to keep us here at all? Why not just push a button and close down the exits?"

Hazel looked at me skeptically as I paced around the room, trying to figure out what I was getting at.

"What are you saying? You think someone else made this place?" Hazel said, perplexed.

"I don't know, but M.E.G has been here for a long time and we triggered something within the operation talking about finding an exit." I said, shaking my head. "What is even the point of their group? Just to research this place? Getting out of here seems like a pretty universal goal for everyone."

"Maybe they are just careful about letting rumors about an exit proliferate through the group." A voice said from behind me, causing me to spin around and see Vata leaning up against the doorway. I jumped backwards towards Hazel, standing in front of her as if to guard her from any consequences from our discussion. Vata remained composed in the doorway, leering at me as my wide eyes searched for what his next move would be. He was unphased at my panic, and then sauntered into the room and sat down in the chair across from where I guarded Hazel by the bed.

"You really won't give it up, huh Jeff?" Vata said, shaking his head. "I saved you from level 55, put in a good word with Vex and gave you a place to stay at the Hub, but you still are here trying to convince Hazel to run away with you."

"I never signed up for endless missions and getting gassed." I snarled, causing Vata to smirk.

"You just don't get it; there is NO way out of here." he asserted.

"You're lying!" Hazel chimed in, jumping up and nestling behind me. Vata looked up at the two of us from his seat, letting out a big sigh as he shook his head.

"You two are exactly what the Dream Palace is for; delusional wanderers who can't cope with the reality of The Back Rooms." Vata accused. "Listen, nobody wants to go on these missions and contend with hazardous environments and entities, but it's our only hope."

"It's not, we know a way out now." I said confidently,

causing Vata to shake his head at me.

"You are not the first person to go down this path, Jeff." Vata said firmly. "Many have gone completely mad with delusions of escape, and it is why we handle rumors so forcefully. When they spread, our organization shatters because people turn on us."

"That doesn't even make sense. People talking about an exit makes them crazy? Give me a break." I said in disbelief.

"Countless wanderers have relentlessly pursued theorized exits, but not a single escape has ever been found. Many expeditionary groups were lost in the early days of M.E.G because of these supposed exits, so the archives were established as a way to give people an accurate idea of what was really out there." Vata explained. "Everything we know is in those books, and they are free for every member to read. We are not hiding anything; we are just trying to keep people safe and methodically work towards a greater understanding of this strange place."

"Suppression of speech and involuntary service; those are your techniques here?" Hazel scoffed. "No wonder people turn on you guys."

"When someone comes along and sings about an exit, the weak minds jump on it. It's a glimmer of false hope for them, and only leads to disappointment and reckless missions. That's why we shut down talks about it; it harms our new members' psyche's and takes away from our actual work." Vata said, leaning back in his seat.

"Then how do you explain Tommy telling us that he entered and exited on a specific level and can get us out?" I interrogated. "And what about Ivan? He disappeared after looking into my story."

"Ivan mentioned your encounter with Tommy; I talked to him after you deployed. He wanted to confirm the level links that you discovered to see if you had been hallucinating, but I bet he's back by now." Vata replied. "He's more studied than me and can answer more of your questions, but that's what this whole thing is about? Tommy telling you there's an exit?"

"Not just an exit; he told us everything about how his job was to get people in and out of The Back Rooms." Hazel chimed. "We told Vex everything, but she didn't believe a word of it.".

Vata crossed his legs and cocked his head at us. His brow was furrowed and while he appeared skeptical, I could detect a touch of curiosity in him.

"You two do realize the implications of what you're saying, right?" Vata asked before pausing for a moment, seeming to want a reply. Hazel and I remained silent, causing him to sigh before answering his own question. "You expect M.E.G to believe the word of *one* person about an exit—a person who had been lost for days and was obviously suffering from delirium—do you see why that's hard for us to get on board with, particularly in a place where paranoia and delusions run wild?" Vata said with raised eyebrows, before shaking his head. He then stood up and put his hands on hips, staring at the two of us. "If you two want to stay with M.E.G, you're going to have to keep quiet about this. It's not good for anyone."

"Can't you at least send a group to investigate that level just in case Tommy *is* right?" I begged.

"All missions need to be signed off on by Vex before being approved, and I doubt she would spend resources on investigating such a well-documented level." Vata replied. "I can try to draft something up if it will get you two off this crazy idea, but there is no guarantee it will be approved."

I glanced at Hazel, who appeared just as uncertain as I, but going along with Vata felt like our only real option. It was that, or get kicked out of M.E.G and be right back at square one. This could very well be one elaborate scheme by Vata to get Hazel and I off M.E.G' true sinister intentions to keep people here, but it felt like we were powerless in the matter. Vata seemed to notice we were coming around, though, so he stepped towards us and said:

"For what it's worth, I'm here because I like you two. Vex already has you both on a watch list, and if you continue causing problems, she'll have you discharged."

"So what? We're stuck in The Back Rooms one way or another?" I said despondently. "What's even the point?"

"The point is to learn as much as we can so that we can find an exit one day." Vata said confidently. "But you don't have to believe me. Hell, if you two want to go charge headlong into oblivion towards wherever you think there's an escape, be my guest, but I can tell you with near complete certainty that it's not going to be there. I'm just trying to save you both from getting lost in there forever."

The three of us lingered in silence; together in this cold concrete cubicle, a thousand miles away from home. The feelings of despair had crept back in with the death of the dream of an exit. Here I was being forced to replace my prior ideas of escape once again with the grim reality of hopelessness, just as I had done countless times before.

"We all want out of here," Vata said sympathetically. "But the reality is that nobody knows the way out yet. Paranoia, delusions, and pursuing false-exits all get in the way of our mission to get home. That's why M.E.G deals with these sorts of things so harshly."

I shook my head in quiet disbelief, rubbing my face while trying to figure out what this meant for the future. Hazel and I's plan to run away had dissolved as quickly as it arose, not because M.E.G had shut it down or threatened us, but because they *hadn't*. They weren't trying to hide anything or even keep us here; they were just trying to keep people safe.

"I guess that's why Vex told me it's easier to believe someone put us here than to accept whatever *this* reality is," I said glumly, causing Hazel to rub my back consolingly. Vata nodded slowly with an earnest expression, seeming half satisfied by the fact that I had once again given up hope.

"Can you at least get Vex to put us back together again?" Hazel pleaded. "We won't talk about Tommy or running away anymore; just let us be in the same group. Please?"

Vata shook his head, causing a fury to bubble in my chest.

"It's the LEAST you can do! Come on! I'm not going anywhere without her!" I bellowed, bringing a surprised look to Vata's face.

"I'll. . .see what I can do," he said with a nod, panging my heart with joy. Despite home seeming further away than ever, being back with Hazel was just enough to keep me from giving up entirely.

"Now," Vata started. "Vex has already taken an interest in this Tommy character, as has Ivan. Let them work on it; if they have questions for you, they will ask. Until then, focus on your missions." Vata warned, looking at me with raised eyebrows. I nodded in agreement, bringing a smirk to his face before he said "Good, glad to have you two back. I'm going to smooth things over with Vex now and see about getting you two back in a group together. Just sit tight in the meantime." Vata then left my cubicle, leaving Hazel and I alone.

Though a sinking pit of dread about being stuck here had reintroduced itself in my heart, the pain was quelled as I looked into Hazel's eyes. Brown and gold, they sat perfectly next to her round cheeks and below her silky brown hair. Every moment together felt precious since we had been separated, and as we sat down together on the edge of my bed, we held each other in embrace. The dream of running away with her had been intoxicating, and as I felt her tender body pressed against mine, everything seemed okay. We were taking refuge in one another, and as I caressed her soft cheek with my fingers and began to go in for a kiss, I was jolted by the sound of someone shouting as they entered the cubicle.

"Jeff!" they said, pushing into the room. It took me a moment, but as I came out of the daze of almost kissing Hazel, I recognized who it was; Ivan. He was alive!

"Yes! Hi!" I stuttered, still dazed by my intimacy with Hazel being so abruptly broken.

"Vex told me you were starting to lose it! Are you two busy? I have something to show you that might help." Ivan said excitedly.

"Uhm," I mumbled, before looking at Hazel who gave me a gentle smile and nod, as if she was okay with talking to Ivan. The only thing I wanted was to be alone with her, but if she was okay with it, I couldn't deny that I was curious about what Ivan wanted to show us. He insisted that we come to the archives with him and said he would be waiting outside the cubicle to give us a minute to get ready. Once he left the room, I glanced at Hazel and thought for a moment before gently taking her face in my hand and giving her a long and slow kiss. Her lips were soft and inviting, and I savored every second of what might be our only moment of romance.

"I guess we better go," I said, helping Hazel up before walking with her towards the door. Then she grabbed my hand and pulled me back, pressing me into her bosom and whispering,

"I don't want you to have any doubts, Jeff." she said, with a voice like honey. "I want to be with you, whether we make it out or not."

A delighted sigh jumped out of me as I smiled, and as I looked at her and thought about forever together, a fire of determination roared in my chest. We had to get out; our future together demanded it.

"We're gonna make it out of here," I whispered. She looked up at me with eyes of love, wrapping her arms over my shoulders before giving me a long kiss.

"We'd better not keep him waiting any longer." she said with a smile.

I let out a half-flustered sigh, desperate to hold onto the moment, before reluctantly nodding in agreement. We then left my cubicle and joined Ivan outside before following him through the laboratory and into the car tunnel. As we entered the archives, I noticed that Ivan's desk had five different books open and scraps of paper scattered about. He motioned for us to sit down and then slid one of the dusty, old books towards Hazel and me.

"What's this?" Hazel said curiously, peering down at the

page.

"An old mission report from Vex," he replied, looking over his glasses at the two of us. "Take a look."

The note was handwritten in cursive and had blotches of ink and yellow coffee stains.

M.E.G Report #109 - 10/6/2000
Commander Jeremiah Black

Gamma Group, composed of Units 43, 50, and 52, deployed on 9\23/2000. Their mission objective was to investigate level 1, The Parking Ramp, for links to any additional levels. They deployed to level 3, The Electrical Station: the closest known link to level 1 from The Hub

The group was making good progress towards level 2, however, approximately 18-24 hours into their mission, the trio was attacked by an entity swarm. Unit 43 was subsequently separated from the group. Units 50 and 52 never successfully made it to level 2, returning to The Hub with injuries and severe symptoms of psychosis.

A rescue party was sent out to search for Unit 43, but the search was called off after two weeks of failing to make contact with the individual.

"Who is Jeremiah Black?" I said, looking up from the paper at Ivan.

"One of M.E.G's founders. He served as commander until 2005 when Vex took over after he passed." Ivan replied.

"Anything ring a bell in that report?"

"Uh, I don't think so. Why?" I asked as Ivan slid a small stack of papers across the table towards Hazel and I. They looked familiar.

Member Intake #43 - 10/14/2000

Name: Thomas Freid
Entry Date: Unknown
First contact with M.E.G: Level 3 - The Electrical Station
Psychological State upon arrival: Paranoid Delusions
Characteristics; 6'4", ~250lb. Bald. Brown eyes.

"Oh, the notes I found in the mall; Vata must've given you them." I said curiously.

"You found these?" Hazel said, thumbing through the notes.

"Yeah, it looked like someone had gone crazy. They got lost in the creepy nostalgia level; 18." I replied, before noticing that the unit number on the report from the mall, #43, matched the one in the report Ivan had just shown us. "Huh, I guess it's the same person." I exclaimed.

"Indeed; M.E.G reports generally do not leave The Hub, though." Ivan said seriously. "The documents you found were stolen."

"Strange, but this report is from over two decades ago. . .What does this have to do with us?" Hazel questioned with a shrug,

"Well, have a look at this intake." Ivan replied, opening another big, dusty book.

Name: Thomas Arbile
Entry Date: Unknown
First contact with M.E.G - Level 2 - Pipe Dreams
Psychological State upon arrival: Paranoid delusions
Characteristics; 6'4, stocky build. Bald. Brown eyes.
Visit notes: Claviceps Liminus treatment failed to resolve psychosis. Thomas fled from The Hub sometime after treatment.

I stared down at the document; suspicion percolated in my stomach while Ivan looked at me with a sober scowl.

"They sound like the same person." Hazel said curiously. "Oh, I see. There are two intake reports because the one Jeff found was stolen, so they made another one for the same individual."

"Precisely," Ivan said mysteriously. "And now we get to why I've brought you here. The description—6 '4, stocky and bald—does that sound like Tommy?"

"Yep, that's Tommy." I replied, still trying to unpack the implications of what Ivan was saying. "So. . .Tommy was here then? All the way back in 2000? And again in 2006? Did nobody recognize him? And why is his last name different in the reports?"

"Well, his second intake report was done with Vex," Hazel replied, squinting down at the papers. "So yeah, she wouldn't have known him."

"6 years is long enough for a lot of. . .member turnover, we'll say." Ivan said grimly. "The way that I see it, Tommy probably gave a different last name because, for whatever reason, he didn't want M.E.G remembering him."

"Why would he be worried about that?" I said, perplexed.

"For the same reason you two tried to run away; our practices are a little. . .heavy handed here." Ivan replied, causing Hazel and I to look at each other, nodding in agreement. "Well, that's one explanation, at least." Ivan said. The room grew silent.

"What's the other?" Hazel asked, shaking her head.

"If Tommy's story about getting people in and out of The Back Rooms on level 1 is true," Ivan started, his composure still stern. "Then M.E.G would be a major threat to his business."

"That doesn't make any sense. He wanted us to bring him here; to The Hub, so that he could show everybody the way out," I challenged, shaking my head. "Why would he care if M.E.G members escaped?"

"Think about it, Jeff." Hazel interjected. "If M.E.G made it out, with their power and members, Tommy's unique ability would no longer be unique. M.E.G would be the way people could explore and escape The Back Rooms."

I scowled at Hazel and then down at the papers, trying to decide if Tommy could truly be that evil. The more I thought about it, the more plausible it became.

"You're right." I said, standing up from the desk. "Tommy never mentioned M.E.G to me, only The Hub. I bet he wanted to fly under the radar if we got here; act like it was his first time." I exclaimed, growing more disgusted with the story by the second. "I bet it was him who stole those intake documents in 2006; wanted to erase the info on himself, otherwise Vex would've asked him a lot of questions about the prior 6 years he'd spent in The Back Rooms."

"That's why he gave her a different name. . ." Hazel said quietly.

"I'm glad I'm not the only one who saw it," Ivan said with a frown. "My best guess is that he discovered the exit after his first deployment and then proceeded to monetize his abilities. His encounter with M.E.G in 2006 was probably a mistake; the report lists him as suffering from paranoid delusions, and I'll bet that's because he was talking about an exit."

"Un-fucking-believable." I spat. "What do you figure, he planned to slip out at The Hub after we brought him back, leaving us all here while he took one of the doors back to the exit on level 1?"

"More than likely," Ivan said soberly. "And I'd even go as far as to say that this isn't the first time he has gotten lost. I'll bet that's his plan when he gets too deep; find The Hub, give a new fake name for his intake report, and then leave while no one is looking."

"We have to find him then," Hazel said, half cheerfully. "He's our only way out; we're going to find him and force him to lead everybody home."

Her voice seemed to quell the torrent of rage I felt bubbling beneath my skin. As much as I wanted to kill Tommy, she was right; we had to find him. He was everybody's ticket out.

***

Hazel and I spent three days in company together at The Hub while Vex, Ivan, and other senior M.E.G officials drafted up a plan to search for Tommy. It would be a mass expedition, with groups assigned to all possible links to the Infinite Mattress store level. The group's overall operation was not really changed; M.E.G would still be sending out expeditionary groups for set periods of time before they were required to return and report their findings. The main objective, however, was established; get Tommy safely to The Hub and then use him to guide every member of M.E.G to the parking ramp level for escape.

Hazel and I had been assigned a new group member named Alucard after more details came out about Rich's insolence during our last mission. This was mostly thanks to Ivan and Vata putting in a good word with Vex for us. Alucard was a relatively strange and brooding character, but he had over a year of experience at M.E.G. I thought our personalities might clash, but he was a huge upgrade from Rich.

Our group would be searching for Tommy on a few key levels, but the one that made me most nervous was the anomalous after-party rooms on level 90. From the book's description, it was a complex series of rooms that all had red tinted carpet and were reminiscent of a child's birthday party room, with balloons, birthday cakes, board games, plastic silverware and colored wallpaper. It had a high psychological risk hazard, along with level specific entities known as party goers. These were described as wanderers infected with a unique virus that causes jaundice, abnormal bone growths around the face and mouth with a particular lengthening and sharpening of the teeth, along with jaw and mouth growth that produces a perpetual gape and appearance of a third row of teeth.

Aside from the horror of level 90, the other levels we would be searching sounded relatively calm, with one of the best ones being the lukewarm hotel on level -33 that was described as a matted-neon hotel with turquoise pools and potted tropical plants, along with soft-blue lighting and a starry, planetarium-like ceiling. We would also be exploring the abandoned tennis courts on level 176, an abandoned airport, an empty high school, and level 126, which, despite having a low entity account, was staggeringly large. This level was described as a labyrinth of corridors illuminated by changing colors of neon light coming through a wall of glass-blocks, with rectangular halls that could apparently stretch in one direction for miles while seemingly leading nowhere. It was not the worst level someone could ask for on a mission, but what weighed on my mind about it was a description in a short side bar on level 126. The risk was extremely low, but there was a chance of coming across:

> *"A large no-clip zone in the halls that leads to an undocumented level, described as an expansive, flat void dotted with giant pillars of monolithic, gray rock where the only exit is through the Hallowed Gate; a 50-foot-tall pair of baroque era doors made of silver and marble that lead to pristine rooms that appear similar to Mayan caves."*

These were the levels we would be looking for Tommy on, and despite the ever-present risk of eternal damnation to this place, at least I was with Hazel, and I could say that we were taking real steps towards escape. The threat of never getting out and losing her would weigh ever-present in my mind, but the love we shared transcended even the most treacherous of fates. We were in love, and though I was going to fight like hell to get us out of here so that we could spend our life together, revenge quietly drove my ambition. Tommy had betrayed me, like no one ever had before, and I hid from Hazel just how much I longed for justice.

A new frontier, like the first European expedition to the Americas, awaited us. I wasn't afraid anymore.